Warwickshire County Council

NEW 9/14 4L			
16-10			
24-10			
30-10			
08-11			
14-11			
25-11			
21-2-15			
8/5			

This item is to be returned or renewed before the latest date above. It may be borrowed for a further period if not in demand. **To renew your**

- **Phone the 24/7 Renewal Line** ...73 or
- **Visit www.warwicksh**ire.g... ...aries

Discover • Imagine ... *with libraries*

Warwickshire County Council

Working for Warwickshire

014003085 6

When
we were
Sisters

"When
we were
Sisters"×

Beth
MILLER

EBURY
PRESS

1 3 5 7 9 10 8 6 4 2

First published in 2014 by Ebury Press, an imprint of Ebury Publishing
A Random House Group Company

The Random House Group Limited Reg. No. 954009

Addresses for companies within the Random House Group can be found at:
www.randomhouse.co.uk

A CIP catalogue record for this book is available from the British Library

The Random House Group Limited supports The Forest Stewardship
Council® (FSC®), the leading international forest-certification organisation.
Our books carrying the FSC label are printed on FSC®-certified paper.
FSC is the only forest-certification scheme supported by the leading
environmental organisations, including Greenpeace.
Our paper procurement policy can be found at:
www.randomhouse.co.uk/environment

MIX
Paper from
responsible sources
FSC® C016897

Printed and bound by CPI Group (UK) Ltd, Croydon, CR0 4YY

ISBN 9780091956301

To buy books by your favourite authors and register for offers visit:
www.randomhouse.co.uk

For John

Melissa

I turn on the stairs when I hear that name.

Miffy.

Not my real name. A nickname. No one has used it for more than twenty years.

Laura stands framed in the doorway of her room. I'd know her anywhere. I try to focus on her face, on her dark eyes with their thick lashes, but against my will my own eyes keep sliding down to her stomach.

She raises her hand as if she's going to wave, then the hand changes direction and smoothes her hair, the lovely sleek black hair I used to envy. Cut shorter now. She's still beautiful, though not the way she was at fourteen.

Last night I deliberately avoided her. Said hello but nothing more. It didn't look too obvious. After a death, normal rules don't apply.

She says, 'Do you want to come in for a minute, Miffy?'

I knew being here would mean facing Laura. She was once such a significant figure in my life; a symbol of everything that went wrong. Now I know she's just a person who did some stupid things.

And haven't we all, as Dad would say if he were here.

Laura

You know those women who say, 'Oh, I only take five minutes to get ready'? I always want to say, 'Yes, darling, I can see that, but what did you do for the other four minutes?'

I take my time. Always have. Hair, make-up, clothes. It's so important to do it properly. You can tell when it's been rushed.

Huw says I'm high maintenance. Used to mean it as a compliment. Now it's: *Laura, what have you been doing for the last hour?* Now it's: *Laura, you look no different from when you went upstairs.* Thanks, honey bun; love you too.

Don't tell him, but tonight's session *has* been a bit of

a marathon – nearly two hours. Partly because of my sodding chin and its plucking hair (ha!); and partly because it's been hard to get the exact blend of foundation to disguise the bruise.

The crowd is roaring on the TV downstairs. You know what? Huw should be pleased. He didn't want to miss the football, and now he's had time for the game *and* the inevitable post-match recriminations. Dopey Paige is down there too, doubtless staring at the telly with her mouth open, drool trickling from her lower lip. The only nineteen-year-old in Wales with no plans for Valentine's, bless her hefty backside. I know it's a waste, paying her to babysit while we're still here. But my chin hairs have started to instantly replace themselves, like a sustainable forest.

'What's happening, *cariad*? Was wondering if you'd died up here.'

Huw's face looms behind mine in the mirror. Eleven years my senior, but looks fresher than me. His silvery blond hair flops onto his forehead, giving him a boyish air. Slim, clean-shaven, eyes the same bright fall-in-love-with-me blue I fell in love with.

I know I look older than thirty-seven. My hair's cut in what passes for a sharp bob in North Wales: basically a straggly bob. I used to think my Spanish heritage was a gift: thick black hair and olive skin, like my mother and

Frida Kahlo. But these days I'm more of a flabby old peasant-type, whose key resemblance to Frida is the facial hair.

'Can you see the bruise?' I ask.

Huw peers at my forehead. 'No, it's hidden under a trowel-load of cement.'

Did I mention this bruise? It's all right, it's not hurting that much any more. I put on some more smouldering purple eye-shadow. My big brown eyes, once my best feature, have so many lines round them I've been considering Botox, even though it's just *not done* here in the back arse of beyond. Not done because if you bother with your appearance beyond wearing matching socks, everyone thinks you're trivial. And literally not done, either, because there aren't any proper clinics. You'd have to go somewhere metropolitan, like Liverpool. I once mentioned my interest in Botox to Ceri, and she reacted as if I'd told her I was considering having my boobs grafted to my head. Which I will do, if they slide any lower. That's the bit I don't like about being pregnant: the way your tits just kind of sit on your stomach, reminding you that the gravity-defying part of your life is over.

'Come on, *cariad*, let's go, if we're going. You look fine.' His Welshy sing-song accent used to charm me, but he surely knows by now that I find it irritating.

'I do not look fine! I look like a fucking dog's dinner!'

'Dog's bollocks, more like. Well, you could maybe try

a different colour on your eyes. What with the bruise, people'll think I took a swing at you.'

'*Daaa*-ddy!' The Ruler of the House is calling, demanding an immediate audience with her most favoured subject. Huw trots off to attend to Evie, and I squeeze into what used to be my reliable going-out dress, before my tummy began to resemble a bowling ball.

Did I mention I'm pregnant? Memory like a sieve. Well, I am. Keep your congratulations low-key. No one but me is particularly happy about it.

I pause outside Evie's door. 'I don't want you to go out, Daddy.'

'Well, darling,' Huw says in his talking-to-children voice, 'it's important for mums and dads to go out together, isn't it? To talk, and enjoy each other's company.'

Doesn't sound like any evening Huw and I have had for a while. But now I'm ready, I want to go. I'm starving, and Jenny-and-Paul are good cooks. Which almost makes up for them holding hands and droning on about how fucking happy they are.

I look into the living room, where Dopey Paige is staring – yes, mouth open – at the telly. I pull on my coat, and hover at the bottom of the stairs. Huw takes his time, being extra patient with Evie to get at me.

It's a fifteen-minute drive to the dinner party – time enough to fit in a good row.

Me: 'Just don't embarrass me tonight, that's all I ask.'

Him: 'Why should I embarrass you?'

'Let's see. Hmm. How about snogging some *girl* in front of everyone. Yes, I think that qualifies as embarrassing, don't you?'

'One fucking kiss!'

'So there was fucking as well, was there?'

'Hilarious! You should be a stand-up. One fucking kiss in fifteen years!'

'What do you want, a long-service medal?'

'I want you to stop going on about it.'

'I'll stop going on about it when you tell me why you did it.'

'Why does anyone do anything? I was pissed, I suppose.'

'Yeah, right. Just a coincidence.'

'Just a coincidence, what?'

'That it happened when it did.'

'What, on New Year's Eve?'

'Fuck New Year's Eve! It was two days after I told you I was pregnant.'

'It was New Year's Eve! The traditional time for getting pissed and snogging people! It's practically obligatory!'

'Just a coincidence, then.'

'Will you stop saying that?'

'I'll stop saying that when you stop snogging other women!'

And so on.

We don't always argue like this. You're not seeing us at our best. We've had our ups and downs: marrying too young (me); a broken marriage (him); then step-children (me); then Evie, our very own home-grown dictator (both of us). Then the miscarriages (me again). Not to mention both having come from complicated family lives. Though who doesn't?

Till recently, we had a strong marriage.

Not lately, though. As I'm sure Huw would put it to the girl from New Year's Eve, or any other totty he has hidden away, we are 'going through a rough patch'.

We're so late, Jenny-and-Paul have assumed we aren't coming and have removed our chairs to make more room. They squeeze us back in, but they're very much not thrilled.

'We should have called,' I say.

'Never mind, you're here now,' Jenny says tightly. 'There's some lamb left.'

She's only gone and decorated the room with red hearts. Spent this morning cutting out crêpe paper, bless her girlish little soul. I wouldn't exactly say she is a friend, in case you're wondering. I met her through Ceri, my boss. For a couple of years, Huw and I, Jenny-and-Paul, and Ceri-and-Whoever-She's-With-This-Time have taken it in turns to host a monthly dinner. I used to fantasise that it would be a sophisticated salon-type thing, but forgot where I was and the sort of people I was dealing with.

Ceri's all cosied up next to Rees. Since her divorce she's been through most of the single men in Gwynedd, so I felt obliged to set her up with Rees, the last man standing. I've known him since my student days. Despite not being bad-looking, he's never been married. Soon as he opens his mouth, you know why. 'Well, hellooo, curvy lady,' he says, leering at me.

Ceri shoves his arm; Huw pretends not to hear; I say, 'Yes, Rees, a baby-belly is this season's must-have accessory.'

Jenny plonks a sparse helping of dried-up lamb and potatoes in front of me and Huw, and we respond with stratospheric cries of gratitude. Jenny sits back down and pushes her dessert bowl aside. She hasn't noticed the stain on her blouse. 'We were worried about you,' she says. 'Wondering if something had happened' – stage whisper – 'with the baby,' indicating my stomach with her eyes.

'Oh, no, everything's fine.' I improvise: 'The sitter was late.'

'Thought you'd decided to have a romantic Valentine's night in,' says Paul.

Rees gives me a creepy wink.

'Can't stand Valentine's,' says Huw. 'Commercial shite.'

'Rees agrees with you,' Ceri says. 'Thinks giving flowers is playing into the hands of The Man.'

'Rip-off, yeah?' Rees does his Woody Woodpecker laugh. 'They double the prices on February fourteenth.'

'I'd be happy getting flowers on the fifteenth,' says Ceri.

'White, red or fizzy, Laura?' Paul says. Thank God, I thought he'd never ask. I'm not drinking but I really need something to get through this.

'Paul!' Jenny cries, miming an enormous stomach. 'She's pregnant!'

'I can have half a glass.'

Jenny shakes her head at Paul, and he pours me some water.

'Better safe than sorry, right?' Jenny's one of those fascist Americans, the sort that tells complete strangers to stop smoking or eating brie if they happen to be pregnant. Ceri makes a sympathetic face at me. I make one back; she needs it more than I do. She's the one dating Rees.

'Nice decorations, Jenny,' I say.

Ceri gives me a tiny smirk.

'Are you all right?' Jenny mouths across the table at me, touching her head. This time it's about my forehead. I suppose the mark's started to show through the foundation, damn it.

'Fine.' Nothing a glass of wine wouldn't help. Cow. 'Slipped.'

'Oh, walked into a door, yeah?' Rees laughs, moronically.

'No,' I say, just as Huw blurts, 'She was literally banging

her head against the wardrobe.' He's already drunk a few while watching the football. 'So pissed off about nothing fitting. Said to her, "Well, *cariad,* if you will insist on getting up the duff…"'

People laugh nervously.

'Huw! Just ignore him.' I smile. *I'll kill you later, you bastard.* 'I slipped and banged it on the edge of the sink. Centre of gravity's shot to shit, you know.'

All right, so I did hit my head against the wardrobe. You're thinking I'm a psycho, but I'm not. It wasn't about nothing fitting. Huw knows that. It was about everything. Valentine's Day. He never even buys a card. Him snogging that girl. Him not wanting the baby. And, yes, about feeling fat as well. I really want this baby – you've no idea how much – but it doesn't mean I'm totally cool about my weight. I'm not one of those wanky hippy chicks who don't care what they look like. Anyway. That's a pretty long list of upsetting things. Some venting is normal, isn't it?

Jenny, sitting next to me, turns and breathes Rioja into my face. 'Changing the subject slightly, we were trying to work out the gap between Evie and the new baby.'

'Well, Evie's eleven.'

'Twelve by the time the baby comes,' says Ceri, grinning at Jenny. The look they give each other makes me realise our arrival has interrupted a delightfully bitchy conversation about us.

11

'You *are* brave,' says Jenny, holding out her glass for Paul to refill. 'It's like having two only children, really.'

'It'll be fine,' I say, watching the lovely red wine glug into the glass. 'I can concentrate on the new baby, and Evie will help.'

'But such a big gap will be very challenging. They're in two completely different places,' says Evil Jenny.

'Ours are the opposite extreme,' says Paul. 'Only eighteen months apart.'

'They play together so well, don't they, Paulie? We were lucky, though. Not everyone can have babies when they want to, can they? Paulie only has to look at me, and bam!'

Rees says, 'Good on yer, mate!'

Ceri discreetly makes a puking face that only I see.

Jenny now completely oversteps the mark, not that she hasn't already. Leaning her head to one side to indicate deep understanding, she drops into a counsellor-type voice. 'I know you've had some fertility problems, haven't you?'

'Who'd like coffee?' says Paul.

I catch Huw's eye, willing him to rescue me, and the bastard just looks right through me before draining his glass. I hate Huw, but I hate Evil Jenny more.

I picture Jenny in a documentary called *Women Who Live A Lie*. She's being interviewed by a thin, blonde, faux-sympathetic journalist. Jenny is wearing her horrible stained flowery blouse.

Faux-sympathetic Interviewer: Why did you pretend you were happy?
Jenny (*weeping*): I wanted everyone to envy me. I'm so ashamed. Everyone thought Paul was such a stud. No one knew he was gay and went out every night as a male escort. (*Sobs louder.*)
F-s Int: And the children...
Jenny (*wiping her eyes, suddenly looking evil*): Mail order from Thailand. Little brats. Wish I could send them back like I'd send back this hideous M&S blouse, if only I hadn't spilled tiramisu down it.

Ceri says, 'Just because you have them close together doesn't mean they'll be friends. Look at my step-kids. Two years apart, fight all the time.'

'So do Huw's boys,' I say gratefully. Now, finally, he looks at me, and raises his glass in a sardonic toast. I toast him back with Jenny's wine glass and take a long, deep, lovely drink before she says, 'Erm, I think that's mine.'

'Yes, we've had a minor fertility problem,' I say. 'Couple of miscarriages, nothing unusual.'

'Did anyone say they wanted coffee?' says Paul, louder than before.

'Well, darling,' says Huw, and I think, no, don't say it, don't tell them there were five miscarriages, don't tell them we'd agreed not to try again, don't tell them I changed my mind without consulting you. If you say any of that in front of these horrible people, I will walk out of here and I will walk out on you and never come back.

'Well, darling,' he says, 'at the very least, it was a happy accident, wasn't it?'

He smiles, and Paul relaxes, and Ceri asks if they have decaf, and I unclench my arse because now I don't have to cause a scene. The rest of the evening passes off boringly with a long anecdote from Rees about the personnel department at Welsh Water, during which he twice flicks out his tongue at me in a manner which some fool – not Ceri, I hope – has told him is sexy.

I drive us home. We're both under-fed, and Huw's over-wined.

'Well,' he says, 'that was a predictably shitty evening.'

'Yes, it was.' I'm glad we can agree on something.

'I hate those people. Let's never do this again.'

'We're sort of committed to this monthly dinner thing. And Ceri likes us there for moral support. Jenny-and-Paul's loved-up scene intimidates her.'

'Well, now she's got the fascinating Rees.'

'She won't be able to stand him for long.'

'No, boyo, then it'll be a sad day down the Llandudno Junction branch of Welsh Water, yeah?' Huw takes off Rees's voice perfectly.

The house is quiet. Evie's asleep and Paige is still in front of the telly. She looks as if she hasn't moved at all, but the chocolate digestives have disappeared from the plate in the kitchen. I pay her and she gets up slowly.

'Come on, Paige,' says Huw, 'I'll drop you off.'

'I'll take her; you're way over the limit.'

'Worried I'll embarrass her outside the Halls of Residence?'

'Huw, you're only embarrassing yourself. Why don't you get some coffee? I'm terribly sorry, Paige, he's had too much to drink.'

Paige, wakened briefly by this outburst, clambers into the car and gazes at me with spaced-out eyes. 'Dr Ellis isn't normally like that in lectures.'

'Yes, well I should hope not. He doesn't drink at work. I don't think.'

'Do you know if you're having a boy or girl?'

'Not yet. Evie wants me to have a girl.'

Big lie. Evie doesn't want me to have anything. I lapse into silence, thinking how separate Huw, Evie and I are right now. We were such a strong unit when Evie was little.

As she levers herself out of the car, Dopey Paige says, 'Oh, there was a phone call for you. Your mother, I think. She said can you call back no matter how late?' She wanders off in her vague student way. I go through my bag for the mobile phone before remembering I ran out of credit yesterday.

Back home, Huw's sprawled on the sofa watching telly, a glass in his hand.

'Oh, good idea, more alcohol.'

'Piss off.'

I ring Mama, but when she picks up the phone I can't hear her. I say, 'Hello, hello?' like an old-fashioned telephonist until finally I realise she's crying.

'Can't hear you properly, Mama. Shit! I'll come down straight away. Tomorrow. Try to get some sleep. No, well some rest, then.'

I hang up, and Huw looks at me questioningly.

'Michael's been rushed to hospital. Heart attack.'

'God, I'm sorry, *cariad.*'

My make-up has been gently melting all evening, and in the living-room mirror I look like a worried clown. Huw puts his arms round me. I move my head so I can't smell the alcohol on his breath. I used to find this smell a turn-on but now it just makes me nauseous. The pregnancy-enhanced sense of smell, I suppose.

'Poor Olivia, how is she? She must be in a right state.'

'I could barely make out a word. Poor Michael, too. He's not all that old. Sixty-five. God, though. Mama will completely fall apart if he, you know.'

'I'm sure it won't come to that.' He strokes my back and says, 'Would you mind terribly if I didn't come with you tomorrow?'

I walk to the mirror, start rubbing at the mascara under my eyes. 'Luckily, half-term starts on Monday, so I can get Evie out of your hair, too.'

'Oh, Laura, that isn't what I meant.' He tries to touch me, but I sidestep away. 'Of course, I'll come if you really want, like a shot, just say the word. But I'll be in the way. Your mum needs you. You can focus on her and your stepdad.'

It's just another little let-down from Huw. I'm getting used to them. My mind races through lists of what I need to organise. It helps to make lists. It's better than thinking about Michael, frail in hospital, Mama distraught at his side.

'I'm just saying it would be handy if I didn't have to cancel that devolution group meeting thing on Tuesday.'

'Can't have you missing a meeting. Must get our priorities right.'

'It's not a meeting, it's *the* meeting, the one I've been working towards for months.'

Is he still talking?

'I already said, you don't have to come.' I'm working out what clothes Evie will need, and whether we can share a holdall, when I think of something else, something bigger, and sit down abruptly on the floor with an 'Oh!'

Huw kneels next to me. 'What is it, *cariad*?'

I go dizzy for a moment; the room tilts and bleaches out. I bend my head forward. Huw puts his arm round me, saying, 'Hey, hey, hey,' in a soft voice. It takes me a minute to recover, then I sit up slowly and look into his worried face.

'I was just thinking,' I say, 'that if Michael's really bad, they'll send for...'

I haven't said their names for a very long time, and can't seem to bring myself to say them now.

Miffy

1979

Flowers All the Way

Laura and I planned our wedding flowers this evening. Laura's having pink roses and yellow mimosa. I'm going to have red carnations. And flowers all the way after I get married, too. I asked Laura what happens after a wedding, and she said you went on honeymoon and had non-stop sex, but I think she was teasing.

My perfect husband would be tall and handsome, like Bob Geldof but with neater shirts. Kind, witty and clever. Gentle and romantic. He'd bring me flowers every day.

Laura said I am naïve. Well, of course I am, next to her. She's nearly two years older than me. She'll be fourteen in March.

Dad did bring Mum yellow chrysanths once, after the four-broken-plates row.

My perfect husband would be Jewish, obviously. And not shouty. In fact, as long as he isn't shouty, he can be short and fat and bald.

Maybe not fat.

After Laura went home, I took Danners a cup of tea. I'm trying to be nice to him because of his friend Towse at the youth club. I don't think that's his real name, but they all say, 'Hey, Towse!' He is incredibly gorgeous, but I don't think sixteen-year-olds go out with people who are twelve. Though last summer Laura got off with a seventeen-year-old man when she was on holiday at Pontins. I'd like to go there this year instead of Brittany again, but Mum said Pontins is full of people called Shirley and Dave wearing sombreros and drinking Babycham. How can she know that, if she's never been? Anyway, Laura and her mum go to Pontins, and as I pointed out, they're not called Shirley and Dave. Mum's just being prejudiced.

Laura

Grim journey. Icy roads, heater on noisy full blast, Evie in a foul mood, me needing to stop to pee every hour. I'm exhausted by the time we pull on to the final stretch of the A47. It's already dark. Seven hours door to door. It never gets any shorter.

As we approach Great Yarmouth, I ask Evie to find my compilation tape. She rummages sulkily through the glove compartment; she knows this is a non-negotiable ritual. It began in the Eighties, long before she was born, when I went to university in Wales. Whenever I came here to see Mama in the holidays, trundling along in

21

my knackered Renault 5, I'd play this same tape: 'Laura's Blues'. Old songs I'd recorded on my Amstrad Hi-Fi when I was fourteen or fifteen. The tape's come with me through every change of car. Evie slips it into the cassette player now, and I smile at the familiar crackles, the sound of the needle being plonked scratchily onto the LP. Christ, I'm a hundred years old. Ooh, I do miss my gramophone and His Master's Voice.

The first song – 'Substitute' by the long-forgotten Clout – blasts into the car, and as always, an image of Miffy singing this in my bedroom flashes into my mind. She's laughing, hairbrush for a microphone, swinging her head from side to side, hamming it up. I sing along with the ghostly Miffy, and feel a little better. When the tape moves on to 'California Girls', Evie, who's been brought up on The Beach Boys, joins in too. I hope this means she's forgiven me for dragging her away from her friends at half-term. It's not as if I like it here either. Great Yarmouth's never been a happy place for me. It doesn't help that it's very off-season, just as it was when I came here for the first time, that rainy September so long ago.

Mama's road is deserted apart from two teenagers sitting on the swings in the muddy playground opposite her cottage. Mama runs outside as we pull up, her face pale and tear-stained. I quickly ask if there's any news, and she shakes her head. Her hair, usually neat in a ballet-dancer's bun, straggles round her face. She pulls Evie into a hug and they stand locked together like statues in front of the doorway, leaving me to squeeze round them with the bags.

While I make Evie and myself a quick tea of beans on toast, Mama fusses round the kitchen, picking things up, putting them down, monologuing about Michael. 'I went twice today, *bebita*; he is very miserable. Evening visiting has already finished, you were so late, but you can go tomorrow morning, they will operate in the afternoon, it is very quick, isn't it? The doctor told me he is no longer critical, but the nurse said he is very poorly, I don't know what to think.'

Once Mama finally stops talking, we lapse into an uneasy silence. It's weird Michael not being here. He's usually the one who keeps the chat light. Then Evie steps into the gap, telling Mama about the TV likes and dislikes of every girl in her class. It seems like light relief for once.

Later I take our bags up to my old bedroom. My posters still cover the walls. The Beach Boys, of course, and a few Eighties bands I can barely remember. The hours I spent in this room! It was my haven, my retreat, when we moved here. Starting a new school in a new town at fourteen – you tell me why I expected to fit in. I had a London accent and was pretty. I was totally asking for it.

I sit at the dressing table in front of my old three-way mirror, and look at my mobile, which has been oddly quiet throughout the journey. I discover this is because it's on vibrate and I've missed several calls from Huw. His voicemail messages increase exponentially in irritability, asking firstly where the pasta is, then where the pasta sauce is, then why the bloody cheese grater isn't in the cheese grater cupboard. I didn't even know we had a cheese grater cupboard. I dial our number and settle back for a nice relaxing row.

You might think I let Huw get away with a lot: being irrationally angry about trivia while I'm dealing with a family crisis; snogging other women; not being able to make pasta without supervision. And you might be right. Because on one level – not that I'd ever tell him – I suppose he's entitled to be pissed off with me. I do feel bad about it. I'm not really the sort of woman who'd get pregnant without discussing it with her husband. But if I'd waited for him to be on board, we'd never have done it.

These are some of the things Huw has said about the baby these last weeks...

I thought we'd agreed to stop trying.

Okay: after all the miscarriages, *Huw* said we should stop trying. *I* never said it. He said it puts too much stress on me and on my body. He's even said he's too old for a baby, which for him is a pretty big deal. He still thinks he's twenty-five.

I thought we'd agreed that one child was enough.

I know Huw would never consider couples counselling, but if we *were* to go to Relate, I'd say: 'No, Mr Counsellor, we never agreed this.' While Evie is Huw's third child, she's only my first, and I always wanted more. I don't want her to be an only child, like me. So much responsibility when you're the only one. So much shit to carry.

Everyone agrees that a twelve-year gap between children is ridiculous.

Only Evil Jenny at that stupid dinner party has ever said this. '*You* don't think so, do you, Mr Counsellor?' Thought not.

It was a unilateral decision on your part to keep the baby.

I admit it. Guilty. (Though is it so very wrong? Let the counsellor be the judge.) I kept my pregnancy completely to myself for more than three months, while I waited to see if this one would stick around. By the time I told Huw, I already knew I was keeping it. His fault, really, for not noticing I'd become a bit of a chubster.

The baby's not usually the official reason we argue, though it lies shipwrecked at the bottom of all our rows. Today Huw wants to complain about me hiding food and utensils. Usually when I go away I leave carefully labelled meals in the freezer. Ceri says that's pathetic, that I've coddled him, encouraged him to act like a dusty old History don instead of a proper twenty-first-century 'partner'. Thing is, he's got no aptitude for cooking at all. He's even intimidated by the microwave. I've always done the cooking, and he's always done the earning; that's just how it is. It was the same when he was married to Carmen, though from what I've gleaned from Glynn and Burl, her idea of cuisine centres entirely round the chickpea. I know: fucking Burl. I'm used to it now, but when I first heard the name I nearly died laughing. Carmen had total freedom to choose whatever she liked by that point, of course. I've always assumed she got Burl Ives confused with Burt Reynolds.

I remind Huw how to work the microwave. I describe the meals in the freezer and the whereabouts of the grater. Gradually he calms down, and even remembers to ask after Michael. I smooth it over, like I always do. I want things to be all right between us. I want him to come round to the idea of the baby. While we talk, I angle the three-way mirror to see what I look like when I'm looking away. I spent hours in front of this in my teens, trying to imagine what certain boys would think of my profile. Whichever way I face now, I am old and tired. Even my elbows look ancient.

After we've hung up, I rummage in the dressing-table drawer and pull out a cracked plastic ice-cream tub full of old eyeliners and lipsticks. I open a sticky purple mascara tube. The brush is brittle, would have dried up a couple of decades ago, but I can see the colour and a brief admiration flares up for the girl I once was, who had a phase of pink mascara for everyday use. I go to push the tub back but there's something in the way, scrunched at the back of the drawer. A crumpled Valentine's card, yellow and faded, featuring two purple elephants, trunks entwined, framed in a heart. As I open the card and see the message scrawled inside – 'You didn't dance with your true admirer' – a folded piece of paper falls out. Paper torn from a school exercise book. Soon as I see it, I know what it is, and I put it back inside the card without unfolding it.

I lie on the narrow bed, breathing in the familiar scent of Mama's sheets. They smell exactly the same as they did in Edgware; the move to Great Yarmouth and the passing of the years have made no difference. I think about sheets, because there are too many other things I don't want to think about.

Two children crouch together in the mud, heads so close they are almost touching. They are digging with trowels. Huge white sheets billow on a line above them, thrown almost horizontal by the force of the hot wind. The sheets move in front of the children, hiding them. When they next flap away, the children are standing. Two girls. They squint into the sun. One says clearly, 'I don't want this any more.'

Next thing I know, Evie's crouching by my head, telling me to stop snoring. Mama stands smiling in the doorway. 'You were lying on your back because of the *bebé*, growling like a lawnmower.'

I struggle to a sitting position and lick my dry lips.

27

I haven't even taken off my shoes, and I notice Mama frown. She's always such a stickler about things like shoes on beds, folded towels, dusted shelves. She used to change the sheets three times a week. Perhaps she still does. I'd never dare tell her I leave mine a fortnight, sometimes more. When Mama pads off to the bathroom, Evie flops down next to me on the bed, her body touching mine. An unexpected honour. She points to one of the teenage posters of a mullet-haired band and says, 'Who's that?'

I dredge up the name from a dusty file in my brain. 'Tears for Fears.'

'They look rubbish,' Evie says, but not antagonistically, so I reply, 'They were, they were crap really,' and she giggles.

'When did you get The Beach Boys' autographs, then?' she asks.

'I didn't,' I start to say, then realise there's some faint writing on The Beach Boys' poster. I get up for a closer look. The writing is in felt-tip and says, 'I love you with all my heart, Laura, please marry me, Brian xxx.' I smile as I remember Miffy autographing my posters one lazy Sunday in Edgware. So many Sunday afternoons lying on the floor on our tummies, filling in quizzes and discussing which pop stars we would marry.

Mama comes back to report that Michael is asleep and 'comfortable'. She says goodnight and I hear her close her door.

'Will Granddad die?' Evie asks.

'Heavens, I hope not. The doctors are going to try and make him better.'

Evie looks at me sceptically. More robustly I say, 'It's quite a routine op.'

Not looking at me, she says, 'And are you and Daddy getting divorced?'

The word 'divorced' hangs in the air like the echo after a shout.

'What on earth makes you think that, darling?' I try to cuddle her but she hops off the bed and starts picking at the curling edge of Tears for Fears, prising off the ancient Blu-tack, which comes away with a hard coating of paint and plaster. Into the poster, she mumbles, 'Shouting.'

The walls of old Gwynedd cottages are three-feet thick, but Huw has a magnificent pair of lungs. Arguing with him is like being on the sharp end of a Welsh male voice choir. I wonder how much Evie has heard. I put my arms round her as she fidgets with the Blu-tack. She doesn't move into my embrace, stiff proud little girl. I tell her everything is fine, that Mum and Dad sometimes argue, but they love each other and Evie very much. That we are all going to love the new baby very much. I suspect my explanation is as pitiful as my 'doctors will make Granddad all better' gambit, but I don't know what else to say.

She is silent, so I ask, 'Do you feel any better now?'

'Yes, thank you.'

I kiss her on the cheek, and smile as she wipes it off with her sleeve, just as I used to when kissed as a child. As I go downstairs for a glass of water, the phone rings. I snatch it up in case it disturbs Mama. I'm assuming it'll be Huw claiming I've deliberately hidden the spatula, but it is another male voice.

'Is that Laura?'

He sounds exactly the same.

'This is Danny.'

I know.

'Sorry to call so late; I had to wait till *Shabbos* was out. How's Dad doing?'

Oh. My. God.

'Should be with you fairly early tomorrow; we're leaving first thing.'

What do you look like now? How have you changed?

'It will be good to see you – how long has it been?'

You know how long it's been, Danny.

'Has your mum managed to get hold of Lissa? I mean Miffy?'

I haven't heard her nickname said out loud for years. The baby whirls around and I lean against the wall, clutching the receiver to my ear.

Miffy

1979

Bedspread

It was a terrible mess, and it was all Laura's fault.

She'd just taken a massive swig of Coca-Cola when I told her about my cousin's wedding music, and out it came, out of her mouth, a great frothy brown spray, splashing everywhere, all over her face, her hair and her school shirt. And a great spreading sticky stain, right in the middle of my cream bedspread.

She practically wet herself, she was laughing so much. I was too worried about Mum killing me to join in. I only managed a fake 'Ha! Ha! Ha!' Laura wriggled off the damp patch and sat on my pillows, away from the mess, school skirt bunched up to her knickers. Even with tears and Coke down her face, Laura was still beautiful. Her black hair was so long and silky. Her legs went on for ever. Her thigh on its own was nearly the same length as my whole leg.

'Of all the music in the whole wide universe, all the brilliant songs, they decided on *that*,' she said. 'You're standing in your white dress and your whole family's there and everyone's looking and then...' And she sang the chorus of 'If You Leave Me Now' in a sarcastic voice, using my hairbrush for a microphone. Then she got hysterics again.

No way was I going to tell her that I'd cried at the wedding when the music started and Cousin Alisa appeared. She was so pretty in her veil, hair piled up inside a sparkly silver crown, wearing one of those gravity dresses with no straps. They stood under a lacy canopy and Simon tried to smash a glass with his shoe. It took him five goes and he was bright red in the face by the time it broke. Everyone yelled, '*Mazel tov!*' with relief. Uncle Kenny said loudly, 'That's the last time he'll get to put his foot down.'

It was much more romantic than Auntie Leila's wedding three years ago, when I was nine. That was in a register office and was all over in five minutes. Mum was upset

Auntie Leila didn't get married in synagogue, wasn't even in white: she wore a flowery purple maxi-dress with matching headscarf. Mum said her sister always did have to be different. Actually, Auntie Leila got divorced from Uncle Ray last year, so it was a very quick marriage and they were probably glad they didn't have a big do after all.

Laura and I have talked a lot about whether we'll wear white or ivory, how she'll thread jasmine through her black hair, how I'll have one of those pretty blue garter belts. Laura's going to wear false eyelashes and a stick-on beauty spot. I'll hopefully have contact lenses by then. And Laura will have a Beach Boys song for her music, of course, as it's her best band. I'm still not sure what music to choose, as my favourite group is The Boomtown Rats, and none of their songs seem very suitable.

We've planned all the details of our weddings, but we never talk about the months and years that come after. When I get married – which won't be for ages, not till I'm quite old, maybe twenty-three – when I get married, it's going to be flowers all the way. Romance and presents and cuddles and laughing. For always.

I knew Mum was going to give me hell about Laura's spilled Coke. It was bad enough last week when Danners splashed kosher wine on the tablecloth.

Laura was still giggling. She sat at my dressing table and tried on her new lipstick, which was called Electric

Plum. I got some cleaning stuff from the bathroom but it didn't help: the patch was lighter but still sticky and twice the size. In the end I turned the bedspread over and prayed Mum wouldn't notice.

Laura said, 'Just tell her your period started,' but the stain didn't look anything like blood.

Then we heard Laura's mum, Mrs Morente, arrive to collect her, and we ran out onto the landing. She was down in the hall talking to Dad. They didn't see us. Mrs Morente was wearing a flowery orange dress with thin straps, even though it was freezing outside! One strap was off her shoulder, a little way down her arm. Dad was laughing, in a different way from normal, and they didn't hear us come down the stairs.

Laura

I am prepared for a stranger, a bearded Orthodox Jew in long black coat and furry hat, the sort I saw so often, back when we lived in Edgware. But when Danny steps through Mama's front door, a suitcase in each hand, he looks uncannily like the boy I loved nearly twenty-five years ago. He's tall and skinny, just as I remember; clean-shaven, wearing ordinary clothes.

But from my hiding place at the top of the stairs, I see a reminder that he is definitely not the same: a red and gold embroidered skullcap nestling in his hair.

I haven't seen him since I was fourteen, but there are

plenty of photos around. Michael keeps Danny's wedding picture in pride of place on top of the telly. Mama and I weren't invited to the wedding, of course, and Danny asked Michael not to come either. He reckoned Andrea Cline, poor wounded soul, wouldn't be able to cope. The photo shows Danny aged twenty-one, handsome in a dark suit, in contrast to his incredibly plain bride, who's wearing a high-necked, whiter-than-white cover-it-all-up dress and stunned smile. Yeah, Hella, we couldn't believe it, either. Mama and Michael were shocked at how religious Hella was, but I was taken aback by the way she looked. Now, finally, here she is, in the flesh. And what a lot of flesh. Short and square in a floor-length black tent, she's more hobbit than woman. It's clear that, if anything, the wedding photo is flattering, poor cow. She's holding a baby, and is surrounded by numerous Hella-lookalike kids from toddler to teen, filling every inch of Mama's hall. Michael seems to get a 'new baby' card from Danny every other year.

Something about Hella makes me want to laugh, and though I try to stifle it, a tiny squeak comes out. Danny looks up, and several things happen at once. First, I see that he is still gorgeous. Second, I have a brief flashback to our last awful meeting. And third, a crazy voice in my head says, *You still love him. You've always loved him.*

'Laura!'

I put my hand on the banister for support. It's probably just the pregnancy hormones, but the sight of him makes me feel quite off-balance. 'Hello, Danny.'

'Oh, helloooo,' Hella moos up at me, and I instantly re-name her 'Heifer'.

I walk down carefully, trilling, 'So nice to see you,' more high-pitched than I'd intended. Danny goes into the kitchen with Mama, asking her about Michael, so my welcoming party consists of Heifer and her thousand children. She kisses me on my cheek, then holds me at arm's length, looks me up and down and says gruffly, 'You're looking blooming!'

'Blooming huge, anyway,' I respond, and she laughs uproariously as though I was the star turn at the Catskills. I'm unable to think of a plausible compliment for her, so turn my attention to the baby, a plucked chicken. 'Oh, isn't he cute!'

Heifer's genes must be incredibly strong to so consistently over-ride Danny's in the production of these hideous children. Our baby – Danny's and mine – would have been far more beautiful than these weird creatures. They're spookily obedient, but it still takes quite a while, under Heifer's insistent guidance, for each of them to say hello and tell me their self-consciously biblical names: Chanah, Micah, Atalia, Asher and Ravid, plus baby Ishmael. Almost makes me appreciate the secularity of dear old Burl.

By the time I get to the kitchen, Danny's already chatting with Evie about computer games as if they've known each other all their lives. He throws me a heart-stopping smile. Jesus! Despite the *cuple* on his head and the laughter lines round his eyes, I see so clearly the boy he once was that I feel breathless. I hope and pray he can see the girl I used to be, because she was quite something, and he was once very keen on her indeed. I move towards him, expecting a hug, a kiss maybe, but he somehow makes it very clear, without really doing anything, that we are not going to be embracing. I know his religion prohibits him touching random women, but I'm family, aren't I? I sit down, feeling extremely conscious of my body: my stomach pressing against my clothes; my hair on my shoulders; the weight of my wedding ring.

Heifer plonks herself down next to me, and says, 'Dan-Dan, have you got the wipes? Ishmael's done a little sickie down my front.'

Poor old Dan-Dan. I'd love to know what he's told Heifer about me. I imagine how their conversation might have gone, if they'd had to face each other on one of those confrontational daytime TV shows Ceri's always watching in the back room at the shop.

Aggressively Moral Host: So, Hella, when did you first become aware that your husband had had sexual

relations with the girl who later became his stepsister?
When she was underage, might I add?
(*Audience boos*)
Heifer (*red-eyed; no make-up*): I only found out last
week. And we've been married for seventeen years! He
said – this is horrible – 'Since Laura, I have never prop-
erly loved, have never had such excellent sex.'
AMH: You bastard, Daniel.
Danny: I'm so sorry.
AMH: How did hearing this make you feel, Hella?
Heifer (*stands, throws chair*): I want a divorce.

Mama puts biscuits on the table, and as I bite into one I
realise our guests must have brought them.

'Kosher.' Heifer grins at me, and I have to eat the whole
tasteless thing.

Mama takes the plucked-chicken baby from Heifer,
cuddles it affectionately and says, 'I hope Laura's baby
will be as sweet as little Ishy-wishy.' My mother, the short-
sighted traitor.

'Well, Dan-Dan and I do have gorgeous kiddies, don't
we, darling?' Heifer smirks, totally deluded. 'Are you
looking forward to having a sister or brother, Evie?'

Evie nods.

I say, 'She's putting on a brave face. She loves being our
only princess.'

Evie says, 'I don't love it, actually.'

The grown-ups all laugh a little uncomfortably, and flail around for a subject change. I ask Danny about his work, Danny asks Mama about visiting hours, and Heifer asks me where my husband is. Evie wanders off to see what the other, bizarrely quiet, children are doing. Praying, probably. I offer to go and see Michael, hoping Danny will suggest accompanying me, but he doesn't. Mama says she'll join me once she and Hella have sorted out the sleeping arrangements. Even the words 'sleeping arrangements' give me a frisson when I glance at Danny. Must get a grip!

Michael's in the James Paget, which Mama and I still refer to as the new hospital, even though it's been here more than twenty years. It was still being built when we first moved here, so I had my termination in the old-fashioned Victorian hospital on the other side of town. The JP, by contrast, is all white paint and chrome, and the nurses look like Gap models in their little shirts and chinos.

Michael's in a side ward of eight beds. He waves when I come in, a Thunderbirds puppet with tubes sprouting from both arms. He's pleased to see me, though I expect he'd look this thrilled to see anyone. I kiss his papery cheek and he puts his hand on mine and squeezes it. Leaves it there longer than I expect.

'How you feeling, Michael?'

'Bit beaten about. Bit bruised.'

I sit on a metal chair. The woman in the bed opposite is chatting to a nurse at top volume: 'Maybe it will be warmer tomorrow, Nurse. You could go to the beach!' Once the nurse has moved up the ward the woman mutters, 'Don't know why they're so cheerful. They should try being stuck in here for six weeks,' and clamps huge headphones over her ears.

'Talking of bruises,' Michael says, 'what's this?' He reaches up and very gently touches the mark on my forehead. Typical Michael – he notices everything. Mama didn't mention it, but to be fair, she is in a bit of a state.

'Oh, it's nothing. Looks worse than it is. Just slipped over.'

'Are you looking after yourself? Huw taking care of you?'

He looks at me intently, but I'm saved from having to answer by the arrival of a young black nurse – Amanda, according to her name-badge – who scolds Michael for yanking his drip about. She uses his first name, which he flirtingly grumbles about. She deftly reconnects the drip and winks at me. 'He's a stroppy bugger, ain't he?'

Michael's a charming man; he's probably already becoming a hospital character. When the nurse has gone he says, 'They're all *schwartzas*, you know. Barely speak English, some of them.' Under the grumpy face he looks exhausted and frail. It's no small deal, is it, waiting for a triple-bypass, a 'nil by mouth' sign above your head?

I give him some letters Mama asked me to bring, and

he flicks swiftly through them, scanning the handwriting. Whatever he's looking for isn't there, and he drops the envelopes onto the bed without opening them.

'Danny and Hella arrived this morning, Michael, with a ridiculously large number of children.'

He laughs. 'Danny's brood! Go forth and multiply. Took it literally. Did you see Micah? Going to be bar-mitzvahed soon. Can't believe it.'

'Yes.' I sort of saw him, anyway; one of the black-clad mass. 'And they've got yet another new baby – don't suppose you've seen him yet?'

'Ishmael? Yes, met him when they were here. Few weeks ago.'

How cosy.

'So. Was it all right, Laura? Seeing Danny again?'

'It was fine. He seems very settled.'

'So do you,' Michael says, moving his hand back onto mine. In an abrupt change of tone, he says, 'Want to thank you. For being such a good girl.'

Oh, shit. Is he revving up for a sentimental monologue about Life? I say briskly, 'Well, I haven't always been such a good girl.'

He nods. 'Yes, you did have wild times. Before we moved here.'

I take a surprised breath. We've never talked about that time... never.

'And I know,' he says, looking down at the bed, 'you were very angry with Olivia and me, for a while. For uprooting you. We should have taken your feelings more into account, Laura. Yours, Danny's and Lissa's. I'm really, truly, sorry.'

Why is he saying all this now, after all this time? And anyway, shouldn't it be coming from Mama? Not that she ever would. She doesn't really do sorrys.

I say hurriedly, 'You know, don't feel you have to talk, if it's a strain. I don't mind just sitting with you quietly.'

He ignores me. 'Another little one on the way. Hope I live to see it.'

'Of course you will! It'll be here in four months.'

'Tell you one baby I'll never see, though,' he says, and then, thank God, another nurse ('Patty') comes to take his pulse. She ought to take mine; it's jumping about all over the place. Which baby does he mean? The one I aborted? One of my miscarriages? Or the one Miffy has never had?

Nurse Patty gives Michael some tablets. 'Here we go, Michael. Swallow them down for me, chicken!'

'It's Mr Cline, Nurse. We don't know each other well enough for first names and endearments.'

She pops a pill into his mouth and flutters a hand at me in amusement. 'Oh, Mr Cline, you must drive your poor daughter mad.'

Michael says quietly, 'I drive both my daughters mad.'

When she leaves, he closes his eyes. In less than a minute his breathing is steady. Exhausted, no doubt, by his unprecedented outpouring. I watch him as he sleeps. Only his blue-veined hands, lying limp on the bedcovers, their skin puckered and stained, make him seem old. His hair is thick. He's still recognisable as the handsome man Mama fell in love with. Danny will probably look like him one day.

The machines he's hooked up to thrum and buzz. A few beds down, something beeps every couple of seconds. Nurses at the top of the ward are laughing. I haven't noticed the continual low noise till now, but once I have, it's hard to block it out.

God, what will Mama do if he dies? She's always been so sensitive, so vulnerable. The exact opposite of the feminist maxim, 'A woman needs a man like a fish needs a bicycle.' She needs a man like a fish needs water. As an adult looking back, I'm impressed she threw my father out. Even though he hit her, that still took guts. Mind you, my father hadn't been gone long before she brought home the first of my 'uncles'. Steven, was it? Or Keith? They all blend together in my mind. I remember Anthony, though – another one like my father: quick off the mark with his fists. She was seeing Anthony when she fell in love with Michael.

One time when Miffy came over to play, I overheard

Michael say to Mama, 'You need someone to protect you.' And to his credit, he did.

A nurse smiles at me as she walks past, and I see what she sees: the dutiful daughter. I imagine I'm in a TV documentary about visiting relatives in hospital.

Laura (*voice-over, as on-screen Laura smoothes Michael's sheets and wipes away a tear*): My life feels very complicated right now.

CUT TO: **Huw** at work, with his arms round that tart from New Year's Eve.

Huw: My wife's insisting on having another baby.

CUT TO: **Danny**, staring at **Heifer**.

Danny (*voice-over*): I'm glad we have all these children; they mean I never have to talk to you. Laura is even more attractive than I remember. Oh, God, help me. Thou Shalt Not Commit Adultery, but…

I nearly jump out of my skin as the real-life Danny appears at the other side of the bed and says, 'Oh, he's asleep.'

Mama sits next to me. She's wearing her grey fur coat, which always makes her look incredibly dramatic and glamorous.

Michael opens his eyes and smiles at me and Mama. Then he sees Danny.

'You're here!'

'Hello, Dad. How you feeling?'

'Can't complain. Bit thirsty.' He turns to Mama and says, 'Sweetheart, could I have five minutes with Danny?'

Mama raises her eyebrows. 'Alone, do you mean? But I only just got here.'

I stand up. 'Come on, Mama, let's get coffee.'

'Five minutes, Michael, okay, but I want to spend time with you before they take you to *theatre*.'

The way she emphasises 'theatre' makes it seem exciting and life-threatening. Which it is, I suppose. Mama and I go to the canteen and sip horrible coffee. She is furious with me.

'You interfere too much, Laura.'

'Sorry, Mama. How's Evie? Is she okay with those children and, er, Hella?' Nearly called her Heifer out loud.

'Evie is fine, Laura. She likes being around other young people. Only children do. You did. Hella is *excelente* with them, of course. She is very experienced.'

'What are they doing?'

'*Dios mío*, Laura! My husband is in hospital, about to have his heart chopped up, and you are asking me non-stop questions. Do you want to know how I feel? I feel that Michael will not make it through the operation.'

'Of course he will!'

'He won't make it, and I will be left *sólo*. I will not cope.'

Tears pour down her face, though her mascara stays put. Cleverly, she has used waterproof.

'You won't be alone, Mama. *I'm* here.'

'I cannot drink this, it's disgusting.' She stands up, leaving me to throw the cups away and hurry after her. When we get back to the ward, there are nurses round the bed and Danny is sitting to one side.

'I am his wife!' cries Mama, rushing forward.

'We're just doing his pre-meds, Mrs Cline,' a nurse says, 'ready for surgery.'

Mama leans over Michael, hugging him and crying onto his head. Danny and I both turn away from the scene, and in so doing, look at each other instead.

17 FEBRUARY 2003

The baby rolls over and over, waking me up. It makes me want to laugh out loud; there have been plenty of times when that movement's never come. Plenty of times when the midwife's put the ultrasound on my belly – smile smile chat chat – then it all goes quiet and she can't look me in the eye. I stroke my tummy and talk to my wriggling baby, quietly, so I don't disturb Evie, who's sleeping on a camp bed at the foot of my bed.

'You're excited today, baby. So am I. It's exciting being so near Danny, isn't it?'

The baby thrashes about, and I realise I need the loo. Right now. I creep into the bathroom. It's five and still dark outside. As I wash my hands I notice the huge jumble of children's toothbrushes at the side of the sink. How come Hella gets all the child-producing luck? How amazing to need so many brushes, so many pyjamas, so many combs. Next to the pile lie two unfamiliar adult toothbrushes: one green, one pink. I take the green one and gently rub my fingers over the bristles. Damp. I use it to brush my teeth, working Danny's saliva around my mouth. I'm about to go back to my room when I realise the significance of the brush being damp. I tiptoe downstairs and, yes! He *is* up, and alone in the living room. Well, not quite alone – he's bottle-feeding the baby. But still, it's a God-given opportunity.

He looks up as I enter, closing the door behind me. Those eyes; that curved mouth. I blink away an image of two young eager bodies in a sunlit barn.

'You're up early.'

'I always get up with the babies so Hella can have more sleep.'

Oh you perfect man.

'What about you?' he asks.

'Babies as well. This one.' I put my hands on my stomach. So glad I brought my silk kimono. 'His acrobatics keep waking me.'

He laughs. 'They're such amazing little creatures, aren't they?' He rubs his eyes with the back of his hand. More tired than you're letting on, hey?

I sit next to him and coo over the chicken baby. 'Such a cutie!' Not.

'God willing, Dad had a good night. I'll try to contact Lissa again today.'

'Where is she, exactly?'

'Still in Africa, I think. Last time I spoke to her, a couple of weeks ago, she was in Sierra Leone. You know she took a year off to travel round the world?'

'Michael mentioned it. Kind of a belated gap year?'

Danny lets the baby fall asleep on his lap. 'She just wanted to get away for a while. Actually, the year's nearly up. She was planning to be back for Micah's barmitzvah in a couple of weeks.' He stretches to put the bottle on the coffee table without waking the baby. His arm brushes mine, making my heart leap about. I feel strange, not myself at all.

'So, what's Miffy like now?' I say. The nickname feels clumsy on my lips, an old toy I ought to have outgrown. 'Is she completely unchanged, like you?'

'Oh, I think I've changed a bit.' Then he gestures to the shelves. 'Well you've seen photos of her, of course?'

But, actually, there are no recent pictures of Miffy amongst Mama and Michael's old-people collection of family portraits, which covers every horizontal surface. Danny and Heifer's wedding photo on the telly, of course, and numerous photos of their interchangeably plain kids, poor buggers. Danny, scrumptious in his graduation robes. None of my graduation, obviously, as I never finished my degree, though there is a huge print of my wedding photo. Huw looks like Terence Stamp in it, staring into the camera with his blue eyes. I'm so young and pretty, gazing adoringly at him. I feel a pang for how much in love I look. Oh God, I'm going to start singing 'The Way We Were' if I don't get a grip. I resolve to make things better with Huw when I get home.

There are actually only four pictures of Miffy. A school portrait in her early teens, looking just how I remember her: chubby, great mass of hair frizzing out from her head, squinting through her glasses. The poor thing's not helped by our school uniform. It's a wonder any of us got boyfriends at all, wearing that hideous ensemble. There's a group shot of an older Miffy with college friends, but the sun's behind them and the young women are bleached out, their faces indistinct. I only know the central figure's Miffy because Mama told me. You can see her backlit mane of hair. Weirdly, she is the tallest of the group. I wonder if she's standing on something, because she was always a short-arse when I knew her. In her graduation photo – so smart, these Cline kids – her face is obscured because she's throwing her mortar board into the air, head flung back, one of those annoying action shots. And in her wedding photo she's kissing the handsome dark-haired groom, so you can only see a cheek, some eyelashes – no glasses – and a lot of white veil.

Danny stands next to me to look at this picture, the baby sparked out on his shoulder. I inch closer, so that if Danny turns to me my lips would almost brush his face. The instant I have this thought, he moves away and says, 'Well, these photos aren't very enlightening, are they? Let's see, what can I tell you about Lissa? You know she got divorced last year, of course.'

'Yes, Michael said.'

Mama told me Michael had sleepless nights worrying that Miffy's divorce was somehow to do with him having left Andrea Cline all those years ago. Like the two things were connected! I don't think Mama let him wallow in that notion for long.

'It was really sad it didn't work out,' Danny says. 'Her husband's a great guy. Lissa went abroad when they separated. I never thought she'd leave her job for so long.'

'She's a child psychologist?' I ask, though I know this from Michael's boasting.

'Yes. She's very good. I sent a friend of mine to see her. His son couldn't stop wetting the bed. Transformed the boy overnight. Fascinating, what she does.'

Heifer comes in, looking super-attractive with flattened hair and pillow scars pulling down her eyelids. 'Where's Ishy-wishy?' She waddles between us, taking the baby from Danny's arms. 'Who's so fascinating? Me, I hope!'

Heifer's definitely one of those women who say, 'Oh, I only take five minutes to get ready.'

Mama appears in the doorway, wondering if it's too soon to ring the hospital.

'They said after six, Olivia,' Heifer says, before I can even open my mouth.

'Shall I make us some coffee?' Danny asks.

We three women sit while he serves us. He knows where everything is, and I watch him as he moves gracefully around the kitchen. I look from him to Mama, red-eyed and silent, and wonder what they think of each other. Mama's never said much about her relationship with Danny and Miffy, even when I complained about my own step-kids. She did reveal a small chink a couple of years ago when she said they were all polite to one another 'now'.

Heifer's in the middle of a monologue about the scandalous price of kosher food – don't buy it then, bat-brain! – when the phone rings. Mama rushes into the hall to answer it. Some of the youngest Cline kids wander in, and Heifer shushes them; we all strain to hear what Mama's saying, but she hardly says anything. When she comes back her face is white. Michael's had a bad night and is 'rather poorly'.

Heifer pulls her into a hug. It's so fucking annoying how she always has to be at the centre of the action. Mama sobs into Heifer's ample bosom. 'This back and forth, he's okay, he's not okay. It's a damn *montaña rusa.*'

Danny looks at me, and I translate, 'Roller coaster.'

He drives Mama and me to the hospital. I sit in the back, force myself not to think about Michael. Focus instead on the shuttered houses we flash past. Focus on the way Danny's hair curls into his nape.

The hospital is a centre of activity, brightly lit against the still-dark morning sky. Trolleys are pushed noisily, crowds of people move purposefully about, others stand outside chattering on their phones. The curtains are round Michael's bed, which makes Mama gasp, but it's only because he's asleep. A nurse opens the curtains to let us in. Michael seems to have lost half his bodyweight overnight. He looks much older. We sit awkwardly, staring at him, not looking at each other, listening to his slow, rasping breath. Three nurses come in separately to check the machines. Each time Mama asks how he is and they all say, 'He's rather poorly.'

Danny says he'll fetch coffee, as we didn't get to drink ours at home. I offer to help, but when we get into the corridor he turns and says, 'Coffee was an excuse.' For one wild moment I think he's going to say, 'I can't stop myself any longer,' and kiss me passionately. But he actually says, 'I've got to try and get hold of Lissa.'

We go outside so he can use his phone. Who knew Orthodox Jews were allowed such tiny state-of-the-art mobiles? We sit on a bench, and while he taps away I watch my breath make foggy clouds into the sky. It's still not properly light.

'Sent it. Really hope she sees it soon.'

'Does she email from abroad?' I want to see grown-up Miffy's words. And I want to keep Danny out here with me.

He presses some buttons. 'This is her last one, from Liberia.'

Where the fuck is Liberia? I thought it was an Arab-y sort of place, but he said she was in Africa. Danny keeps hold of the phone so I have to lean in to him, and for a moment I can barely see whatever he is showing me.

Danners, never take flushing loos for granted. Miss you. Miss J too. You were right. But all things must pass. Including my time with these hole-in-the-ground bogs. Tomorrow, Sierra Leone. Love to you and H and kids. L x.

'What does she mean, you were right?'

'I told her she'd miss Jay when she was travelling.' He smiles. 'I'm always right. She knows that. I'm the sensible one.'

'That's so weird; I always remember her being sensible. You were wilder...'

He stands up. 'I'll ring Mum, see if she's heard anything.'

Andrea Cline still lives in the old family house with her new husband. Which means that Danny is ringing the same number I used all those years ago, the dozens of times I called Miffy.

'I know, Mum. I'm really sorry to keep on.'

It's clear from his end of the conversation that Andrea still hasn't forgiven her husband for having left her four million years ago. I can't hear her words, just a rhythmic babble.

'But I just want Lissa to have the chance to see him. He's not doing at all well.'

A great outburst of jabber jabber jabber follows, during which Danny stares at the sky, then gives me a thumbs up.

'Yes, please, that'd be great. Thanks, Mum.'

He clicks the phone shut. Sits next to me and blows out his cheeks. 'That's good news. I didn't realise she's got an emergency phone number for Lissa. Someone's relative on the Ivory Coast.'

'Well, her daughter's bloody father is dying! Isn't that an emergency?' I know I shouldn't swear in front of him, but honestly! That fucking woman!

He turns to look at me. 'Mum didn't realise how ill Dad is, Laura. Of course she'll leave a message. Though we don't know how long that will take to reach Lissa, either.'

'What about Miffy's home in London? Maybe someone's collecting her messages from there?'

'There isn't a home any more. It's been sold, and her stuff's in storage.'

Abroad and homeless! Miffy's elusiveness is infuriating – and intriguing. Who is this strange woman?

When Danny puts his phone into his jacket pocket, looking defeated, I can't stop myself. I hug him, press my face against his shoulder. He smells of a long time ago. 'Don't worry,' I whisper. 'We'll find her before anything happens.'

For one glorious moment Danny is in my arms. Then he pulls away, mumbling, 'Please, don't.'

'Oh, Danny.' I point to my belly. 'I haven't got my period or anything! I'm not unclean!'

'It's not that.' Danny stands up, face red. 'We'd better get back.'

The curtains round Michael's bed are pushed to the side, and two doctors are talking to Mama. They are all smiling, an unexpected sight. Michael is out of immediate danger. The hospital staff tell us there's no point staying. They encourage us to go home, get some rest and come back later when he's conscious. So we go. Mama chatters repetitively all the way back about the look on the doctors' faces when they realised Michael was responding to treatment. Meanwhile, I think about the look on a different face: Danny's when he pulled away from me saying, 'It's not that,' and what that means.

We send Mama to bed; she doesn't even put up a token protest. Heifer offers to make Danny and me some scrambled eggs. I open my mouth to refuse, but find I am starving and say yes, please, instead. While she cooks I check on Evie, who is still asleep in her usual position, arms flung high above her head. I smooth her hair from her forehead and quietly close the door.

In the kitchen Danny smiles at me. I wish he'd stop doing that. No, I don't. He waves his phone. 'An email from Lissa!'

I read it quickly.

Danners. Bad re. Dad. Sorry not with you. Somewhere near Bo. Coming back asap. Waited all day for internet. Send this now before lose connection. L x.

'Thank God she knows now, anyway,' I say.

Heifer serves us breakfast as though we are the couple and she our housekeeper. I like it. Danny eats with one hand, starts typing a reply. Upstairs, their baby wakes and cries. When Heifer lumbers out I say, 'Danny,' intending to see if I'm brave enough to say something about what happened outside the hospital. But when he looks up I lose my nerve as quick as Miffy's internet access, and say, 'Where is Bo?'

'Sierra Leone, of course.' He grins. 'Don't worry, I had to look it up.'

'Miffy's become very adventurous. The kid I knew would never bomb off round the world on her own.'

Danny nods. 'Well, she's changed a lot since then, I guess.'

'Have I?'

He pushes his plate away. 'I'm exhausted. Think I'll go back to bed for a bit.'

'Have I changed, Danny?'

'Laura. We're both tired.'

'I'm only asking. You haven't seen me for more than twenty years; of course I must have changed. You still look just like yourself. Still nice. What about me? Is it all for the worst, do you think? I know I look a bit older.'

He stands up, blocking the light. I can't see his face.

'You tell me,' he whispers. 'Have you changed?'

He closes the door quietly, and I hear him climbing the stairs.

After a minute to calm my breathing, I go up too, and crawl into bed. It's only seven o'clock. I want to get back to sleep, especially as the baby is calm, for once, but instead of my stomach it's my head that whirls about. All the things I should have said, whether he fancies me at all, whether I have a little hormonal crush or am full-blown in love. Have I lusted after him all this time without real-ising, or has it just been re-ignited now I've seen him again? Would I even have these feelings at all if things were better with Huw? I hear children's voices, and Heifer talking quietly to them. Do I hear Danny's murmured voice? I strain to listen but I'm not sure if it's a person or just the wind outside.

Now there is dappled sunshine, and two girls digging in mud. They flit around, sometimes disappearing momentarily. They resemble those little Victorian girls who photographed fairies. The mud they are digging in starts to make a noise, an insistent noise, and I am dragged out of the depths by the phone ringing, and by someone running downstairs to answer it.

My alarm clock says it is ten-forty, and I already know that Michael has died.

Miffy

Girl's World

Evenings like this, just Laura and me, are the best in the world. She called me Miffy the whole time, her nickname for me. Some people call me Missy, which I hate, and others call me Mel. Mum always calls me by my full name, Melissa. Daddy calls me Lissa. One time I asked Laura if I was like the real Miffy, the children's book rabbit. She said Miffy and I were both small and sweet. She did a drawing of me with rabbit's ears and a cute dress, which I stuck on my wall.

Laura had got one of those doll's heads Mum won't let me have that you can style its hair. And she had loads of make-up because her mum's friend Anthony East works for Max Factor. Laura showed me how to put on eyeshadow. When I tried putting it on at home it looked like I'd got the lurgy. I need it for the Valentine's disco at the youth club, which I am praying will be when I get off with Towse. Laura said I should wear strong make-up because of my glasses, and when I put them on you could see the colours really clearly.

When we went downstairs for Coke, Dad was still there, sitting at the kitchen table drinking whisky, which he doesn't do normally except when he is ill. Mum never drinks, except for one glass of wine at Passover, when she gets all giggly. Mrs Morente was wearing a dark-red flared-out skirt with tight pleats. Her black hair was piled up on top of her head with curls hanging down. She was drinking whisky too. Laura asked Dad if he liked my make-up. He said, 'Very nice.'

Mrs Morente told us to go and play. Then she said something to Laura in Spanish that I didn't understand. Laura looked at her feet and nodded.

'Aren't they good girls?' Mrs Morente said to Dad, and he said, 'They sure are.'

We went back upstairs and did a quiz in *Patches* about our ideal boy. Laura likes dangerous boys whereas I like romantic ones. It got pretty late so I had to tell Dad it was time to go.

Mum opened the door before Dad had got his key out. She stared at my face and said, 'Oh, are you planning to join the circus?'

I yelled at Mum that she was horrible, and ran upstairs. Then I realised I needed her cleansing cream. I listened at the top of the stairs to hear if she was in a better mood, but she was shouting at Dad, so I went into her bedside drawer in the dark. I could feel some papers, shoved in at the back. I found the cream, and some nice perfume. I'll put it back after I've had a try.

Leg

School today was crap: Maths, Geography, then Domestic Science with the Dreaded Miss Gibbs. Sasha said she would stick her head in the oven, but we pointed out it was electric. She has got very carried away with Sylvia Plath, who we are reading in English, but Sylvia had a gas oven, obviously. Colette Fitzgerald suggested Sasha try electrocuting herself, but I said as her cooking partner, it would be me who'd have to clear up the mess, so she just crushed an egg in her hand instead. It was the one funny moment in a draggy day. I kept drifting off while making my scotch egg, thinking about seeing Aron at *shul* on Saturday. He is so nice; his hair is really pure blond, almost white. It looks as soft as a baby's hair.

I think Mum knows I like him. Last week I was in the loo after the service and I heard her come in and say to someone, 'Isn't it interesting how many young women are coming to *shul* since the student rabbi joined us!' and they both laughed. I nearly died of embarrassment. I had to wait in the cubicle till they'd gone, and then Mum had a go at me for holding her up.

Batmitzvah class with Max after school this evening. Yuck. Max is so old he dribbles over the books. He sits right next to me, running his finger along the words. He sometimes puts his hand on my leg while I am chanting my Hebrew.

I read in a magazine about a man on a tube train who started touching a lady's bum. She turned right round and said, 'Would you mind not groping me?' Everyone in the carriage stared, and he got off the train, covered in shame. Every time Max touches my knee I want to say something, but I just can't. We can hear Mum clattering along with the tea tray for ages, so he always has his hand back by the time she comes in. I did tell her after the third time he did it. She was in a foul mood and just said, 'I'm afraid that's a typical bloody man, Melissa.'

Laura always has loads of brilliant stories – things are always happening to her – and this was the first properly exciting thing I'd ever told her. She was more interested in Mum than Max and my knee, though. She said, 'What's made The Charming Mrs Cline such a man-hater?'

Mum did have a quiet word with Max, and for about a month there was no touching, but then he started to do it again. At least it proves I am not ugly.

Skimpy

Laura and I went shopping for her Valentine's disco outfit. She tried on the whole of Chelsea Girl and finally chose a pink dress with tiny roses. You could see a lot of her bosom in it. Fifteen pounds! I've never spent that much in my life. I hope my jeans will be all right. I didn't know we were supposed to wear dresses. Back at her house she showed the dress to her mum. Anthony East was there, too. He had black hair, slicked back, and was wearing a navy suit. Mrs Morente had on very high orange sandals and was laughing when we came in. She stopped laughing when she saw Laura, and told her the dress was 'too skimpy'.

Anthony East said, 'She's all right, Olivia, it's the fashion.'

Mrs Morente smiled with all her teeth. 'Showing her knickers is the fashion, is it, Tony?'

Laura burst into tears and rushed out of the room. I was left standing there like a lemon, except lemons don't tend to be bright red, so actually more like a tomato. When I went back up, Laura was putting on lipstick in front of her three-way mirror. I said, 'Anthony East is very good-looking,' thinking she would be pleased.

She blotted her lips. 'God, I think he's hideous. He made Mama cry last week.'

To cheer her up I did impressions of teachers at school. After a while she was sobbing with laughter, holding her stomach and begging me to stop. We both ended up lying on the bed gasping for breath and cuddling. It was lovely. But Laura said we had better work on our dancing for the disco. She turned on her record player and we spent ages doing routines for songs from *Grease*. The one for 'Greased Lightning' was brilliant. I jumped into her arms and she swung me to the left then the right. By the time Dad came to collect me, I was dead on my feet, and spent the evening watching telly cuddled up on the sofa with Mummy.

Disco Day

I tried to get out of *shul* this morning, because I wanted to start getting ready, but Mum was in a mood over the Coke-stained bedspread, which she'd just discovered at the bottom of the laundry basket. She snapped that not even film stars needed ten hours to get ready and I was going to *shul* and that was that. Laura says I'm lucky I only go to synagogue once a week, because she has to go to church three times on Sundays. But her church sounds miles more interesting than *shul*; it has candles and confessing, and even incense, which Dad won't let me have in case I burn the house down. Actually, *shul* was okay because there was a new family with a nice-looking son.

After lunch Laura came over, and we showed Mum and Dad our 'Greased Lighting' routine. They clapped. I did the splits, and nearly got right down to the floor. Then Laura did her make-up, and tied her hair into a ponytail at the top of her head. She looked beautiful in the pink roses dress and high shoes. I felt even shorter than usual. By the time Dad drove us and Danners to the club I was really nervous. I couldn't hear what Danners and Laura were talking about because I was in the front with Dad, who kept going on about his 'first dance'. *Dance!* No one calls it that.

I signed Laura in and we went through to the hall, which was dark with proper flashing lights. The music was really loud and I couldn't see where it was coming from. Laura yelled in my ear, 'It's "Le Freak"!' and pulled me into the middle of the floor. She started dancing straight away, smiling and flicking her hair. We hadn't done a routine to this song so I tried to follow her, but every time I got the hang of a move she started doing something different, so in the end I copied a girl who was just moving from one foot to the other. Then Laura pulled me over so we were dancing near Danners and his mates. Towse was there, and my heart began thumping. He was wearing skintight jeans and a black T-shirt. I thought about the Valentine's card I'd got him, hidden in my jacket pocket, and wondered when I would give it to him. When we finally sat down, Danners and Towse came too, which was amazing because normally at the club Dan pretends not to know me. Both of them were talking to Laura, though I couldn't hear what they were saying because of the music. But I was happy just to watch Towse. I was chatting to a girl called Shelley when 'Greased Lightning' came on. I looked at Laura but she hadn't noticed, so I tapped her arm.

'Ow!' she yelled. 'Why did you hit me?'

'Sorry, Laura, I didn't mean to. Shall we do our routine?'

'I don't feel like dancing any more.' She rubbed her arm where I'd touched her, and turned back to the boys. It got quite late and they turned off the lights. Shelley said, 'Oh no, it's the smoochy songs,' but straight away a boy came up and asked her to dance. I watched them to see how you did it. It didn't seem too difficult. I was in a trance watching Shelley's feet moving slowly round when Laura came over and whispered, 'Towse has asked me to dance. Do you mind?'

I shook my head, and Towse pulled her onto the dance floor. Danners asked a blonde girl to dance. I waited for a while but no one came over, so I went to the loo. I put

Towse's card in the sanitary towel incinerator; first time I have ever used one of those. Then I sat in a cubicle reading a leaflet about the Green Cross Code that someone had left behind.

At ten o'clock I left the toilet to see if Daddy had arrived. He was at the entrance talking to Rosa Spiegel. It was so lovely to see him. He gave me the car keys and I let myself into the front seat. About ten minutes later, Dad came back with Laura and Danners. Laura asked where I had got to and I said I was 'around and about'.

Everyone was quiet on the way home. When we dropped Laura off she said, 'I'll call you tomorrow.'

I said, 'Okay,' and did the best smile I could.

Laura

Knee to knee round Mama's kitchen table, so squashed together that Heifer's upholstered bust keeps bumping my arm. She is weeping, as she has been pretty much since Michael died, presumably to show everyone how wonderfully sensitive she is. Evie is subdued, smart in a navy dress, sitting on her father's lap. Huw wriggles uncomfortably, runs his finger round the neck of his shirt. He keeps telling me his suit's shrunk, accusingly, as if it's my fault. Mama bustles about, as much as one can in such a cramped space, obsessively brewing pots of coffee. Her eyes are red and her skin is blotchy. I tried to get her to put on some make-up this morning but she waved me away.

Danny, sitting next to Huw, is beautiful in a dark-grey suit. His eyes are glistening, eyelashes black and spiky. He holds the chicken baby on his lap. Two of his other children crouch at his feet, colouring in poorly executed drawings of bible scenes.

Heifer went out first thing this morning, and when I opened the door to her, she presented me with a box of eggs and a bag of flour. I have literally no idea why. She's also put tea towels over all the mirrors. I took off the one over the bathroom mirror, but the cheeky cow crept in and put it back!

For some irritating reason, Mama seems to find comfort in these Jewish rituals. I'm reminded of when she first fell in love with Michael and told me we were going to become Jewish. Mama even played the organ at the Clines' synagogue for a few months. The conversion never happened, though. After we left Edgware, Mama stopped going to church, but that was all, and Michael pretty much gave up being a Jew. Now Heifer's convinced Mama that Michael must have a proper Jewish burial. This began yesterday when Mama said she would scatter Michael's ashes on the beach. Heifer went mad: apparently, Orthodox Jews don't allow cremation. Who knew? I kept saying that Michael wasn't religious, but no one wanted to hear. Danny made some phone calls, and now we're burying Michael in a Jewish cemetery in Norwich. The only thing Mama's decided for herself is that I am to ask for a prayer to be said for Michael at my church back home. She's in such a state she hardly knows what she's doing. When I rang Julie Owen, her friend up the road, to tell her about Michael, Mama grabbed the phone from me and started sobbing, 'I knew he would leave me, Julie. He was *mi amor,* love of my life.'

I've been wondering if Mama will turn to me; if I'll get her back now Michael's not here. I was very fond of him, don't get me wrong. But between my father leaving and Michael coming along, there were a few years when it was just Mama and me, give or take a few boyfriends. I liked it just us. That feeling of us girls against the world.

I scrape my chair a few millimetres away from Heifer's. But her enormous shelf-bust still reaches me. What a disjointed little group we are. How would we be described in a documentary about complicated modern families?

This man here, intones the sombre voice-over, *is Laura's husband, and she is grateful he is with her at this tragic time, though luckily the funeral is the day after his very important devolution meeting. Laura wonders what he would have done in the event of a clash. Laura and her husband have not had sexual intercourse since she revealed that she was unexpectedly pregnant with his child. He has, in fact, been behaving like an asshole.* The voice-over man wouldn't usually use such strong language but he thinks it appropriate here. *Despite this, Laura is trying to make things right between them. The other man at the table is Laura's stepbrother, though once, long ago, he was her lover. And Laura wouldn't object if he were again. His huge milch-cow wife is also here, her bosom taking up half the kitchen. Here we have Laura's mother, consumed by grief and consequently making some odd decisions. Here, Laura's daughter, in denial about her murderous feelings towards her forthcoming sibling. And absent, yet very central, is the man they are here to bury: Laura's stepfather.*

I haven't felt like crying since Michael died. Hopefully everyone assumes I'm so grief-stricken that I'm beyond tears. But it feels more like the death of an uncle than a father. Which I guess is fair enough. He was 'Uncle Michael', at first, and although when they married Mama wanted me to call him Dad, it never felt natural. I've always thought I was lucky to get a second chance at having a dad, to make up for my own crappy father. Now it turns out that, after all these years, he still feels like 'Uncle Michael'.

The voice-over man continues:

So. Everyone in the family is here. All except Michael's daughter, Melissa. Despite leaving messages everywhere, with all her friends and acquaintances, the family have heard nothing since a brief email. They don't know if she is aware of her father's death.

My skirt, the only dark elasticated-waist one I own, is unevenly short at the front, twisted round by my bump. Very attractive. I go upstairs to sort it out, and to get away from Heifer's snuffling and her boring anecdotes about Michael. I want to grab her flabby arm, shout in her face, 'He wasn't even your dad!' But then, he wasn't mine, either.

Huw and Evie's things are strewn all over my room. All the other rooms are occupied by the Clines and their five million kids. I step over the debris, sit at the dressing table and pull the fucking towel off the three-way mirror. Can you believe she's had the nerve to come in here? Mind you, I almost put it back on again when I see how horrendous I look. I scrabble round in the drawer for the old make-up I found the other day. I take the cap off a dusty lipstick – 'Stupid Cupid' – and sniff the sweet ruby stub. The smell plunges me back.

Miffy and I are in my old house in Edgware, in front of this same mirror. Her face is done up in pink and blue candy colours. We both watch my reflection as I apply lipstick, the deepest crimson: cock-sucker red, we call it reverently, I having got that name from an older girl at school and passed it

on to Miffy. Neither of us has the faintest idea what it means,
though we guess it's something naughty, and I pretend that
I know. Again and again, I glide the sweet-smelling goo over
my lips – three, four, five layers – then blot it hard against
a tissue. We examine not my lips or their reflection, but the
round red mouth I have made on the tissue. This, we know,
is the mark of a woman. 'Perfect,' says Miffy.

There aren't many mourners apart from us. Michael
and Mama weren't much for socialising. Just Mama's
mate Julie, and a few of Michael's friends, relics from his
working life and his polytechnic days. They still think of
him as Michael-and-Andrea, even though Michael and
Mama were together for twenty-four years: longer than he
was with Andrea. They're from the generation before the
one that is cool about divorce. They avoid Mama's eye,
look at her feet while they say how sorry they are. They
don't know what to say to me, either. They gaze past my
ear, muttering sorry, sorry, sorry, till I want to grab their
faces, twist their heads, force them to look at me.

They're only slightly more comfortable with Danny.
On the one hand, he's Michael's boy; on the other, he's
a mad Hassidic Jew with a mad Hassidic wife. We're all
relieved when an usher asks us to take our seats. The men
stay downstairs while we women troop obediently up to
a gallery. A woman with a tipsy wig hands us each a little

booklet with the stark legend *Prayers For the Dead* printed on the front. The Cantor starts to sing in a deep chocolaty voice, and I follow the words in my *Dead* pamphlet.

'*El malei rachamim shokhen ba-m'romim...*

God full of mercy, who dwells on high...'

I've been in a synagogue before, of course, back when Mama played the organ at Miffy's synagogue. It was kind of a wishy-washy progressive place. Men and women sat together: often, I sat next to Danny. The whole building was make-do-and-mend, a converted scout hut with folding chairs and electric plug-in heaters. The sacred Ark of the Covenant had previously been a wardrobe.

'*Ha-m'tzei m'nuchah n'khonah tachat...*

Grant proper rest on the wings of the Divine Presence...'

The Ark here is an expensive mahogany box, and the everlasting light hanging above it looks like it's made from Murano glass. It makes me think of our honeymoon in Venice, of how I dragged Huw round every single glass shop in search of the perfect vase, how he never complained, how he bought me an ice-cream the size of a baby's head. Hard to believe sometimes that we are the same two people.

The tiny windows are so high up that the little sun they let in stays near the ceiling, floating above us like a layer of smoke. This synagogue suits Heifer's fundamentalism: dark and cold. We could do with some of those electric heaters. Everyone keeps their coat on, apart from the Cantor, who presumably is used to it, or else warmed by an inner fire. I sit back, and let the Hebrew wash over me.

'*V'yanuchu b'shalom al mish'kabam v'noma.*

And may he repose in peace on his resting place'

Like most of the men sitting below us, Huw is wearing a borrowed cotton *cuple*. He keeps putting up a hand to check it's still there. I scan the heads till I find Danny. His is a special mourning *cuple* made of rich black velvet. He is skinny in his black coat, too big for him, like a boy wearing his father's clothes. I fantasise that I can smell his lemony scent. I imagine his lips moving as he mumbles the words along with the Cantor. It's all meaningless sounds to me, but of course he can hear something profound in it.

'Amen.'

Ooh, a word I recognise.

Now the Rabbi begins speaking about Michael. Mama weeps quietly at my side. Heifer's wedged in tight on my other side, bust akimbo; Christ knows why we have to keep getting so cosy. She clasps my hand into hers, which is hot and clammy. I stare at her sleeve against mine. Although her dress looks identical to all her other black tents, this one seems to be a blacker black.

The Rabbi is an uninspiring elderly man in a dark-blue suit, going through the motions, white prayer shawl round his shoulders. As he'd never met Michael, I presume

Danny has briefed him, but the person he describes could be anyone. In broad strokes he tells us of a good man, a devoted husband, a loving father. These things are prized above rubies. He says that Michael performed the sacred duty of family man to the best of his ability. Hey, it was better than that, Rabbi: he performed that sacred duty for *two* families!

For some reason, I remember the good-looking young Rabbi at Edgware, someone I haven't thought about for years. Miffy was madly in love with him. I smile, thinking of it, and Heifer squeezes my hand harder. I pull it away on the pretext of getting a tissue out of my bag.

Mercifully this interlude about some bloke called Michael is brief, and after a final prayer we're on our feet, jostling politely down the stairs to get the hell out. In the foyer the Rabbi wishes Mama and me long life. We both mutter 'thank you'. Heifer leads us away, and as I turn, I see Danny say something to the Rabbi. The older man looks over at us and nods. Outside, Mum hugs Julie Owen tightly, and Danny shakes hands with Michael's old friends, then just the family set off for the cemetery. For some reason, the gender divide continues in the cars. I'm driving Mama's big old Peugeot, and on the way here I had Mama, Evie, Huw and two of the Cline kids, but now Huw's somehow been swapped for Heifer; she squats, toad-like, in the back with the children, baby asleep on her lap, and spends the fifteen-minute journey babbling about the service, the fabulous rabbi and the general superiority of Judaism over everything.

'He was such a learned man. He spoke from the heart. It was almost like he knew Michael, don't you think, Olivia?'

Evie asks me if we can have some music, but before I can reply Heifer says, 'It's not appropriate, Evie. Today is a day of mourning, not a day of music and festivity.'

Mama frowns at me, so I say nothing. I don't want to upset Mama, though I'd very much like to upset Heifer.

Heifer babbles on and by the time we pull into the cemetery car park, the wheels crunching across gravel, I'm in a trance, Danny and Miffy flitting in and out of my thoughts. I turn off the engine, undo my seatbelt and say, 'Ready?'

Mama and Evie open their doors and Heifer cries, 'Where are you going?'

We all stop, twisting in our seats to look at her.

'Where are we going?' I repeat, and Mama says uncertainly, 'To the cemetery?'

Heifer looks so outraged there's a mad moment in which I wonder if one of the superior things about Judaism is drive-through burials, and we're all meant to stay in the car until a signal instructs us to move slowly forward in first gear.

'Women can't go to the cemetery,' Heifer says. 'I thought you knew.'

So that's why Heifer infiltrated our car! She wanted to make sure we didn't break any orthodoxies.

'How would we know?' I ask.

Heifer says, 'It's common knowledge.'

'Not amongst *shiksas*, it's not.'

Heifer winces at my using the rude word for non-Jewish women. *Shiksas* aren't meant to know that Jews call them that. My brain must have dredged up the word from my Edgware days. Heifer's girls – fifteen-year-old Chanah and eleven-year-old Atalia – stare at their shoes.

Mama says pitifully, 'I want to say goodbye to Michael.'

'Of course you do, Mama.'

Heifer says, 'Honestly, Olivia, it's better for women not to be there.'

'Better for who?' I ask. I know Huw would tell me it's better for *whom*, but he's not here. Yes, why isn't he bloody here? What a wimp, letting Heifer muscle him out of the car.

Heifer fixes me with her piggy eyes – if ever a woman could use a little mascara! – and says, 'Pregnant women must avoid situations where they might meet the evil eye.'

I give Heifer the evil eye in the mirror, but she doesn't notice. 'If we can't go into the cemetery, why are we here?'

'To support the men. And pay our respects. We can pray just as well for Michael here as anywhere.'

I know Mama doesn't want a fight, but I do. I really bloody do.

'Mama, Evie, out you get.' I say this in Heifer's own bossy tones, and they comply immediately, scurrying out of their seats.

'Please, Laura!' Heifer says.

I stare at her, astonished all over again that this ugly old cow is married to Danny. To Danny! How is this possible? If nothing else proves there is no God, this alone is enough. All the rage I've suppressed since meeting her comes bubbling up. I lean towards the back seat, slightly impeded by my bump, and under my breath say, 'Hella, my stepfather has just *died*. My mother wants to say goodbye to her husband. So do you think you could do us a big favour, and just shut the fuck up?'

Heifer jerks away from me as though she's been shot, her face puffy and startled. The baby stirs on her lap, waves an arm in its sleep. Her daughters gape at me, their mouths little circles of shock. I get out of the car and slam the door. Mama clutches my arm. 'What did you say? What did you say?'

I'm so angry. I say, 'We're late, let's go.'

We walk quickly across the grass to where the men are standing. Our breath steams into the frosty air. I remember Miffy and I, one dark winter on our way home from school, buying sweetie cigarettes and blowing pretend smoke into the sky.

As we approach the grave I see from the sombre faces that they're not thrilled to see us. Despite my fury I want to laugh, to yell and shout, that painful feeling of forbidden giggles welling up, like in school assembly or church. I push my freezing hands into my coat pockets and spike nails into palms to stop myself laughing. I nearly slip on the silvery grass, and only just get my hands out in time to grab Mama by the sleeve of her soft fur coat. Danny glances at me for a moment, then looks down. He and the other men stand under a kind of canopy formed by bare-limbed trees. In his oversized black coat, if you didn't know him, if you didn't look at him properly, you would think he was like all the other religious men here. An image of his younger self flashes into my mind: Danny at fifteen, beautiful, reaching for me with a persuasive smile. A long lean body. I don't feel like laughing any more.

Huw walks over to us, having no idea that anything's happened. Stupid bastard, it's all his fault. I shake my head at him and he gives me a 'what have I done now?' look. I put my arm round Mama. She whispers, 'What did you say to Hella? I hope you haven't upset her, Laura. I hate any kind of bad feelings.'

I take my arm away.

The Rabbi starts reading a prayer and all the men join

in, swaying and intoning at different speeds, which makes me feel properly upset, as if everyone is mourning in their own way. Mama cries as though her heart is breaking.

'Yit'gadal v'yit'kadash sh'mei raba…'

If this were a film, this would be the big reunion scene. Miffy appears at the last possible minute, screeching up to the gate in a fast car. She runs towards us, as we stand waiting at the graveside. She wears something black and chic, dark glasses covering her eyes.

'Oseh shalom bim'romav…'

In truth, if she's anything like the Miffy I remember, she'd probably pull up in a knackered old taxi, the diesel engine drowning out the sound of prayers while she fumbles for change and drops her purse. She'd be wearing a hideous olive-green hat like the one she had at school, with tassels and earflaps. The thought of it makes me smile. But the smile hurts my face.

'Hu ya'aseh shalom…'

She would embrace everyone, then turn to me last, and linger. She'd remove her sunglasses and we would look into each other's eyes, all the absent years forgotten.

'Aleinu v'al kol Yis'ra'eil v'im'ru amen.'

The men finish chanting, bow their heads; the Rabbi starts to sing in a clear deep voice. Huw turns to me and whispers gently, 'Are you okay, cariad?'

Because now, finally, I am shedding unstoppable tears.

23 FEBRUARY 2003

So we're having a full-blown, week-long *shiva*. What's a *shiva*, boys and girls? Well, I'm not entirely sure, despite being on the fourth day of it. Mainly we sit in the living room crying, and people come and visit, and bring food because we're too upset to cook. Sounds a laugh, right?

Mama has handed Heifer responsibility for all the arrangements, to make up for my behaviour. 'I feel so bad you went against her wishes.'

'It wasn't just me, Mama!'

'We are going to do everything right from now on. *Todo.*'

I tell Heifer that I don't mind cooking; it'd give me something to do. But she says in a patronising voice that I'm in shock, and should rest. Presumably 'shock' is how she's making sense of the incident in the cemetery car park.

'What about the kids?' I ask. 'They have to eat.' She opens the freezer to show me it's packed with delicious kosher ready-meals.

I don't know who all these people are that are going to come round. A couple of neighbours did pop round the day after the funeral. They were visibly puzzled by the tea-towelled mirrors and the low stool Mama was perched on – actually a pouffe, if we're still allowed to call them that. Old Mr Henderson from next door was so thrown by the seating arrangements that he stayed for two hours, long after we'd run out of small talk. I asked Danny the significance of the stool but he said Heifer – he didn't call her that, unfortunately – is the one who knows the traditions: she was brought up with them. But I'm not sodding asking *her*.

On the third day, Huw told me if he sat through another minute there would be a new death to mourn. I wasn't sure if he meant himself as a suicide, or Heifer as a murder victim. I was trying to be good for Mama's sake, and felt obliged to stick it out, but I suggested Huw took Evie to the cinema. He jumped up faster than Mr Henderson when he realised he could leave. I realised too late, seeing the look on Heifer's face when Huw offered to take some of the Cline kids along too, that it was Saturday, so we were breaking all the Sabbath rules as well as the *shiva* rules. The poor kids gazed longingly at Evie, prisoner on day release, as she skipped out the door.

After they'd gone, Heifer told me proudly that neither she nor her children had ever been to the cinema. I glanced at Danny, who'd taken me to see *Life of Brian* when it came out, and put his hand on my tit in the back row. I wondered if he was remembering that too.

Today it's pouring with rain; the boring Sunday to end all Sundays. Huw takes Evie to a pottery-painting place they found yesterday, but once again the Cline kids aren't allowed to go out. Their shrieks upstairs indicate some desperate kind of torture game. Mama, Heifer, Danny and

I sit around doing nothing. Danny is calm and composed, says little. Perhaps he's meditating, tuning Heifer out. She keeps trying to encourage us to talk about Michael, tell stories, but Mama's too sad, and looks increasingly uncomfortable perched on that damn pouffe, and I don't want to indulge any further Heifer's notion of the ideal family bereavement.

A spine-chilling yell makes us all jump. Heifer leaps to her feet and starts shouting in Yiddish, though who it's directed at, I'm not sure. Danny takes hold of her, talking gently, trying to calm her down, and it's left to Mama and me to check no one's been murdered. One of the smaller Cline children is floundering in the bath, fully clothed and soaked, a sibling having turned the shower on him. Mama towels down the sobbing child and asks me what we can do to distract them. For some reason I think of the flour and eggs Heifer brought, and suggest to the children that we make pancakes. The poor things are so deprived of fun that they greet this idea with whoops of joy, and hurtle down to the kitchen.

Heifer, having finished her tantrum, comes in to see what's happening. For a moment I panic that pancakes aren't kosher, but then remember that she brought the ingredients. She says, through tight lips, 'That's fine. They can do cooking. *If* they are incapable of playing quietly, or just sitting still.'

She sweeps out, leaving behind the clear implication
that if even adults such as myself are incapable of sitting
still (or playing quietly, come to that), how can she expect
children to know better? I give her the finger as she leaves,
but I'm pretty sure none of the children see. They are
enthusiastic cooks. Only one pancake ends up somewhere
it shouldn't (stuck to a curtain). The cooking and eating
is a big hit, and I congratulate myself as I watch the row
of Heifer-like heads, bent over the table, chewing the cud.
When they've finished, I shoo them out of the kitchen,
on the basis that it's now someone else's responsibility –
who knows, even their parents'! – to entertain them. I go
to clean myself up, and bump into Danny as he's coming
out of the bathroom. I fall against him, perhaps a little
more enthusiastically than necessary. His body is warm
against mine.

'Oops!' I say.

He sidesteps me. 'Don't, Laura, please.' He sounds like
he's going to cry.

'It was an accident!' I say, but he turns and gallops down
the stairs.

I can't remember why I've come up, so I go and sit in
my bedroom. What does he think of me? Is he still angry
from all those years ago? We were just kids, after all. I
root around in my dressing-table drawer till I find that
old Valentine's card. Danny sent it, the day after I danced

with someone else to make him jealous. 'You didn't dance with your true admirer.' It was the first time he'd said anything about liking me. I sit there a long time, staring at the card. I can only recall fragments. Danny sitting staring. Me slow-dancing with – who? I can't think. Was Miffy there? I can't remember.

The front door slams, and a few minutes later Huw appears in the doorway. I shove the card in the drawer.

'How was pottery?'

'Shite. Listen, I'm really sorry for Olivia and everything, but that's bloody enough now. We need to go home.'

I don't argue. Even the secret compensation of being able to gaze at Danny all day is wearing off. I've done all the fantasies to death, my favourite one being that he and I are the only two people in the house and he strides over and sticks his hand up my skirt. Heifer usually puts the kybosh on that little daydream by starting off on one of her inane streams of consciousness. Or unconsciousness, in her case.

Huw sits down on the bed. 'I only brought enough pants for two days.'

'I wondered what that whiff was.'

He sticks out his tongue at me. 'I didn't realise Jewish mourning rituals took so long. Or that we'd be doing Jewish mourning rituals, come to that. Anyway, Evie's back to school on Tuesday.'

'We could offer to take Mama home with us?' I say, expecting him to protest.

'Laura! You are fucking brilliant. It gets us out of here, without making us look heartless. And she'll be company for you in the evenings, too. You look charming with batter in your eyebrows, by the way.'

'Why, where will you be in the evenings?'

'I *told* you,' he sighs, in his usual tone. 'I've got weeks of deadlines, tons of papers to finish, conference stuff to prepare, theses to read and...'

'Yeah, okay. Mama and I can be widows together, you're saying.'

'I'm still alive, aren't I?' he says.

'For now.'

We go downstairs and I ask Mama if she'd like to come back with us tomorrow.

'Oh yes, please, *bebita*.'

Heifer frowns. 'But we won't have the full week, then, Olivia.'

Huw and Mama immediately start in with explanations and reasons, and I can see they'll be fine so I go into the downstairs loo to clean myself up. The worst is off my face but I'm trying to wipe the batter from my hair when there's a knock at the front door. I hear Heifer go to answer it, lecturing Mama as she stomps down the hall. 'This is why you have a week of sitting *shiva*, Olivia, to give everyone time to come round.'

I come out of the loo, trying to undo my apron ties.

Mama says, 'It's probably Julie Owen, she said she'd visit again today.'

But when Heifer moves back from the door, the tall elegant woman who steps over the threshold is definitely not Julie Owen. She is a completely different species from both her and the dumpy Heifer hopping up and down beside her. The new woman wears a cherry-red coat, speckled with rain. Her hair is a long curtain of gold. I take all this in, and Heifer's strange expression, but it still doesn't click who she is until Danny runs into the hall and hugs the woman tightly, calling out her name.

24 FEBRUARY 2003

I sit down. I stand up. I sit again, in a different chair. Mama watches me. 'Ah yes, I remember that well.'

She thinks I'm uncomfortable because of the baby, and I don't contradict her, but the reason I can't sit still is because I've got ants in my pants, as we used to say at school. We once actually did put ants in Fiona Bryan's knickers – she was a willing participant – but they wouldn't stay in long enough for her to report back. Now I know exactly what it feels like.

Mama hands me some lukewarm tea, then the door

opens and I jump, spilling tea down my trousers. But it's just Heifer. After nearly a solid week, I already wish her a long way from me, and right now I wish far worse things than that. She pulls a dubious-looking tissue out of her sleeve and starts mopping me down against my will. 'Oh, these will stain; you'd better change. I'll give them a quick hand-wash.'

I manage not to shove her away, really hard. 'They're just old maternity jeans. Please. Don't. Worry.'

'I'll make more tea, shall I?' she says. 'I'm doing brunch soon, and if we're all leaving today' – a pointed look at me, instigator of the *shiva* shutdown – 'I'd better wake Lissa up.'

I raise my eyebrows at Mama once Heifer's left the room, but she pretends not to see. She says, 'Did you get a chance to speak to Melissa yesterday?'

'I barely said hello.'

Miffy spent ages talking to Danny in the kitchen, and later Heifer monopolised her, huddled her into a corner, trapped her against a wall. I couldn't take my eyes off Miffy, trying to see the messy-haired little kid I'd known, but she was unrecognisable. If I'd met her in the street, I wouldn't have known her.

Mama and I don't really talk about our life in Edgware, our life before we came here. Miffy is a big part of that unspoken history. But Mama has seen Miffy regularly, knows about her life since Michael left Andrea, and right now all the things I've ever vaguely wondered about are of the most pressing importance.

'Mama, do you know why Miffy got divorced?'

Mama, fumbling with a hankie, wipes her eyes. 'Michael did not discuss the details with me. If he even knew them. He was devastated, I tell you that much. It made him cry.'

'That's sad.'

'Life *is* sad, *bebita*. People divorce. People die.' She blows her nose, an elephant honk. 'It's a shame you and Melissa lost touch. You were such nice friends.'

Michael's death has completely addled her brain.

'Yes, Mama. It *was* a shame, wasn't it?'

Heifer crashes in with a tea tray before I can say anything else. I grab a cup and take it upstairs, my hands shaking, slopping tea on the carpet. Fuck it. I swap my stained jeans for my brown cords, sit at the mirror, do some antenatal breathing to calm down. I touch up my foundation and give myself a pep talk. What's the matter with me? There's no need to be stressed. It's just silly little Miffy, who looked up to me when we were kids. Plain little Miffy with her bushy hair and Bessie Bunter specs. There's no need for me to get all worked up: not about her, nor about the way my mother seems to think we could somehow all have been friends. Miffy's the one who should be feeling anxious. Seeing me again after all these years is bound to be difficult. I'll let her do the fretting for the both of us. I will be calm, cool and sophisticated.

Since the moment I realised I might see Miffy and Danny again, some long-forgotten memories of my early teens have resurfaced, catching me unawares. One floats into my mind now. A missing piece of the Valentine's card jigsaw: Miffy and I dancing for her parents. Where has that memory been hiding all these years?

We were at Miffy's house, getting ready for the disco. Michael was just Miffy's dad then, but I knew he was Mama's special friend. I liked him too. He was a slim, good-looking man, gold-flecked brown hair falling over his forehead. Hair like Danny's.

Miffy and I danced for her parents. I showed off, flicking up my short dress. I remember the knickers I was wearing: my favourites, soft pink lace, a present from Uncle Anthony. He worked for a make-up company and loved buying gifts for women. Lots of women, not just Mama, it turned out.

Miffy's parents clapped, and I kicked my legs up high, again and again, feeling all eyes on me, Miffy trying to keep up, until Andrea Cline abruptly turned off the tape player and asked Miffy to get her a drink of water. Then Andrea turned to me. 'You're becoming a sexy young lady, Laura. Like your Mama. Isn't she Michael?'

I knew it wasn't a compliment. Neither Michael nor I spoke.

Andrea went on, 'Michael loves looking at pretty ladies, don't you, choochie? But you know what they say: most likely to look, least likely to stray. They'd have to drag you by the hair, wouldn't they, darling?'

I didn't understand Andrea's meaning, or why her eyes didn't match her smile. Then Miffy ran back in and said, 'I can do the splits, look!' Practically did herself a mischief in a doomed attempt to get both legs flat on the floor.

Michael stood up. 'Time I took you girls to the disco.'

Colour me stupid – it's only now I realise she intended me to tell Mama her comment about Michael straying. But of course I didn't.

I hear steps in the hall and open the door to see Miffy going downstairs. I call her name – her nickname – and she turns. She looks up at me, her expression unreadable, and gives a sort of nod. Her appearance is still utterly unfamiliar. So different from that eager splits-performing kid. She's tall, for starters; when did that happen? Her hair's silky and fair, when I remember an unruly brown cloud. Beautifully dressed in a cream linen shirt and dove-grey trousers, she looks like she's just walked off the set of *Heat And Dust*.

Finally she gives me a hesitant smile, and for the first time I see that it *is* her. The old Miffy is there in the smile, the cats' eyes crinkling up, the straight white teeth. She used to say her perfect teeth were what she had in common with Marilyn Monroe.

I say, 'Do you want to come in for a minute?'

She shakes her head, so that I think she means no, but then she walks back up the stairs towards me. She still has a slight limp. Almost unnoticeable, unless you're looking for it. Unless you know it's there.

And now here we are in my bedroom. Different room, different town, twenty-four years later. But here are Laura and Miffy, still hanging out.

'This is weird, isn't it?' I say.

She sits down on the bed and leans back against the headboard. I sit upright on a chair facing her, all Miss Prim. Now I look at her properly, she's not conventionally beautiful. Her eyes are small without her glasses, her nose too long. But there's something about her. The eye is drawn towards her. Plain little Miffy, who'd have believed it? She wears silver bangles which jingle when she moves. That could get annoying. She's barely wearing any make-up. She looks so young. God, you'd think she was twenty-five, though she must be ten years more than that, at least; she's only a little younger than me. I feel mumsy and fat in my flowery shirt and maternity cords.

'When's your baby due?' First thing she's said to me, other than hello.

'Bit less than four months now. June.'

'A June baby. How lucky.'

We used to tease her about her low husky voice. It never occurred to me it might be appealing. The dads who bring their kids to her office – 'fascinating, what she does' – must all want to get into her pants.

'Is Evie looking forward to the baby?'

I'm definitely not going to give anything away to a child psychologist. 'She's very excited, of course. And she'll be a great help. It won't be like having two only children at all.' Shit, saying too much. Shut up, Laura.

'Dad often spoke about Evie. He was so fond of her.'

Michael's presence is suddenly between us in the room. 'Listen, Miffy, I'm so sorry we weren't able to get you here before he died.'

'It honestly doesn't matter,' she says.

There's a knock on the door and Mama sticks her head in. 'Would anyone like coffee?'

'Yes, please, Olivia. It might help me wake up. I've never had jet lag before. I was wide-awake in the night, and now it's gone eleven. Crazy.'

'I too was awake all night,' says Mama, 'but without having need of air travel.'

She goes out and Miffy and I grin at each other. All day – actually, all week – to be honest with you, for twenty-four years, I've tried not to think about the last time I saw Miffy. But I've never been able to completely wipe it away.

'So will it be strange? Going back to nappies, after such a long time?'

God, can't she talk about anything else? 'I guess so. I wanted to have lots of children all close together, but it didn't work out that way.'

'No,' she says. 'These things don't always work out.'

'Miffy, did you...'

'No one else calls me Miffy.' She smoothes a strand of hair away from her face. Her nails are bitten, ragged round the edges. Good to see something's not perfect.

'Doesn't Danny?'

'Oh, not for years. Not to my face, anyway!'

'What would you like me to call you, then? Lissa?'

'Actually, Miffy's okay. I kind of like it.'

I look down to hide my smile, examine one of my own nails. Not bitten, neatly shaped, but covered in what I now realise is a tacky shade of candyfloss pink.

'You look just how I remember you, Laura.'

'Oh, I can't do! I've aged so much. I certainly wouldn't have recognised *you*.'

She laughs. 'Perhaps that's a good thing. My early teens weren't my best look.'

'When did you get so tall?'

'Growth spurt when I was fifteen. Went from being the smallest to one of the tallest in a few months.'

'Must have been weird.'

'It was brilliant.'

Mama returns with the coffee, and Miffy invites her to sit down. Mama perches stiffly on the edge of the bed.

'I wanted to ask you both something,' Miffy says. 'Danners, Hella and I want to invite you to a party we're having next month.'

Mama jumps in, all affronted. 'Thank you, but no. What an extraordinary time to be thinking about parties.'

'I know what you mean, Olivia,' Miffy says gently. 'But it was arranged a long time ago. You know Dad was going to come.'

'Oh! For Micah's barmitzvah,' says Mama. She gives a long shuddering sigh. 'Michael was looking forward to it.'

'I'd always planned to throw Micah a barmitzvah party, as he's my oldest nephew,' Miffy says to me. 'Then my friend Amy wanted to give *me* a welcome home party, so we're combining them. Amy's hosting it; her house in Sussex is pretty big.'

'It sounds great,' I say. 'We could use it, after all this sadness.'

'Exactly. And we thought it could also be a celebration of Dad's life, Olivia.'

'That is a nice gesture. But it sounds a bit much right now, to my mind.' Mama assumes I'll agree, but to my surprise, the phrase *sod it* jumps into my head.

'I'd love to come,' I say. I'm mystified to be invited, but I'm going to go if it kills me.

Mama says, 'I'd better see if Hella needs help in the kitchen.' She goes out without looking at me.

Miffy says, 'Maybe I shouldn't have mentioned it. But you know. Life goes on.'

'Was Micah named for your dad?' It's only just now I've noticed that their names are alike.

'Yes. Unusual. Jews don't usually name a baby after someone who's living.'

'So why did they?'

'Um. I don't know. I guess at the time Danners felt that Dad was, well, sort of dead to him.'

'Oh.'

'Just got to nip to the loo,' she says, and slips out with a jingle of bracelets.

I check my face. Great: my lips are all dry and granny-mouth. I put on a conditioning lipstick and pretend to read a magazine. When Miffy comes back she says, 'Do you still smoke, Laura? When you're not pregnant, of course.'

'Me?' I can barely remember smoking at all. 'No, not since we were kids. Why, do you?'

'Can't you smell it?'

I sniff the air and realise there *is* a faint smell of smoke. 'Miffy, have you been smoking in your room?'

Hand over her mouth, she giggles like a schoolgirl. 'Out the attic window,' she whispers. 'Don't tell your mum!'

After this I find her easier to talk to. I tell her about my life, about Evie and the new baby, Huw's kids, the shop and Ceri, about *La Vida Boring* in North Wales. Every time I stop, she asks another question, but finally I manage to ask her about her travels.

She stretches her arms above her head, and rattle rattle go the bracelets. 'Only impulsive thing I've ever done. Everyone said, be sensible, buy a flat, don't leave your job. But I'd never been anywhere before. Jay, my ex, wasn't into travelling. I visited Australia, Hong Kong, South America, Africa. It was so exciting. I wish I'd done it years ago, before university, when everyone else went to India and I was...'

She stops abruptly.

'You were...'

'Stuck at home with Mum.'

I ask, 'What's he doing now?'

'Jay? Same as before, I guess. He's a surgeon. Vascular. Works hard. Tennis Sundays. Wine club Thursdays. Probably glad to be back at his mother's for a while.'

'Are you and he Orthodox too, like Danny?'

She laughs. 'No, not at all. Danners is a one-off. I hardly even go to *shul*. Just for the festivals, you know. Jay and I would try and do Friday night candles, though he usually got back too late. And I still love chicken soup. That's about it. What about you, do you still go to church?'

'Oh, yes. Well, once a fortnight. Huw and Evie don't come so it's a chance for some peace. And I still go to confession.'

'I always thought that was such a brilliant idea. Cleansing.'

'I'm surprised you're not so into Jewish stuff any more. You always seemed more keen than Danny. With your batmitzvah and all that.'

She shrugs. 'I think the batmitzvah kind of knocked the religion out of me.'

'It's just . . . I don't get Danny. Were you surprised when he went religious?'

She stares at the ceiling. 'I used to think he'd change back, but he's totally immersed.'

'How come he doesn't wear the black hat like I used to see in Edgware?'

'And the long curls? No, Hella was brought up ultra-Orthodox, but she and Danny are more modern.'

'When I think back to what he was like . . .'

'I know. But I do understand it, even though it's not for me. Danners really needed some certainty in his life back then, after, you know, everything that happened.'

My throat feels dry and I sip my coffee. Cold.

She says, 'The Orthodox have a rule for everything, and Danners likes that.' Then she grins. 'Well, most of the time he does. This morning he's bunked off. He reckoned he had to go to Norwich to discuss the gravestone, but I think he could have done it just as easily by phone.'

Without thinking I say, 'So is Heifer sitting *shiva* all by herself down there?'

Miffy explodes with laughter at the nickname, reminding me vividly of when we were kids and she used to almost wet herself having hysterics.

Mama calls up, 'Food is ready!'

Miffy says, 'Be serious, Laura!' and we go downstairs, still giggling.

Brunch is a strange meal made of everything Mama wants to use up, cooked in Heifer's inimitable style. I seem to have toast spread with marge, fried eggs and a portion of kosher chicken.

Evie is fascinated by Miffy, makes sure to sit next to her. When Miffy turns to talk to her, Evie, embarrassingly, reaches up and strokes her hair. Miffy is unfazed. 'Hey, Evie. Did you ever know your mum when she had long hair? I was so envious. I grew mine to be the same.'

'I think she cut it when I was little.'

'It got in the way,' I say. 'Evie was always pulling it when she was a baby.' I miss my long hair.

Huw eats standing up, old-fashionedly letting the ladies and children have the chairs. He chats to Miffy about her travels and they discuss the history of various places. He's doing his urbane lecturer shtick to impress her. Mama watches me watching Huw and Miffy.

'Maybe it is best we are leaving today, *bebita*,' she whispers.

Furious at the implication – I wish to fuck I hadn't told her about Huw and the New Year's Eve tart – I look her straight in the eye and say, 'Why?'

She's shocked. It's the second time I've been off message today. She's always prided herself on our great understanding. 'Like sisters.' She tells friends, strangers, everyone, how close we are.

'We are maybe just a bit too crowded here,' she says, scraping her uneaten food into the bin.

Miffy disappears after the meal, and when she comes back to the kitchen, smelling of peppermint, she is dragging her enormous rucksack.

I can't help it; I am so uncool. 'Oh, you're not going already, are you?'

She smiles. 'Well, you're off today too, and I want to get the one-fifteen train. I must go and see Mum.'

Mama is standing at the counter. Her back stiffens at this reference to Andrea Cline. Miffy carries on, 'I haven't seen her yet. I came straight here from Heathrow. She'll be upset about Dad, despite everything.'

I ask Miffy why she doesn't travel with Danny and Hella, and she laughs. 'Danners did offer, but they're already breaking the rules about how many people you should have in one Volvo. Have you not experienced his kosher driving?'

'His what?'

'Oh, he thinks he doesn't need to pay attention to the road because God's keeping an eye on him. So far, God does actually seem to have been paying attention, but I don't want to be there when He turns away to sort out a war or something.'

Danny comes in while she's talking, and grins. 'You're letting me drive you to the station, though.'

'I've weighed up the odds of how much damage you can do in such a short distance, and decided to risk it.'

Outside the cottage, Miffy kisses us all goodbye, including me. I catch the scent of mint.

'Will you let me know about the party?' I ask.

'Of course!' she says. 'I got your number from the notice-board in your Mum's kitchen.'

This gives me the same thrill I once felt when boys used to secretly copy down my number from Mama's old dial-phone in the hall.

When Danny's driven her away, I go to help Mama pack. I feel very restless.

'Stop pacing, Laura. If you want to help, help. If not, please do something else.'

'Sorry, Mama. Just thinking. Hasn't Miffy changed? I'd hardly have known her.'

'She is changed, in some ways,' Mama says, crypti-cally, 'but in other ways she is still that same little *niña* from before.' She doesn't say any more, a Spanish Confucius, and I can't think how to continue the conversation without wading into treacherous waters. So we work together in silence, other than Mama's sighs and little sobs, folding her old-lady cardigans and pleated skirts into Michael's battered brown leather suitcase.

I go to my own room to pack, but am drawn to the window, where I can watch the Clines' attempts to get all their kids into the car at the same time. Heifer keeps having to go and look for shoes and coats, dispensing snacks like a vending machine, while Danny straps suitcases to the roof. Every time he ties an elastic cord to one side, he has to stretch to tie it to the other, revealing a flash of flat stomach. Very nice.

When at last they're ready, I try to get away with an air-kiss for Heifer, but am pulled against my will into a full-blown hug. By God, she's strong.

'Look after yourself,' she gasps, all moist-eyed. 'And this little one.' She clumsily pats my stomach, then trots off for a final trip to the loo, leaving Danny to settle the children into the car. I pretend we're married and the kids are ours. Bloody hell, the number of them: clearly we can't keep our hands off each other.

Laura: Well, Danny darling, long drive ahead.
Danny: Yes, my sweet, but once we've got the little ones

to bed, I won't be too tired to give you another marvellous seeing to.

Laura: Ooh, yes please! (*Giggles happily.*)

Think how old our child would have been – twenty-
two! Unbelievable. I wonder if Danny ever thinks of it.

There's a mad moment when the children are seated,
Heifer's still in the house, everyone else has wandered
off, and just Danny and I stand together by the car. I
say, 'Drive carefully, won't you? Miffy says your driving's terrifying.'

He smiles, looking down at me. I reach up and snake
my arms round him, skin of my arms against skin of his
neck. To my surprise he lets me, even bends his body
slightly towards me, exhales a breath against my face. I
feel a rush of blood to all my most interesting places. My
nipples actually ping out.

Now he pushes me gently away, but not before I have
felt his erection against my belly. The sky darkens momentarily, and I can't focus. He won't look at me. He opens the
boot and reorganises some bags, though they are packed
fine, unzips one then zips it up again. Says, 'Ah, here's
Hella now.'

I stand back to let his fat wife take her place in the passenger seat. Mama rushes out with something one of the
kids has forgotten, and we stand and wave. Mama goes

inside once the car is down the street, but I stay for I don't know how long, watching the space where he was.

What the fuck just happened?

The house is very quiet when eventually I go back in. I open my bag to put my sunglasses away, and on top is a note from Miffy. It's scrawled on notepaper torn from the pad by Mama's phone, but it smells of Miffy's scent. 'Good to see you, Laura. I'll be in touch soon. Love—' and instead of her name she has drawn her old trademark signature: a rabbit's head with floppy ears.

Miffy

1979

Melinda

Rabbi Aron is gorgeous to look at, but his sermons are so boring. This morning everyone was doing those hiding-yawns where you keep your mouth closed and stretch out your face. Nat Samuels fell asleep. I tried blocking out what Aron was saying, and concentrated on his face, but it wasn't easy. The man's got to be able to talk interestingly, as well as look sexy, hasn't he? Otherwise once you're married and used to his face, it's going to be a lot of dull evenings listening to him drone on.

After the service, Aron was mobbed by a bunch of old people. I stood behind his elbow for about a million years, tapping his soft jacket, until finally he turned round and I blurted, 'I'm not doing too well learning my portion.'

I was hoping he'd offer to take over my teaching but he said, 'Max tells me you're doing brilliantly, Melinda.'

Who the hell is Melinda? I said, 'It's Melissa.'

'Oh, yes, of course, I'm so sorry.' He turned back to talk to Rosa Spiegel, who was standing very close, her sticky pink lipstick stretched round her great fat smile.

On the way home I told Mum my views about how a husband has to be interesting as well as nice-looking (not mentioning Aron, just as a general opinion on marriage). She said I had hit the nail on the head. Dad was driving so I didn't think he could hear. But he looked at us in the mirror and said, 'Don't forget to tell Lissa about women and their bloody boring nagging, will you, darling?'

None of us said anything else for the rest of the journey.

Flirting

Laura came over today to discuss the guest list for her birthday party. When she wrote down Towse's name, I asked if she fancied him. She said, 'Of course not! He's your bloke, isn't he? Anyway, between you and me, he was a crap snogger.'

Mum was out shopping with Danners, and Mrs Morente stayed and drank wine with Dad in the garden. Laura and I watched them through the French windows. They didn't know we were there.

Laura said, 'Isn't Mama pretty?'

'Yes.' Mrs Morente was wearing a red shirt with a wide-open collar and tight black trousers, with her high orange sandals. 'My mum's pretty too.'

'Mmm. The Charming Mrs Cline has some good points. Her hair's a good colour. Mama says her hairdresser earns her money.'

Dad put his arm round Mrs Morente's shoulder.

'Isn't it sweet the way they love to flirt?' Laura said.

I didn't know exactly what she meant. She said, 'Sometimes I think your dad is really my dad too.'

I didn't like her saying that. I said, 'What about your real dad?'

'I haven't seen him for two years.' She laughed. 'He probably won't even bother to send me a birthday present.'

Dad shook his head, and Olivia Morente put her hand on his cheek for a moment, as if to say, 'don't worry'. Then they both stared at the ground and looked sad. If this was flirting, it didn't look that much fun.

Laura said, 'Let's pretend your dad is my dad too, then we'll be sisters.'

I don't want to share my dad, but it would be brilliant

to have Laura as a sister. For the rest of the day, we kept calling each other 'Miffy-sister' and 'Laura-sister'. It was really nice.

The Kiss

Dad took us to Laura's party early, so he could help. Mrs Morente told me I was looking very nice, though Mum had insisted on me wearing my horrible yellow blouse from Helene's Paris Fashions. Laura was looking gorgeous in a new pink swirly skirt. The room was decorated with bunting and a poster Laura had made of a huge '14' decorated with photos of all her friends and family. There was one of me in the middle of the four. I gave Laura a big packet of Maltesers and a jewellery tree I'd made from pipe cleaners, painted gold with Danners' Airfix paint. I pretended I'd bought it at a craft fair, but actually I'd got the idea from *Blue Peter*. She said the Maltesers were brilliant, but didn't say anything about the tree.

I helped Anthony East put out the food while Dad and Mrs Morente arranged Coke and lemonade on the bar, which was really a kitchen table. When the doorbell rang we all squealed. Some older boys, who all knew Danners, came in. Then the bell seemed to ring every minute until the room was full. Dad was serving people drinks in an embarrassing way, saying, 'What would sir like?' and, 'We have a fine array of beverages here.' Danners and I were just dying, but Mrs Morente was really laughing. She asked Anthony East to go out and buy more orangeade. Then she and Dad stood behind the bar, talking and smiling. Was *this* what Laura meant by flirting?

I went over to where Towse was standing, hoping he'd talk to me. This worked, sort of – he asked me if Dan was there. I pointed to where I'd last seen him, but he'd gone. Then he asked where Laura was. I really wanted Towse to stop asking me about other people. So I asked if he'd seen any good films lately, a suggestion for chatting up boys I'd got from *Patches*. He just shook his head, so I gave that suggestion nought out of ten. I decided I'd tell him my best film if he didn't speak for thirty seconds (which I was timing on my watch), but then he said, 'See if I can find Dan,' and walked off.

I went back to the bar, which had turned into self-service because Dad and Mrs Morente had disappeared. Then someone turned out the main lights. 'Hey!' I said, but no one else seemed to mind, and straight away the room was filled with snogging couples. Someone turned up the music. I groped my way back to my chair. As my eyes got used to the dark, I could see Laura's friend Fiona kissing a huge black boy. He was holding her chest.

Then a boy squeezed himself onto my chair. We were so squashed together that when I turned my face to say something, he hardly had to move to put his mouth against mine. He smelled of TCP. I opened my lips and he put his tongue inside my mouth and turned it round and round like the spin cycle of a washing machine. My first proper snog! I had my eyes open, and I could see he had fair hair and was quite good-looking, though he had a few spots. My tongue started to get tired and I wondered how long you could kiss without breathing properly. This is the sort of thing they should have in *Patches*, not useless chat-up lines that don't work.

Suddenly the lights were snapped on and everyone groaned. It was so bright that for a moment it was hard to see. Fiona called out, 'God, sorry, I accidentally leaned against the switch.'

Two people on the other side of the room were kissing so passionately they hadn't even noticed the lights go on. I realised it was Laura and Danners. I turned to the boy I was with and he said, 'Whoops, sorry – thought you were someone else.' He got up and so did loads of other people, and everyone started getting ready to go home: finding shoes, doing up shirts, looking for jackets. I said goodbye to Towse, but he didn't hear, and pushed right past Laura and Danners, who had stopped kissing and were holding hands. Nearly everyone had gone by the time Dad reappeared.

Laura kissed Danners on the cheek as we left, and

said, 'It was brilliant, wasn't it, Miffy-sister? I'll phone you tomorrow.'

Dad teased Danners about Laura's kiss, but he didn't say anything.

'What about you, Lissa?' Dad asked. 'Did you make any new friends?'

'No,' I said. 'No one special.'

No Easter Eggs

So fed up. Mum, Danners and I had been going to visit Auntie Leila in Brittany for a week. But stupid Dan got a stinking cold which he and Mum insisted on calling flu, meaning he was allowed to stay in bed all day, and Mum cancelled our holiday at the last minute. Everyone else was away. Sasha was in Dorset, and Laura was in Spain at her grandparents'. Dad couldn't get any time off work, so Mum was grumpy too.

Even worse than not going on holiday was that it was Passover and the shops were filled with Easter eggs, which we're not allowed to eat. At supper, Danners staggered downstairs wrapped in his continental quilt. He said he would give me money to buy a load of eggs tomorrow and stash them in our rooms till Passover was over. I thought it was a brilliant idea, but Mum said, 'Flu or no flu, I'd better not catch you bringing *traife* into the house, young man,' and Danners went into a sulk. So we were all in a mood. When I'm married to Towse or Aron, I'll let our children buy chocolate eggs and save them till after Passover.

Jay

After *shul* this morning, I was walking past that nice-looking son from the new family when he dropped his prayer book right in front of me. I picked it up and he said, 'Thank you! My name's Jay, what's yours?'

He told me his family had only recently moved here from Manchester. Then Mum, with stunning timing, came over to say we were going. I prayed she would fall into the middle of the earth and disappear, but she smiled at Jay, said, 'So nice to meet you,' though she hadn't met him, and told me to run along.

Cagoule

Daddy took me to the big shopping centre at Wood Green. All the shops were under cover, so you didn't have to go outside. It was nice, just me and Dad. He was in a really good mood and kept cracking jokes. He bought me, Danners and himself these brilliant cagoules, raincoats that you fold up into your pocket.

Laura

The world's most pregnant woman lumbers past, leaning heavily on her scraggy husband. She looks quite deformed. A midwife leads them into a side room, and the rest of us exchange horrified looks.

Huw says, 'Christ, did you see that?'

'I don't remember being anywhere near that enormous with Evie.'

'You were pretty fucking big, now I come to think of it.'

'Oh, God, was I?' I put my hands on my bump, tiny compared to that elephant woman's. Being at the clinic always makes me feel vulnerable. 'Thanks for being here, Huw.'

'We're not in the Dark Ages, *cariad*. Even busy profes-sors are allowed to accompany their wives to scans.'

'I did ask Mama to come but she didn't feel up to it.'

'The Merry Widow's not up for much, is she?'

'Bit harsh, Huw. Michael's only been gone ten days.'

He puts down his magazine – an old *What Car?* 'I know. Sorry. It's just the atmosphere at home's a bit Miss Havisham.'

The young couple sitting opposite us are eavesdropping. The girl's unblemished. She looks about seventeen. Her hair's in a ponytail, for God's sake. The poor boyfriend. Her fresh skin and cute tits will soon be distant memories.

I lower my voice. 'Jesus, Huw, it's not like you're home much. I'm the one who's coping with it.'

I'm really trying to be nice and stay in patch-things-up mode, but God, it's hard.

The elephant woman waddles out, all eyes on her humungous arse, and the midwife calls out, 'Laura Ellis!'

In the tiny room, I climb inelegantly onto the bed. Huw stares at the ceiling while the sonographer puts the cold jelly on my stomach, but then the cliché of the baby on the screen works its magic and we both gaze at it, transfixed. All is apparently as it should be: head circumference, spinal column, etc. I've had a lot of pregnancies, but none of them, apart from Evie, of course, made it anywhere near this far. The technology since her scan doesn't seem to have moved on; you still need someone to point out which of the fuzzy blobs are the head and the arms. But then, unexpectedly, the angle changes and there, clear as anything, are a pair of tiny feet, soles facing us, ten stubby toes. My eyes fill with tears. I wish Huw were happy about this baby. Wish he felt the same as twelve years ago, when we came out of the hospital clutching Evie's scan picture, awash with disbelief and joy. He took me to a jewellery shop and bought me an eternity ring. Beautiful, it was; gold with tiny emeralds right round the band. I suppose it's kind of symbolic that I've lost it.

'Did you want to know the sex?' the sonographer asks.

'Yes!' I say, at the same moment as Huw says, 'No, thanks.'

She says, 'Ohh-kay. I'll let you discuss it for a moment,' and goes out.

'Why not, Huw? We found out for Evie.'

'There's so few mysteries in life, aren't there? It'd be nice if it was a surprise.'

'Oh, how lovely!' I hug him. Maybe he is looking forward to the baby after all.

'Yuck!' He pulls away. 'You've got jelly all over my shirt.'

Walking out to the car park, Huw puts his arm round my shoulder and I feel as if we are like that fresh young couple, just starting out.

'Don't suppose there's any chance of us getting a quick coffee?' I ask.

'Would love to, *cariad*, but we ought to get home. I want to grab a shower before heading back to work. We're taking a visiting professor out to dinner tonight.'

'Can you at least drive me to church and wait while I speak to Father Davies?'

Huw looks at his watch before saying, 'Yes, that should be okay.'

Yes, it fucking should, I say in my head.

Outside the church, Huw leaves the engine running. 'You might as well turn that off,' I tell him. 'We're not doing an armed robbery.'

He sighs, and turns it off.

I'm barely through the door of the church before I have to stop and hold on to the back of a pew as a sudden wave of tummy pain washes over me. It passes quickly but leaves me feeling shaken. Maybe the scanning equipment's done something?

There's a four-bar heater blazing in Father Davies' little office, in sharp contrast to the cold of the church. He takes my hand. 'Laura, I was so sorry to hear about the loss of your stepfather.'

'Thank you.' I sit down and face him across the desk.

'So how are you doing, Laura, in yourself? How's the baby?' He smiles at me.

'I'm fine, really. Baby's fine too, touch wood.' I briefly rest my hand on his desk. God knows why, it's not one of my superstitions. 'My mum's not doing so well, of course.'

'Well, that's natural.'

'Yes.' It's terribly hot. I take off my coat and scarf. 'The funeral was weird. I saw Melissa and Daniel again, you know, my step-family, for the first time in years. And I used to be in love with Daniel and he was a bit funny with me, and he's got a ton of kids, anyway that's not relevant, but we had a Jewish funeral and there are so many rules and I ended up being rude to his wife even though she was asking for it.'

I take off my cardigan. How can he stand it in here? It's a sodding sauna.

Father Davies looks down at his hands. 'Would it be useful if I heard your confession now, Laura? It seems there is a great deal going on for you.'

'Oh, no, Father, sorry, Huw's waiting outside. I just wanted to ask if you'd be kind enough to say a prayer for my stepfather on Sunday?'

'Of course.' He rummages in a drawer, hands me a piece of paper and an old-fashioned fountain pen. 'Please fill in these details, and I'll take it from there.'

The ink runs thick as I write, leaving a string of little blots across the paper.

Congregant's name: *Laura Ellis*

Name of deceased: *Michael Cline*

Beth Miller

Age at death: *65*
Relationship to congregant: *Stepfather*
Other relevant friends/relations: *Wife, Olivia Cline.*
Granddaughter, Evie Ellis

It's the first official form I've filled in for Michael. Mama and Danny dealt with everything else. It makes me realise, properly realise, that's it. That's the end of Michael. I won't see him again.

'I wish I did have time for confession, Father.' Sweat slides down my back. Are there any other layers I can take off without scaring the bejesus out of him?

'So do I. It's been a long time.' He smiles. 'But I understand you're very busy.'

It's a relief to get out. A few more minutes and I'd be down to my knickers. Though Father Davies, being short, balding and the wrong side of 60, is not in any sense a fantasy figure, the thought of stripping in front of him turns me on. It makes me think of Danny's erect prick against my body as we said goodbye, and I feel absolutely horny as hell. I get into the passenger seat and give Huw my best heavy-lidded look. It always used to work. 'Is there time for, you know, uh, a quick lie-down when we get home? You could shower after.'

'Ha ha, good one. Right, let's get going.' He starts the car.

'I'm serious! I really feel like it. That doesn't happen very often these days.' *With you*, I add in my head.

He glances at me. 'Bloody hell, *cariad*, what happened in there?'

I lean my head against the back of the seat. 'Never mind, forget I spoke.'

'Pregnancy hormones, is it?'

'Forget it, I said.'

Evie's at a friend's, so Mama's on her own in the house, and in a grump. She can't stand being alone.

'I organised the prayer for Michael, Mama.'

She nods. 'Good.'

Thank you, Laura.

'Father Davies is so kind. It didn't bother him that Michael wasn't Catholic.'

'I should think not, *bebita*! It would be completely un-Christian to even have such a thought.'

I know I should leave it. 'Quite a few Christians might have trouble with it, Mama. I'm only saying that Father Davies...'

'That's *enough*, Laura! It's obvious who really had the problem with Michael.'

'I don't! I didn't.'

'I think you have always made your feelings crystal clear.' She slams out of the room, and after a moment I hear the telly blaring.

Huw's clothes are strewn across the bathroom floor. His blurred pink body shimmers behind the steamed-up shower door. I raise my voice so he can hear me over the noise of the water. 'Mama just had a right old go at me.'

'Oh dear, what about?'

'It was stupid. She said I had a problem with Michael being Jewish.'

He turns off the shower and steps, dripping, onto the mat. 'That's crazy, you've never minded Yids.'

'Huw! You can't say that.'

'Just trying to cheer you up.'

'What, by being racist? Mama's really upset me, it isn't funny.'

He pulls me close to him, making my clothes damp. 'I'm sorry, *cariad*.'

To my surprise, the stirrings of desire return. I really must be starting to forgive Huw for the New Year's Eve tart; I haven't felt like touching him for weeks, but now I can't stop myself. 'Huw,' I whisper, 'do you really have to rush out?'

He doesn't move, so I unwrap the towel from his waist. Slide my hand down to his penis, slippery from the shower, and stir it into life with my fingers, pressing my face against his neck and kissing the drops of water from his skin. When his breathing gets faster I sink to my knees, a more difficult manoeuvre than I remember, kissing all the way down his chest, till my mouth finds the top of his cock, swollen, clean-tasting. I can easily bring to mind the memory of Danny's circumcised teenage cock, and I kiss and lick it, teasing, before letting it slowly fill my mouth. Huw sighs, puts his hands on my head and pushes me gently, further down the shaft. I close my eyes and take more and more into my throat. Huw groans. The pulse is banging in my cunt, but he makes no attempt to stop and make love as he usually does, so at last it is I who pull away and lie across the floor, awkwardly as there isn't quite enough room. Huw kneels between my thighs and pushes my pants down to my ankles. I arch my hips towards him, but as his cock, wet from my mouth, touches the edge of my thigh, he starts to shrivel. I reach for him with my hands, but he says, 'Shit. Sorry, *cariad*, it's no good, it's gone.'

I struggle to a sitting position. 'Why? What happened?'

'I'm really sorry. I don't know.' He is holding his limp dick, staring at it. 'Useless fucking thing.'

This has almost never happened before. Once or twice back during the worst of the split from Carmen, but he can usually do it even if he's completely smashed.

'Oh dear, poor you. Don't worry.'

We are formal and awkward. He starts to get up and I realise he thinks that's it; that's the end of the session.

'Um, Huw. Can you, would you, I mean, I'm still sort of turned on here.'

'Oh, yes, of course,' he says politely, and pushes me down again onto my back. As his tongue darts in and out of me, I swim back into my mind. This is Danny; this is Danny giving me head. I come violently, a sharp series of spasms. The last one makes my stomach hurt again like it did in the church, and I yell out.

'Was that an ecstatic shout?' Huw sits up on his haunches and wipes his mouth on a piece of toilet paper. 'It sounded a bit weird.'

'It hurt a little. I've had a tummy ache today.'

The pain subsides once I get to my feet, and I sit on the edge of the bath, adjusting my clothes. Huw brushes his teeth.

'We need a bigger bathroom if we're going to start having sex in it,' I say, in an attempt to dispel the weird atmosphere.

He rinses and spits. '*Cariad*, I've been meaning to ask. Carmen's going a bit bonkers with Glynn. Could he stay for a few days? We haven't had him for months.'

Oh, Christ. Glynn moping round one circuit of the house, Mama moping round another. I'm about to say absolutely not when I think of some advantages.

1. Glynn will give Mama someone to fuss over when Evie's at school.

2. Huw will owe me a favour.

'Oh, all right.'

Huw grins at his reflection and pulls dental floss through his front teeth. 'Thanks, *cariad*,' he says, slightly indistinctly. 'I knew you'd be okay with it, so I've told Carmen he can come on Friday.'

'That's the day after to-fucking-morrow!'

'It's not a big deal, is it? He'll be light relief compared to the Merry Widow.'

I force a smile. I am going to keep the peace if it kills me. 'Yes, of course, that's fine.' I'm about to say more but he goes back into the shower and starts washing me off him. For a moment, I don't care, because that's the first time we've had sex since the twenty-ninth of December – not that I'm keeping count or anything. Then as I go downstairs it occurs to me that we still haven't technically had sex, not if you mean actual penetration – sorry to sound like Shere Hite. And Huw, like most men, does only mean actual penetration. Shit, he didn't even come! Now I feel worse than before.

Evie's back and she and Mama are watching the news. Mama's tutting loudly at every item. 'Have you seen this, Laura?' she calls indignantly. 'This business in Iraq?'

'Yes, awful,' I call back, the grown-up equivalent of 'whatever'.

I ring the midwife but she's not there. I'll try again tomorrow. I start making supper. Huw breezes in, wearing a dark shirt I've never seen before and which is far too trendy to have been bought in Bangor. The slate-grey colour makes his eyes seem more blue.

'Where's that from?'

'I got it in some designer place in Great Yarmouth, that day Evie and I went to the cinema.'

'You look lovely, Daddy,' Evie says.

Huw gives me a kiss on the forehead, whispers, 'That was nice, upstairs?' Then says more loudly, 'I'll be back pretty late. See you in the morning.'

The door slams behind him.

10 MARCH 2003

First Mama, filling the place with gloom; now Glynn, six feet two of smelly hormones, lumbering round like Lurch. The house has never felt smaller.

For lunch I heat tomato soup. Glynn's not just a sodding vegetarian; he's a sodding tinned-soup-and-macaroni vegetarian. He mooches in, wearing a bedtime fug and jeans halfway down his arse, and lopes about, inefficiently assembling a cup of coffee. Mama asks him how he slept, in a bright youth worker voice. The answer must surely be 'extremely well' as he's been in bed more than twelve hours, lazy fucker.

'Yeah, good.' He slops his mug to the table and hunches

over his mobile, texting violently. He's supposed to be on a gap year before university, God help us. He had a job at the start of the year in a call centre, but not any more. We're not supposed to mention it.

Mama circles her spoon round a tiny portion of soup. Glynn eats the rest, and I make myself a ham sandwich. I love eating meat in front of him. Childish, I know, but his pained expression amuses me. The phone rings as we're finishing, and Mama starts piling up the crockery. I can't face her stacking the dishwasher all wrong again, so I let the answerphone pick up. Then I hear Miffy's voice and snatch the receiver.

'Hey, Miff!' Too loud. 'Nice to hear from you!' I feel a little unsteady as I take the phone upstairs.

'How's it going?' Her voice is warm.

'Oh, you know, I'm being ground down by vile ungrateful offspring.'

'Offspring plural? Has the sprog come early?'

I explain about Glynn, and she laughs. 'Boy, I've sure missed out on teeming family life.'

I reach my room, puffing, and sit on the bed.

'All went well with the scan, I hope?' Miffy asks.

'Yes, thanks. Everything seems fine.'

'And I hope Olivia's doing okay? She's lucky to have you looking after her. You were always so close weren't you, such a tight little unit of two.'

And now we're back to being two. I say quickly, 'So how was *your* mum?'

'Surprisingly upset. She still calls Dad her "bastard ex-husband".' Miffy laughs. 'But she was really affected by it. Anyway, I was just phoning to give you the details of Micah's party.'

'And your party.'

'Oh, yes, I suppose it is mine too. I keep forgetting. So it's this Saturday. Most people are making a long weekend of it. There's loads of room. Bring Evie and the lovely Huw. Glynn too, if you like.'

I think not. She says she'll email a map, and I'm about to ask her something, anything, just to keep her talking, when she says, 'Bye,' and hangs up.

In the kitchen I see Glynn's gone, leaving a splash of soup on the table. Mama's gazing into space. The dishwasher's running on the wrong cycle.

'That was Miffy,' I say.

'I know. I heard her voice on the machine. Meanwhile your other telephone has been going beep beep, driving me *loco*.' Mama slides my mobile across the table. I've missed three texts from Ceri: *Looking 4ward 2 c u*, *Hop u not 4got,* and *where u r!!* Probably even Glynn's texts are more lucid.

I'd forgotten tonight's grim plan for Huw and I to meet Ceri and Rees for a drink. Rees's idea. I've been putting it off for weeks, worried he's going to suggest a wife swap. I ring Huw to remind him.

'Sorry, *cariad*, no can do. Going straight out from work. Wining and dining.'

'Again?'

'I know, love, but this professor's important. This collaborative work might put our department on the map.'

Yeah, like a Welsh History department is ever going to be on any kind of map. I don't argue. Hopefully Ceri will cancel if we can't both come. When I hang up, Mama says, 'I've been thinking about Melissa's celebrations. Do you think I was too hasty, saying I would not go?'

She is pottering mournfully around, sniffing and making coffee. Oh God, I *so* don't want to have to nurse-maid her at this party. I really need to let my hair down. With Danny, hopefully. Kidding!

'I don't think so, Mama. You felt it was a bit much, and I'm sure your instincts were right.'

'I just had a tiny thought that Michael might want me to go. But it would be silly, it is far too soon.'

Phew.

'I am so glad you and Melissa are friendly again, after all this time. It was so crazy' – she says 'crazy' with a Spanish roll – 'it was so cerrrrrazy for you two not to be friends, and Daniel also, I could never understand it.'

And with that little bombshell, she calmly takes her mug and moves to the door.

'Mama, hang on a sec. Don't you remember *why* I haven't seen them for more than twenty years?'

'Well, *bebita*, that is all water under a bridge, you know.'

'Not to them!'

I stare at her. I don't realise I'm clenching my fist till I register dimly that my palm hurts: my nails are digging into it. I can't remember the last time I felt so enraged. Yes, I can: aged fourteen, dragged away from my life, my friends, my boyfriend, fobbed off with a stack of false promises. *Of course Great Yarmouth will be lovely! Of course you'll be able to go on seeing Danny! Of course Melissa will still be your best friend!*

'It's not water under the bridge to me either,' I say, and still Mama stands in the doorway, ready to run the minute she might have to face up to something.

'I don't think this is the time for arguments, Laura.'

'Oh, yes, it's never a good time for me to say how I feel.'

'That's very rude.' She looks down at the floor. 'It makes me very sad.'

'Yes, well, it *is* sad.' My stomach twinges. '*Fucking* sad.'

Mama starts crying, and her coffee splashes onto the quarry tiles. I take the cup from her and get a cloth, but she says, 'I'll do it,' and pulls the cloth from my hand, as though that's what we are fighting about. Very slowly, she mops up the mess, then drapes the cloth super-carefully over the taps. Finally she sits down. She doesn't look at me.

I try to keep my voice steady. 'Mama, I'd love to have been in touch with Miffy and Danny all this time. As their stepsister, if not their friend. But I couldn't. I'd really like to talk about why.'

There's a long silence, during which I endure a wave of pain, tell myself it feels nothing like a contraction, remind myself to bloody well phone the midwife again.

Finally she says, 'It was all such a long time ago.' Her eyes are dark and wet. She is still beautiful with her heart-shaped face, thick hair, perfect cheekbones. I hope I look like her when I'm nearly sixty.

'I don't want to upset you.'

'Upset? Yes, *I* am upset. You talk to me as though I am a stranger, not your *mamita* who bore you from her own body.'

Yeah, yeah. I make a big effort. 'I don't mean to talk to you in a funny way. Please, can I ask you about it?'

She shrugs, so I carry on. 'When we lived, you know, back in Edgware?'

She gives a theatrical sigh.

'Sorry, Mama. This is hard to ask. Okay. Did you. Um. Did you. Encourage me towards them?'

She says nothing, but I can see from her face that she knows what I mean. I speak fast. 'Encourage me towards

Miffy and Danny. To be friends with them. I'm asking because I remember lots of times. Times I didn't have a choice about seeing them. I seemed to be in my room with Miffy an awful lot, feeling I couldn't go downstairs and disturb you. And I remember, once, I wanted to go to a disco and you wouldn't let me because Miffy was coming over, even though I hadn't asked her.'

'But she was your *amiga*, of course you wanted to spend time with her.'

'And you were always saying what a lovely boy Danny was.'

'So this is a crime now? To approve your daughter's friends?'

'Mama, Miffy and Danny have always blamed me for breaking up their family.'

'Oh, *bebita*, they didn't blame you.'

'They bloody did!'

'Please stop swearing, Laura. They might have blamed *me* for a while, but I'm sure they never blamed you.'

'So why didn't they want to see me all these years?'

'I don't know. It made your stepfather terribly sad.' She starts weeping again, and can't find her tissue. It's on the floor at her feet, and I'm about to pick it up when I decide not to help her. I have to physically stop myself from bending down. I take a breath and say, 'What I'm asking, Mama, is did you encourage me to be friends with them? So that you could, you and Michael could, have an excuse?'

'An excuse? An excuse for what, exactly?'

'I mean a reason. Excuse is the wrong word, sorry. A reason to see each other.'

She is on her feet. 'You are asking me, would I use my own child, would I do such a thing? How can you think it is acceptable to ask me this? *Qué insulto!*'

She is furious, her eyes properly flashing, like a flamenco doll I used to have. I haven't thought about that doll in years. It had a black and red lace dress and lovely black hair. A red comb. A *mantilla*, Mama called it.

'*Mi marido*, he is still warm in the ground and you say these dreadful things.'

She always did have a touch of the melodramatics.

'It's just – seeing Miffy and Danny again, realising that all these years I wasn't being paranoid, they really were avoiding me...'

She snorts. 'You talk like a cerrrazy person. I am worried for your mind. You ought to see somebody, a professional.'

'I'm not crazy, Mama. They always made sure I wouldn't be there when they visited you and Michael.'

'Believe what you like, Laura. I know what I know. And now, if you will excuse me. *Tengo un dolor*, my head aches. I am going to have a lie-down.'

So am I. When she's out of the way, I crawl upstairs and

fall into bed. I'm sure I won't sleep; my head and heart are both racing.

There's a feeling of intense heat. Fiona, a friend from school, runs ahead of me. I call out, tell her to wait, but she laughs, and then we're in a room with an old-fashioned black dial-phone. Fiona has turned into Evie. She reaches for the phone and I want to stop her, but I can't move, my legs are made of water. 'No, don't call her,' I cry, but she says, 'I want to go home,' and picks up the receiver.

I wake up and the real phone is ringing – my mobile. It's Ceri, wondering why I haven't texted her back.

'Sorry, Ceri,' I say brightly, to cover the fact that I've just woken up. 'Perhaps we should cancel? Huw's just told me he's got a work commitment tonight.'

'Hasn't he always.'

Oh, do fuck off. I say, 'I'm happy to rearrange.' Bit of luck, she'll forget about it for a few more weeks.

'I suppose we might as well go ahead tonight anyway. Rees has been looking forward to it. I'd like to have known earlier.'

Bollocks. I make peppermint tea in the interests of tummy-calming, and by the time Evie gets back from school I'm feeling better. She runs upstairs and I follow her, and knock on Mama's door. She is standing by the wardrobe, her face pinched, suitcase open on the bed.

'What are you doing, Mama?'

'Surely that is obvious, Laura. I won't stay where I am spoken to so rudely, so harshly.'

A shrink would say I've spent all my life trying to make my mother happy; it's too ingrained to stop now. 'Mama, please don't go!' I reach for her hand, but she holds hers away from me. 'I wasn't thinking. I just wanted to, oh, it doesn't matter what I wanted.'

'No. You weren't thinking. I have just lost *mi marido*, the love of my life. I come to my daughter's house for a small piece of comfort, and what does she do? She accuses me of dreadful things! I would not have believed it of you, Laura.'

I start to cry. She can always make me cry. 'I'm so sorry. Please stay.'

'As you know, *bebita*, I did not have a happy relationship with my mother,' she says, staring at the floor. 'I always prided myself that we were different. But the things you said to me today . . . I wonder, where did I go wrong?'

'But Mama! You haven't gone wrong anywhere.'

'I hope you will take me to the station, but I am willing to telephone a taxi.'

'A train? What, now? It's an eight-hour journey! You'll get stranded at Stockport! There's at least four changes!'

She hesitates. She's never tried to go anywhere by herself from North Wales.

'At least will you wait till tomorrow, and I can drive you as far as Crewe?'

Beth Miller

With extremely ill grace, she agrees to wait till morning, and goes downstairs to call Rail Enquiries.

There's a burst of giggling from the study, and when I push the door open I find Evie and Glynn lying together on his airbed. They're each wearing one earphone plugged into Evie's iPod. Music seeps out.

'Mum! Haven't you heard of knocking?' Evie sits up. 'It's the latest fashion.'

'Chill,' Glynn says to her, and flashes me an insolent smile. 'We're not doing anything illegal.'

'I'm delighted to hear it,' I say, in Mama's youth worker voice. All I can think to do is leave the door open, but am not surprised to hear it shut before I get downstairs.

Rees suggests a pub on the far side of town called the Ty-Nant, which I've not been to before. At Ceri's subtle suggestion ('If you're not drinking anyway...'), I'm driving. Rees sits next to me in the front, so he can navigate, or that's his story. In the dark of the car, his hand brushes my leg more often than chance alone. Once, he rests it there for a moment, and I abruptly change gears so I have a reason to shunt him off; the car lurches and Ceri screams, 'Ooh, I'm getting all thrown around here.'

Rees turns to her. 'You would if I was back there with you, babe, yeah?'

When we arrive, he sits at a table before Ceri and I have

got our coats off, and says to her, 'I'll have a pint of best, babe, yeah?' He has that North Welsh verbal tic, the interrogative 'yeah?' at the end of every sentence. Wonder if he does it in bed? *Oh, you're so good Ceri, yeah? Do you like it like that, yeah?*

While Ceri dutifully goes to the bar, I try to shake my head free of images of Rees in bed. I sit opposite him but he leans round the table so he can stroke my arm.

'This is nice, Laura. Soft. Cashmere, is it?'

'Polyester, I think.' Actually, it is cashmere. Creepy bastard. I shift a little further away along the seat.

'Ceri was saying you're off to a big fancy party in England. Your stepsister and brother, yeah?'

'*Yeah,*' I say, but he doesn't notice.

'Well, now. If I remember what a little bird told me down the Student Union in 1985, when she'd had too much snake-bite and black — and I think I do — wasn't this stepbrother your first shag, when you was just fourteen, yeah?'

Christ, I can't believe I ever told him that. I can't believe he remembers it, either. I suppose it was that godawful night I ended up on his filthy sofa. Bloody dreadful being young, wasn't it?

'Always liked that story, Laura. Always thought it was a bit kinky, like.'

'Is that a fact?' God, how does Ceri stand it? She comes

back with the drinks. Spills a bit of mine, but as it's orange juice, who gives a shit?

'Is anyone smoking in here?' she says, tilting the ashtray to see if there's anything in it.

'So, you planning to get up close and personal again with him, Laura? Old times' sake, yeah?'

'What you on about, Rees?'

'Laura's stepbrother.'

'What about him?' Ceri looks round the pub for other smokers.

'Nothing, babe,' he says, and winks at me. Christ on a bike. Why's it always the ones you wouldn't touch with a bargepole who fancy you?

'Thing I don't get about this Melissa, right,' Ceri says. 'You haven't seen her for years. Then you meet her and bam, you're bezzie mates, off for the weekend together.'

'It's not that strange. We *are* related. And we used to be brilliant friends.'

Ceri lights her cigarette. 'When you were *kids*. But last time you saw her, your mum had just run off with her dad.'

Rees lights up too. 'Romanian, these are.' He shows me the packet. 'Wouldn't smoke nothing else now.'

My stomach, which has been calm for hours, gives a sudden lurch, and I wince.

'You okay?' Ceri says. 'You look washed out. Doesn't she, Rees? Maybe you're anaemic?'

Rees blows smoke in my face. 'She looks good to me. She looks good.'

I cough, and he says, 'Bloody hell, Ceri, we shouldn't be smoking. The baby, yeah?'

'Think I'll just nip to the loo.' I stand up.

'In that case, I'm going to carry on smoking,' Ceri says.

Rees discreetly strokes my bum. Just once. Just light enough that if I say anything, he can say it was a mistake, he was just moving his arm. 'You're still a bit of a goer, Mrs Ellis, aren't you, on the quiet?'

'What do you mean, *still*?' Ceri stares at him.

I walk round the bar, the pain getting steadily worse. I spot the sign for the toilet at the same moment that I see Huw sitting in a booth with a woman. His back is to me, but I can see her clearly. The good news is she's not that tart from New Year's Eve. The bad news is everything else.

I push open the toilet door and collapse onto a loo, let my mind go blank until the pain fades. I don't know how long. Two minutes? Ten? I count the black and white tiles on the wall. Two hundred and fifteen. I wonder how long it took to tile all the cubicles. Wonder if halfway through they wished they'd chosen more interesting colours. When I wipe myself, there is blood on the paper. This makes me very focused. Everything else is irrelevant, except for the following:

1. I don't want Huw to know I have seen him;
2. I don't want Ceri and Rees to see him;
3. I don't want anyone to know I am bleeding;
4. I want to go home.

I step quietly back into the pub. Huw and the woman are still there. So it wasn't a horrible mirage. She is younger than me. Good skin, blonde hair piled on her head like Brigitte fucking Bardot. She is looking at him from under her lashes. She is the reason he couldn't get his dick up last week.

'You were a long time,' Ceri says. 'Are you okay?'

'I'm fine, but I was taking a call from Evie. She doesn't feel well. I'd better go.'

'Shame.' Rees makes a crying face. 'Thought your mum was with her, yeah?'

'Oh, you!' Ceri hits his arm playfully. 'Typical non-parent. You always want your mummy when you're sick, don't you? You'd better head off then, Laura. We can get a cab back, no worries.'

'Well,' I say, thinking desperately, 'she also wants to see her Auntie Ceri.'

'Does she? Why?'

'I told her I was with you and she said she wished you'd read her a story.'

'Ah, that's sweet,' Rees says, stroking Ceri's arm.

'Well I can do, I guess...'

'How about you both come with me, we pop inside for a quick story, make a sick little girl happy, then you two can go for a drink at that lovely new cocktail bar near us?'

'The Griffin? That's not new,' Rees says. 'I've been there loads.'

Thanks a fucking bunch, Rees.

'Who've you been there with?' Ceri says.

Huw's blonde 'professor' comes round to our side of the bar to order drinks. Rees stares a moment too long, and Ceri puts on her coat. 'Come on, then. Just call me Florence Nightingale.'

Then, thank Christ, we are out of there. Back home, I work quickly, going in first and then nipping back outside to tell them that Evie's already asleep. Ceri and Rees bugger off, and I shut the front door and lean against it, like in the movies when they've outwitted a load of zombies.

Mama comes into the hall. Another zombie. 'There's a train first thing tomorrow, Laura. Only three changes, not your nonsense story.'

'If that's what you want, Mama, fine.'

I'm unequal to any more conversation. Possibly ever again. I crawl into bed, wrap my arms round my stomach, and whisper, *Come on, now. Come on, now. It's going to be all right.*

12 MARCH 2003

No blood on the sheets. None yesterday, either. The midwife said she'd worry if there was any more. Got to stop rushing about after other people, she said. Got to not let things get to me. I told her that my mother had gone home – I didn't say in a huff – and the midwife said, 'Good. Now you could do with shifting that stepson of yours.'

Too right, Nursie. Apart from anything else, I'm anxious Glynn will take advantage of Evie. I must talk to Huw about it. Oh, yes, you're right. Must also discuss that blonde with him. But when? He gets in after I've gone to bed; he leaves before I'm up. An idea comes to me and makes me laugh. Evie, eating cereal, looks at me but doesn't say anything. I drop her at school and go on to work.

I usually love going into the shop, but Ceri's in a bit of a mood today. I tell her I like her jumper (even though it has a picture of Olive Oyl appliquéd onto it), make tea and try to amuse her with Tales of Glynn. When we first started working together, Ceri and I bonded over our nightmare step-kids. We would spend hours analysing the dreadful things Huw's kids said to me, and the vile things Owen's kids said to her. Now she's divorced that wanker and never has to see them, lucky cow. The topic works some of its magic again, as she smiles at my descriptions of Glynn sleeping in till lunch, him saying 'chill' and 'don't get stressy', plus his irritating vegetarian pose.

The shop's quiet as usual, so we sit out the back with the portable telly on, keeping an eye on the door. Today's programme is about men who're in love with their mothers-in-law. It's mystifying how many the producers have managed to round up. Ceri smokes and I passively inhale. I ask if her younger sister might lend me a nice dress for Miffy's party – Rhianna's just had a baby, and her maternity clothes are way more stylish than Ceri's usual wardrobe. Ceri shrugs, maybe, and gives me the phone number.

I politely ask her how things are going with Rees – not that I want to know.

'Okay. I don't know. He's good in bed but he talks a lot of shit.'

I'm amazed to hear this: not the talking shit part but the sexual prowess. He was totally useless when we were students. I'm distracted by a mother-in-law on the telly who looks younger than her daughter-in-law, when Ceri says, mock-casual, blowing out smoke, 'So Rees says you and he used to date.'

What a twat! Why on earth did he tell her?

'Oh, you could hardly call it dating. It was one of those incredibly brief student things, years ago. Before I met Huw. Before you and I were even friends, I think.'

'Thanks for letting me know, Laura.'

'Gosh, Ceri, I'm sorry, but it was, what, eighteen years ago? You know what it was like when we were students. I scarcely remember it.'

'He remembers all right. He can't stop bloody going on about it.'

'How boring of him.'

Ceri stubs out her cigarette on the step and says, 'Looks like it's going to be another quiet day. Why don't you head off? There's no point us both hanging round.'

She stands up, brushes fag ash off Olive Oyl's face, not looking at me.

'Seriously? Do you want me to?' I stare at her.

She smiles. Not properly. 'Yeah, I'll do the stocktake. See you tomorrow.'

It's not yet eleven o'clock. Reluctantly, I get my bag and leave, calling 'Bye!' in a cheery voice. After the row with Mama, the last thing I need is to fall out with Ceri as well. But I feel pretty upset. This not letting things get to me is going well, then.

As I'm in town I decide to act on my idea of this morning to surprise Huw at the university. After all, I need to speak to him, and he's never at home. I haven't been to his office for ages. I used to come here a lot. Ha ha, in both senses of the word. It was so exciting shagging in here when he was still married and I was his student.

I knock, and when he snaps, 'Come!' I stick my head round the door and say, 'Ooh I was just thinking that I'd love to.'

'Laura!' He looks so startled I wonder if he's getting a

blow-job under the desk from that Brigitte Bardot tart.

'Well, hello, honey bun, to you too.' I sit on a chair opposite him. There are photos of me and Evie on his desk, where Carmen and Glynn used to be.

'Why aren't you at work? Is everything okay?' Huw sounds completely rattled. I ought to turn up unexpectedly more often. Keep him on his toes.

'Everything's fine. It's just we haven't had much chance to talk lately, so I thought I'd pop in.'

He leans back in his fancy leather chair, trying to look relaxed. 'So, what can I do for you, *cariad*?'

We're on a new reality TV programme called *Couples Communicate*. Our images freeze on the screen, and over the top a computer writes:

Things to discuss with you:

1. Posh Sussex house party on Saturday;

2. Your son being creepy around our daughter;

3. That blonde I saw you with the other night.

The screen unfreezes and I feel more confident. That's the way to do it: start with the easy, work up to the hard.

'Three things. One, what are we doing about Miffy's party this weekend?'

'First I've heard of it.'

'No, it isn't! I told you about it on the way back from Great Yarmouth.'

'Fucking hell, after that shitty week I wouldn't have remembered if you said we'd won the lottery. No way can I go love, sorry.'

'The professor, right? What's his name again, I keep forgetting?'

'Professor Hartfield. You don't really want me there, do you, *cariad*? It's your long-lost family. You and Evie will have a great time.'

Hmm. No Huw and no Mama. But yes to Danny . . . Maybe this party could work rather well.

'So what else is on your urgent agenda?'

'Glynn. The other day I found him and Evie lying on his airbed together.'

'Were they dressed?'

'Bloody hell! Of course they were.'

'I'll have a word. He's not very good at boundaries.'

'He's a terrible influence on her, Huw.'

'You sound ancient when you say stuff like that.'

'I just can't understand why he wants to stay for so long. You'd think he'd be missing his friends in Kings Heath. He doesn't actually do anything all day, just gets under my feet' – and now I am starting to get worked up – 'and he has to have vegetarian food, which is incredibly inconvenient, and he never even bothers to talk to me, he just mooches round the house like a long streak of piss' – and then proper tears fill my eyes.

'Where the fuck's all this come from?' He pats my shoulder as if I were a student upset about my grades. 'Sorry you're finding him a strain, *cariad*. Carmen's not been coping and I said we'd give her a break for a couple of months.'

That stops the tears all right. 'A *what*? A couple of *months*? Without consulting me?'

'Well, now.' Huw walks over to the window. With his back to me he says, 'I didn't know we had to consult each other about such trivia. For instance, like you didn't consult me about having another baby.'

'Is that what this is about? Are you playing get your own back like some pathetic five-year-old?'

I know I'm supposed to be keeping the peace, but sodding Mother Teresa would be hard pushed here.

He turns round. 'And what was the third thing you wanted to talk about?'

'Fuck off.' I slam the door.

I'm in such a rage on the way home that when a red Fiesta cuts me up, I hoot so vigorously the driver winds down his window and sticks a finger up at me. As soon as I get home, though, my mood lifts. The bliss of a silent house; the unexpected windfall of a few free hours. I sink into a chair, allow my mind to relax, let X-rated images of Danny and me flick across my mind.

Two girls dancing. Sheets flapping on a line. One girl jumps

*right over the sheet, and when she lands, she is a boy. He says,
'A June baby, how lucky, lucky, lucky.'*

I wake with the word 'lucky' ringing in my ears. These repetitive sheet dreams are at least useful in reminding me to change the beds. I go upstairs and rummage in the linen cupboard. When I take the bedding into my room I notice a shoebox of papers I brought back from my old room at Mama's house. I empty it onto the bed and pick up Miffy's recent note, which is on the top. 'I'll be in touch soon. Love—' and the little drawing. It makes me smile. I put it aside to keep, and look through an old autograph book from school in Edgware. The silver cover is cracked and the pages are yellow, but my friends' writing is still legible. I remember taking that book in on my last day. It wasn't at the end of term, of course, but near the start: a Thursday in September. We'd just started a project on the Tudors. I'd been enjoying that, drawing the costumes the Tudor ladies wore. At my new school in Norfolk, they'd already done the Tudors, so that's a gap in my education thanks to Mama and Michael's desperation for a shag.

My friends couldn't believe I was really leaving. Claire cried, promised to visit. In my autograph book she wrote, 'If all the boys lived under the sea, what a good swimmer Laura would be.' But it was Fiona who kept in touch the longest: we wrote to each other till we went to university. I can't remember where she went. Durham or Liverpool or somewhere. A good one, anyway. Wonder what she's doing now. Her page says: '2 sweet + 2 bee = 4 gotten'.

Then I come to Danny's Valentine's card with the elephants on. I open it and the piece of paper falls out. I take a long breath before I unfold it. Torn from an exercise book, and the writing scrawled in pencil, it's faded but it doesn't matter because I remember what it says. Word for word:

'Dear Laura. This is to say goodbye. I thought you loved me but it was just pretend. I will never forgive you. D.'

After all these years it still has the power to shock. When I read it as a child, it pierced my heart. I thought it unbelievably cruel. I couldn't understand what he meant or why he felt compelled to write it. Now, of course, I can see the sorrow in it.

I take it downstairs and set a match to it. When it's in flames, I drop it in the sink.

Miffy

1979

Perfect Teeth

When Laura came round after school today, I told her about Jay, that new boy at *shul*. She helped me go through my clothes, looking for something nice to wear next time I saw him, and said she'd turn up one of my skirts to make a mini.

She sat at my mirror, twisting her silky black hair into a French pleat, and putting on red lipstick. She said, 'If I was blonde, would I look like Agnetha?'

'Oh, no, you'd be much prettier.' Her reflection grinned across at me.

I said, 'If *I* was blonde, I'd look like Marilyn Monroe.'

'Umm...yes...dar*link*. Not quite ze spitting image...'

'Because she had very straight white teeth, and so have I.' I giggled.

She laughed. 'Phew, thought you were being a bit deluded there.' She blotted her lipstick, and we checked the outline of her mouth on the tissue – perfect. Then she examined my teeth and said, 'They *are* really straight. Anyway, guess what?'

I guessed loads of things, but they were all wrong. After I begged her to tell me, she said, 'My mum's going to start playing the organ at your *shul*.'

'But she's not Jewish.'

'So?' Laura opened her eyes wide to put on mascara. 'She only has to learn some tunes. Anyway, she said we might convert.'

Garibaldis

Breakthrough with my batmitzvah study! As usual, Max was sitting too close while I was chanting my portion, saying, 'Pliss try and put a leetle beet of feeling into eet.' He still has his Polish accent even though he's lived here since 1937 or something.

Suddenly, for the first time, I could see the point of what I was saying. The Hebrew made sense, the actual meaning of the words, and I realised what the rhythm should be. It was like poetry, and I knew exactly how to do it.

'That's eet! That's eet!' Max cried, and in the excitement he clutched my knee, and just then Mum came in with the tea tray and he was caught red-handed. He yanked his hand off my leg as though it were on fire. Mum stood there holding the tray and said calmly, 'Mr Kaplinsky, we have spoken about this matter before. Please do not touch my daughter. Now, here's your tea, and there's a choice of bourbons or garibaldis.'

The Belt-Skirt

Dad was working late, and Danners was at Towse's (lucky thing). Mum wanted to go out with her friend Bernice. I told her I was nearly thirteen and would be fine on my own, but she wasn't listening. She phoned loads of people but no one was free. Finally she said, 'I suppose Olivia is always offering.' She stood looking at the phone for a while, till I thought she'd changed her mind. Then she slowly dialled, pausing between each number. I could tell from the conversation that Mrs Morente had said yes. Mum hung up, and stared at me so strangely that I checked my face in the mirror, but it looked no worse than usual.

Mrs Morente brought Laura with her, so that worked out well. Laura had my skirt, which she'd shortened. I nearly died. It was more of a belt than a skirt. Mum will never let me wear it. I was convinced people would be able to see my knickers, but Laura said they'd have to be looking.

Half an hour after Mum went out, Dad came back. I leaned over the banister so he couldn't see my skirt and said, 'I thought you were working late.'

'Yes, wasn't I lucky, Andy didn't need us after all.' He went into the kitchen and I heard him say, 'Fancy seeing you here, Olivia.' Then the door shut.

Back in my room, Laura was looking through my clothes. She held up my old red T-shirt that was too small and said, 'You need a tight top like this to go with the skirt. You've got great boobs, you should show them off more.'

I always thought they were too big. I used to get teased about them. At primary school I was the first in the class to wear a bra. I started being ill on Thursdays because we had Music and Movement, and wearing a leotard was so embarrassing.

'Jay won't be able to resist,' Laura said. 'You won't wear your hat, will you?'

'Which hat?'

'That stupid one you wear to school; the green thing with the earflaps? It makes you look about five.'

I liked that hat. Auntie Leila gave it to me. It was warm and soft and made me think of her. I wanted to cry to think that everyone was laughing about it. To change the subject I said, 'I got Mum to buy some proper Cokes. Let's go downstairs.'

'No.' Laura put her hand on the door. 'I think we should try out your make-up for Friday. Jay will propose on the spot, you'll look so nice.'

After she'd done my make-up, she wrote down my married name in all its different ways. *Mrs Jay Jacobs. Mrs Melissa Jacobs. Lissa Jacobs. Miffy Jacobs.*

Ultra Brite

A truly great day: Max never showed up, and I smoked my first cigarette!

We waited for Max for half an hour, and finally Mum rang his house. She spoke to his wife (amazing that Max is married; it proves that there really *is* someone for everyone in this crazy world), who told her Max had been rushed to hospital. She said he would be out of action for several weeks. Yes! Thank you, God! As if this wasn't enough, Mum said, 'Maybe this is a blessing in disguise after that funny business, not that I'd wish ill health on Max. I'll see if the Rabbi can take over your teaching.'

I thought I'd died and gone to heaven. I gave Mum a big hug.

'You're very fond of the Rabbi, aren't you, Melissa?'

'Not specially.'

'No, you've got good taste; he seems a very nice young man.' She sighed.

Young? He's twenty-two if he's a day.

At Laura's house later, Laura made me close my eyes, and when I opened them she was holding a packet of three cigarettes! Anthony East left them last time he was at her house. We sat on the windowsill and Laura put a cigarette in her mouth. She gave me a box of matches, but my hand shook and it took several goes to light one.

'You scared, Miffy-sister?'

'My hands always shake, actually.'

Finally, I got the thing lit, and Laura took a deep puff. She held the smoke in her mouth for a moment, then blew it in a long stream out of the window. She looked really cool. Then she handed the cigarette to me and I took a puff, expecting to cough, but it was easy. When I whooshed the smoke out, Laura said, 'Hey, you look good!' She moved her dressing-table mirror so I could see myself from all angles, and I did look brilliant smoking. When we'd finished, we sprayed Charlie perfume round the room, and went to the bathroom to brush our teeth. Laura lent me her toothbrush. She uses a toothpaste called Ultra Brite which made my mouth taste funny.

I was sure Dad and Mrs Morente would smell the smoke when we went downstairs, but they didn't say anything. Dad offered to come over the next day and help Laura with her revision for chemistry and physics, as they were topics he did at polytechnic. I wanted to help too, but Dad said I would distract Laura from her work. Which is a shame, because now I don't know when I am going to get my next cigarette.

In Suspenders

I left it till the last possible minute to come downstairs. I thought I'd got away with it, because Mum was arguing with Dad and barely noticed me. Then Danners said loudly, 'I can see your bum.'

My coat was quite short so it looked like I wasn't wearing anything underneath. I gave Danners a filthy look, but the damage was done.

'Melissa,' Mum said. 'What. Exactly. Are. You. Wearing?'

'Nothing.'

'That's what it looks like.' She sent Dad and Danners out to the car, then said, 'Show me.'

I opened my coat like the flasher that hangs round the school field. Mum went mad. 'What the hell happened to that skirt? We're going to a place of worship, not a brothel!'

She gave me thirty seconds to change. Nothing was clean or ironed except my foul Helene's Paris Fashion blouse and skirt, and I started crying while I was pulling it on, great gasps of sobs that hurt my tummy.

No one said a word on the way to *shul*. We were late, Mrs Morente already playing the organ as we crept in at the back. As the music stopped and Rabbi Aron stepped up to the pulpit, I saw Laura. Sitting next to Jay.

Laura ran up to me at the end of the service. 'Where were you? My first time at *shul* and I didn't know anyone.' I started to blub and she grabbed my hand and said, 'Where are the loos in this place?' Once we were squashed in a cubicle, I sobbed my heart out. Laura was lovely and hugged me and gave me tissues. Dad was waiting for us but everyone else had gone. Mrs Morente had taken Mum and Danners home. Laura whispered that she wanted to tell me a secret, and she got me to ask Dad if we could stop off at her house. I hoped she didn't want to tell me that Jay had asked her out.

Mrs Morente was just back, and she offered Dad coffee. Laura and I raced upstairs. 'You mustn't tell. Cross your heart and hope to die?'

'Promise! You know I won't. Hurry up, Laura-sister! I'm in suspenders.'

She looked very serious. 'Danny wants to sleep with me. What shall I do?'

'Oh, my God!' Laura had never asked my opinion before. 'You'd have to go on the Pill.'

'No way! I'm a Catholic.'

'How will you stop getting preggers, then?'

'You suck a Polo mint while you're doing it.'

'Why do you even like Danners? I mean, his feet are so smelly.'

'I've fancied him for ages. But he was a bit slow. Thought it would encourage him if I danced with Towse at the disco. Treat 'em mean; keep 'em keen.'

'So anyway,' I asked, 'what did you think of Jay?'

'Oh, he was all right. I go for the older man myself. He's got quite bad spots, too, hasn't he?'

I asked what she was going to do about Danners, and she said she would 'sleep on it'. This set us off into giggles.

Back home, Mum had forgiven me over the belt-skirt. She made me hot chocolate and we cuddled on the sofa. It was really nice.

Laura

'A pretty big house,' Miffy had said. A mistress of under-statement. Remember the stately home in *Brideshead Revisited*? That's the kind of scale we're looking at here. It's a great white wedding cake of a place, with an absurd number of rooms. I get lost every time I leave the kitchen. One time, trying to find the bathroom, I ended up in a completely new wing. You'd expect Amy, the owner, to be a posh wanker, but she's actually all right: friendly and down-to-earth. She works as a children's psychiatric nurse, which is how Miffy knows her. Weird kind of job for someone who's got a mansion in Sussex. It's her parents' house really, inherited off rich relatives. Another world.

The party's tomorrow but loads of people are here already. Amy's got friends staying; there are Cline kids everywhere; someone else has got three children under five. Or is it five under three? Can't sodding tell.

Miffy's making a huge cooked lunch for everyone in the enormous kitchen. She's standing at the eight-ring cooker frying onions, looking half her age in a strappy vest and denim skirt. She clearly loves the chaos, the noise, the kids running round. Evie, playing Rummy at the long oak table with some of the Cline kids, loves it too. She's smiled more since we arrived than in the last three months.

I sit with my feet up on a chair. My ankles are puffy and I don't feel great, don't feel like talking, but it doesn't matter because everyone else is talking their fucking heads off. Creating more than her share of the noise is my best mate Heifer, labelling bags of food for the freezer and gabbing loudly to one of her cousins. They're wearing matching LBTs – Little Black Tents. They must be boiling. Whenever Heifer catches my eye she sends me a sympathetic glance. She can't get over the fact that Huw has 'let me' drive all this way without him, *in my condition.*

'I go where I want, when I want,' I tell her, but she clucks her tongue, starts riffing about the raw deal women get in modern marriages, how the little wife ends up soldiering on by herself. I love that she can stand there on her stately tree-trunk legs and say stuff like this.

And here, making my heart skip, is her lovely husband, who soldiers on her behalf. Danny comes in from the garden with an armful of wood, flushed from exertion, so sexy as he chucks the logs into the basket and brushes his hands down his trousers. I must be off-the-clock horny, because even the cream-coloured *cuple* on his head looks alluring.

When Evie and I arrived this morning, both knackered after our stupidly long drive through the night, the size of the house was surreal enough. But to make things even weirder, Danny bounded out to meet us, came right up close and whispered, 'So glad you could make it.' Ooh, hello. I get a lurch in my groin just from thinking about it. Being so near him is freaking me out. I feel weird and super-sensitive, as if I'm missing a layer of skin. I feel I could come just from him touching my hand.

Miffy passes plates round, then sits next to me. 'It's so stuffy in here with that Aga thing,' she says, pushing her hair off her face. 'Thinking now that a hot meal was a daft idea. Are you okay?'

I haven't told her about my bleeding episode earlier this week. I don't want her to tell me I shouldn't have come.

'I'm fine, just tired. It's good to get away. And Evie's

having the time of her life.' We both turn to look at her, laughing at something one of the Cline boys has said.

'I don't feel any older than her right now,' Miffy says. 'I feel like when we were kids and dying of excitement about a party.' She sits back in her chair, her food untouched, and hugs her smooth brown knees. I avert my eyes from my own podgy knees, blotchy-white as semolina, and contemplate her glowing face. Surely only a man could make her look like this?

'Anyone in particular you're looking forward to seeing?'

Her lashes sweep down over her reddening cheeks. She can't help smiling as she says, 'Oh, no, not really.'

She's still a rotten liar, I see.

Most of the younger kids have given up on lunch and are running round the table. The adults are drinking and chatting. No one can hear us. On a whim I decide to tell Miffy about Huw and the woman in the pub. She's lovely, says straight away how awful, how sorry she is. 'What was she like? I hope she had the decency to be ugly.'

This is something I'd forgotten about Miffy: she could always make me laugh. 'Alas, no,' I reply, feeling better already. 'Blonde and big boobs.'

'Like Norah Ephron says, "Your basic nightmare." So what's he had to say about it, then?'

'I haven't talked to him yet.'

She raises an eyebrow and lights a cigarette, takes a

deep long drag. Across the table, Amy shakes her head, but she is smiling. 'Amy's being lenient as it's my party,' Miffy says, then sings, 'It's my party and I'll smoke if I want to, smoke if I want to...'

I ask what she's going to wear, and offer to help her get ready.

'You always used to love doing that.' She grins. 'Last time you styled me, you put me in a tiny miniskirt that barely covered my bum.'

'Did I?' I can't remember.

Danny laughs. I turn round, but he's not looking our way. He's dealing amiably, not just with a baby on his lap, but also with two toddlers trying to scramble into his arms, and an older child standing behind, curling her arms round his neck. Look at all the fucking kids crawling over him, and Huw's been making a fuss about two!

'You ought to ask Huw about it, you know,' Miffy says, blowing a row of smoke rings. 'You ought not let it fester. It might not even be anything. She could just be a colleague. It's almost as bad as being unfaithful, I think: not saying what you mean, or what you need, in a marriage.' She doesn't say it in an unkind way at all. She seems genuinely sympathetic.

People start to clear dishes. Miffy offers to take the kids to the local steam railway, and a small group forms around her. Evie goes with them, doesn't even give me a backward glance. Amy starts allocating people to shopping and cooking duties.

'Why don't you have a rest, Laura,' Heifer calls across the table. 'You look ever so tired.'

'I'm fine, thanks.' You annoying fucking cow.

Danny tells Amy he'll fetch some champagne.

I quickly say, 'Oh, I'll give you a hand. I always like anything to do with champagne. Not that I can have any, of course.'

There's the briefest of pauses. Heifer looks at Danny.

He says, 'Why not? It's a nice walk. The wine shop's in the middle of some gardens.'

My heart pounding, we are somehow outside together – alone – before anyone can stop us. The air is warm and spring-like, so I carry my jacket, relieved I'm wearing my pretty blue empire-line blouse with the long sheer sleeves. We walk along a path at the back of the house which opens out into fields. God, he meant a proper walk. It's one-to-one time with him, so I'm definitely not complaining. I hadn't realised how pretty Sussex is. Rolling hills, lush greens, spring sunlight flitting through the trees, sexy out-of-bounds man beside me. We are walking close enough that our arms touch occasionally, each time an electric shock.

'Will you be okay with stiles?' he asks. 'I had a look at the map, and there's a scenic route.'

'Whatever you like.' Hopefully he'll pick up my subtle double entendre.

We chat as we stroll: about the weather, the party and the house – mansion. Danny says he always jokes with Amy that she should swap houses with him, so all of his children could have their own bedroom. The talk turns naturally from his children to mine, and to my pregnancy.

'Are you hoping for a boy or a girl?'

'I don't mind, I only care about getting it to term.'

He looks so mortified, I realise he must think I'm referring to the abortion. Of course, he doesn't know my miscarriage history. Shit! I can't believe I said that. Before I can think of a way to explain, he quickly starts talking about their latest baby, how moving he found the circumcision ceremony.

We reach a stile and he lets me go first. I stumble slightly and he takes hold of my elbow to help me. I'd never realised before what an erogenous zone this part of my arm is. We walk through a yellow crop. Wheat? Corn? Daffodils? No idea.

I wait till he has finished talking about the joy of watching Micah at his recent barmitzvah, which takes us almost right across through the yellow field. Then I say, 'Danny, can I ask you? When we were kids, you didn't seem that religious.'

'No, you could say that.' He coughs.

'So how did you became Orthodox?'

'It's a long story.'

Another stile – I am, once again, erotically helped over by Danny caressing my elbow. As I land on the other side, a black-and-white cow looks up at me.

'Oh. I'm a bit scared of cows.'

Danny hops over the stile athletically. 'They won't hurt us.'

'What do you know about it, Edgware Boy?'

He laughs. 'We're nearly there. This is the last field before Sheffield Park.'

'If we make it through this rampaging herd of cattle.'

'You'll be okay. I won't let them get you.'

The cows part to let us through. Is he Moses? Will he lead me to my promised land? What with the heat, and the cow anxiety, and the burn of his touch still tingling on my elbow, I lose the sense of what he's saying. Then realise with a thud that he's leapt straight into our joint history.

'Me becoming Orthodox, it goes back to when we were kids. After Dad left. And after, you know. Other stuff.'

I feel the blood draining from my face. He talks fast, stumbling, telling me about his mother, how she had a kind of breakdown when Michael left them.

'She was still right in the middle of coping with that, and Lissa's accident, when she had to deal with me.' His voice drops, almost to a whisper. 'Getting you into trouble.'

I can't help it; I'm so wound up with nerves that I let out a laugh. *Getting into trouble* is just so quaint.

He stops walking, stands there, totally still. Fuck! You should see the look he gives me. 'It isn't funny.'

'No, of course not! Not in the least, it was just the phrase you used. I'm sorry. I'm feeling sort of nervous.'

'Okay, then, if you don't like my phrasing.' His face is red as he spits out, 'After we murdered a baby...'

'Oh, Danny!' I cover my mouth with my hands. How have we got from 'I'll save you from cows' to killing babies in just a few minutes? He looks stricken too.

'Laura, I'm sorry.' He steps back. 'I'm sorry, sorry, sorry. That was awful. I'm such an idiot. Forgive me?'

'Of course. Don't worry.' What else can I say?

We continue walking towards the far corner of the field. The atmosphere is electric. Incredibly exciting. Who knows what will happen, what will be said, what will be done?

Danny (*taking Laura into his arms*): What's the point of fighting this? We both want it.
Laura: But what about...
Danny: Don't say anything. (*He pulls her down onto the grass and puts his hand inside her blue empire-line blouse.*)

At the final stile, we perform my favourite up-and-over

elbow routine again, and we're in the park: a beautiful landscaped garden of weeping willows and lakes.

I break the silence to say, 'Oh, it's lovely! Shall we walk around a bit first?'

'It's a bit naughty, because we haven't paid to get in.'

'Well, Danny,' I dare to say, 'the thing you used to like about me was that I *am* a bit naughty.'

It could go either way and my heart practically stops as he looks at me. Then he smiles; thank you, God. 'Go on, then, bad girl. Let's take a stroll.'

There seem to be no other people around. The vast garden, with its hidden paths and meandering trails, is designed for lovers. We walk round a lake, sparkling with sunlight, and I decide it's time I took control of the conversation.

'Miffy said your mother was very upset by Michael's death.'

'Well, of course,' Danny says. 'He was the father of her children. I don't think she ever really stopped loving him.'

'But she's remarried now?'

'Oh, yes. Morris is wonderful to her. His wife passed away a couple of years ago, and they became close.'

Yes, I can see it clearly: the helpless widower, struggling to cope without his wife; the brash divorcée, shoving to the front of the single-ladies queue with her kosher chickens and honey cake. Poor fella probably never knew what hit him.

'Morris has fitted into our family well. He's a better *Zaida*
– grandfather – to the kids than Dad was, to be honest.'

'I know Michael always loved it when you and your
family came to Great Yarmouth...'

Danny stops walking and snarls, properly snarls,
'Christ, yes. He never stopped going on about it. All of us
getting together for lovely cosy seaside weekends with his
lovely cosy new family.'

He's a different person when he talks like this. I shake
my head and say firmly, 'Danny, don't.'

He stares for a minute as if he has no idea who I am.
Then, in his ordinary voice, he says, 'I have absolutely no
idea where that came from. I am so sorry, Laura. I can't
seem to stop being horrible to you.'

'Well,' I say, lightly as I can, though my legs feel shaky
– it's like Jekyll and Hyde – 'good to see you've got over
it, anyway.'

'Okay, maybe there's still an unresolved issue or two.'

I laugh nervously and he grabs my hand; no mistaking
it, he really means to hold it. His fingers entwine with
mine, flesh to flesh, sparks flying. I'm so confused. Is he
allowed to touch my skin or isn't he? What the fuck is
going on between us?

'I really am truly sorry, Laura.' He almost whispers
it. 'It's so important we get things out in the open. Dad
wanted us to.'

'He wanted you to do what?'

'Wanted us to talk to you. Mend bridges. It was his idea to ask you to the party.'

'When did he say this? He never said anything to me.'

'That last time we saw him. At the hospital. He felt it was my responsibility. Mine and Lissa's.'

So *that's* why they wanted me to come to the party. Michael and his barmy deathbed dreams of reconciliation!

'The Rabbi said this might happen.'

'Said what?!'

'That I'd get emotional. He knows my self-control isn't all it could be.'

I put away for now the very excellent news that Danny has self-control issues and ask instead, 'You talked to your rabbi about seeing me again?'

'Sure. I talk to him about everything.'

'Kind of like a therapist?'

'I suppose so. Except he doesn't think everything has to do with S-E-X!'

He really does spell it out; and perhaps the word makes him remember that he's holding my hand, because he abruptly drops it.

A signpost directs us to the wine shop, and as we walk towards it we meet a couple coming the other way. The woman smiles at me as we pass. She thinks Danny and I are a couple, like them.

'I still haven't answered your question,' Danny says. I can't remember what my question even was any more. 'We changed schools, to a Jewish school. That's where I met Hella. She helped me make sense of a lot of things.'

I don't want to dwell on the subject of Danny and Heifer's hideous courtship, and luckily, before I have to say anything, we reach the shop, a small outbuilding almost hidden by trees. While Danny examines bottles, I sit in a chair and gaze at his lean frame, note the graceful way he moves, his cute backside.

My head's full of unaskable questions. You loved me once, do you still? Did my abortion permanently scar you? Is that why you went religious? Why did you marry Heifer? Why have you got so many kids? Have you only ever had sex with me, and Heifer? Does Heifer know about me? Does she know about the abortion? Does Miffy? Can Orthodox Jews have affairs? What about your hard-on last time we met? What would you do if I kissed you?

I go into a trance with the swirl of thoughts and the horniness and just the general head-fuck of talking to Danny about this sealed-over past, so when he says, 'Ready to go?' I jump a mile into the air.

He suggests we walk back along the road, rather than lug the heavy bags over the stiles. There's a lot of traffic and no pavement, just a verge, so we walk in single-file without speaking. He's such a complicated mystery. This same person:

1. Wrote me that horrible farewell note;

2. Fucked me senseless in a tumbledown shack at the side of the road in Spain, and subsequently in a wide variety of alleyways and deserted car parks;

3. Is an upstanding member of the Orthodox community;

4. Used to cry out 'Jesus, Jesus, fucking Jesus' when he came;

5. Married a hobbit.

After a while I say, 'It was good to have a sit down in the shop.' I say it for no other reason than to make a noise, but it pays huge dividends. Danny asks if I'm still tired and when I say I am, a bit, he suggests a rest. We stop by a detached house set back from the road with a low wall out front. We sit side-by-side on the wall, and he carefully sets the bags of bottles on the ground between us.

'While we're being honest, Danny, I want to say I'm sorry I was rude to Hella at the cemetery.' I'm not really, but it won't hurt to say it. 'Funerals and hormones – bad combination.'

'That's good of you, Laura. I know Hella would be the first to admit to being rather tempestuous at times.'

'I guess you must like tempestuous women.'

An image of Huw kissing that Bardot professor comes

into my mind, and without stopping to think I turn to Danny and press my lips against his. He resists at first, pulls away, but I move towards him the same distance and then some more, and for a few long, slow, beautiful seconds, it's a proper snog and we are kids again, it's twenty-four years ago, our faces hot and damp, the warmth spreading across my chest. Without a doubt the kiss of my life, I melt into it, slide a hand round the back of his head, my fingers fluttering against his neck, catching in his hair. He shivers, breathes in, a tiny gasp. Then he pushes me away.

'For Christ's sake, Laura.'

He says 'Christ' a lot, for a religious Jew.

'What the hell are we doing?'

Well, doh, as Glynn would say. 'I guess we just felt like kissing.'

'Why, Laura? Why did you do that?' His face is red, flushed. I can't tell if he's angry or about to cry.

'I don't know. Raking up the past?'

He doesn't smile. I look into his beautiful severe face. I don't know what he's thinking. I barely know what I'm thinking myself, to be honest.

I say, 'Do you remember when we went on holiday to Spain?'

'Yes,' he says politely. 'It was really hot, wasn't it?'

I don't trust myself to say anything. I stare at my hands. They look old. The freckles look like liver spots.

'It was fantastic,' he says, in a low voice. 'The best week of my life.' He is so quiet I wonder if I have heard him properly. We look at each other. We can see it in each other's eyes. The memory of the first time we made love.

He stands up quickly, kicking over one of the bags, and there is a clash of glass against glass. He takes out one bottle at a time, turns it round, checking for cracks. 'Not broken. Lucky. We ought to get going.' He looks at his watch. 'Sunset's in two hours, and Hella will be wanting me to take the babies off her hands for a bit.'

I look at his hands, the ones that will shortly be dealing with babies. I'm absolutely ablaze; a fire burns between my legs.

'Danny, shouldn't we talk some more?'

He looks down at me, clutching the bags to his chest. 'Think we've said enough for now.'

We walk the rest of the way in silence. The kiss. His body. His hands. What just happened?

Heifer is alone in the kitchen, feeding the baby. Poor old Heifer, with her half-covered droopy boobs. Danny starts telling her about the wine shop and the gardens. To my ear it sounds hasty and garbled, but she just nods. I don't make an excuse; I don't care what it looks like. I leave them there, dash up to my bedroom, which thankfully I find first time, lock the door, and in less than two minutes give myself the best orgasm of my adult life.

15 MARCH 2003

Danny pushes me against a wall. I'm wearing my red dress, nothing underneath. He kisses me, hard. Thrusts a hand up my dress, pushes two fingers into me where I am soaking. Squeezes my breast so the nipple presses against the cloth. His mouth is everywhere, my face, my neck, my shoulders. Our breathing is out of control. He yanks down the straps of my dress, pushes it down to my waist, sucks my breasts, first one, then the other. I am trying to be quiet but I can't. I cry out, I beg him to be rougher, to bite me. I start to come from the feel of his mouth on my nipples. I moan to him to come inside me. I reach for him...

And then I wake up, damn it, gasping, in a sweat, legs tangled in the sheet, nightie halfway up my stomach.

That kiss. Oh, that kiss.

It's after ten, sunlight pouring into the room. I dress quickly and after a few wrong turns into unknown corridors, I reach the kitchen to find Miffy trying to force a bowl into a completely crammed fridge. She smiles and shows me where the breakfast things are. She seems distracted: keeps picking things up and putting them down again. When I say, using our old joking word, 'Do you want me to help with your transformation later?' she looks startled.

'Getting changed, you mean? Well, if you're sure you want to. I won't be getting ready till about six, though.'

Evie's upstairs playing Monopoly with the other children. She barely acknowledges me when I come in; shakes her head when I ask if she wants to go into Brighton. I go back to my room and ring Huw's mobile, but it goes straight to voicemail. I call Mama, but she's still sniffy, and isn't interested in having a nice gossip about the Clines and their rich friends.

On my second circuit of the house I bump into Heifer, trying to manage her crew of children. Somehow I become embroiled as back-up nursemaid: bouncing toddlers on my knee, reading *Sammy Spider's First Hanukkah*, and changing a nappy for the first time in nine years. 'Good practice for the new one,' Heifer says, beaming, as I have my first encounter with kosher poo. Very similar to non-kosher, in case you were wondering.

I ask, a little anxiously, where Danny is, feeling horrified and thrilled at the thought that he might be hiding because of our kiss. Heifer says he's walked to a synagogue in Haywards Heath. I don't ask why he didn't take the car. I remember Michael telling me proudly that Danny never drove on the Sabbath. 'Good God, that's a long walk, isn't it?' No wonder he's so trim.

'Oh, it's only about seven miles. Be good for him. Help get things out of his system. Bracing.'

Help get what out of his system? Me? Have they discussed me? Maybe had a row?

'So Laura,' Heifer says. 'How *are* we today?'

We? Yeah, Heif, you and I are so close we're practically as one.

'Fine, thanks, how are *you*?' I examine a child's drawing – Moses? Santa? Balance of probabilities says Moses – rather than look at her.

'I'm terrific! I'm a lucky woman, you know that?'

You got that right, honey bun.

'Every day, I give thanks to God for my beautiful children, my wonderful husband. I am so very blessed to have such a good man.'

'Well, that's great.' It's definitely Moses – there's the ten commandments – but why has he got a cross in his hand?

'Laura, I want you to know that I trust Dan-Dan completely.'

So they *have* discussed me. 'Oh. Okay. Right. Well, that's good.' It's not a cross, I see now, but a staff. Moses had a staff, didn't he?

'It's so important, don't you think, that a wife can fully trust her husband?' and she whispers the next bit, so that, afterwards, I'm not completely sure I heard right. 'Do you trust yours?'

'Um, sure.' I stare at the Moses drawing until the staff turns into a penis, and I pray to any deity of whatever faith to open up the ground and get me the fuck out of there. Luckily, one child snatches a crayon from another, and an almighty wail goes up, allowing me to escape.

I have a long bath, and ponder how the conversation between her and Danny might have gone after he kissed me.

Danny: I'm sorry, Hella, I've tried so hard to resist, but I'm in torment.
Heifer: It's all right, darling; I give you my blessing.
Danny: Seriously?
Heifer: I know how incredibly, unbelievably lucky I am to have you. I can't compete with her. Do what you have to do. I'll always take you back.
Danny: A night with her and will I want to come back?
Heifer: I'll risk it.

I do my hair and make-up, and remove every single bit of stubble from my chin. Then I take from my wardrobe the world's most beautiful maternity dress, borrowed from Ceri's sister Rhianna. Deep-red silk, very flattering, very low-cut. You might remember it from my dream. Teamed with a necklace which plunges into my cleavage like an arrow, and my black shoes, the highest I can manage with my dodgy centre of gravity, I look like a pregnant Sophia Loren. I haven't looked this good in months. I could give that stupid blonde a run for her money.

On the dot of six, I knock on Miffy's door. She looks surprised and not all that pleased. I say quickly, 'Listen, Miff, I know you probably don't need help, but I'm bored and you've been rushing around all day. I thought you could use a bit of pampering.'

She rakes her hand through her hair. 'Oh, go on, then. You look sensational. Let's see if you can make me look half as good as you do.'

She does need my help. She's wearing her glasses, her hair's frizzy and her cheeks are flushed and blotchy. She looks much more like the Miffy I knew as a child, and I feel a rush of warmth for her.

'Don't worry, honey, I can help you look sensational too.'

She sits on the bed, lights a cigarette. 'Need a fag first. Bit of a busy day.'

'I thought there were fire alarms up here.'

She points to the ceiling, where a smoke detector dangles from its wires.

'You naughty girl!'

She blows a spool of smoke sideways, and gestures to a pile of clothes on the chair. 'Go on, then. Choice of three. I can't decide.'

I smooth the satiny black material of a full-skirted dress, then pick up a lilac shift dress of soft linen. Size eight. The cow.

She goes to take a shower, cigarette still in hand. I get

to work, plugging in her straightening irons and sorting through her clothes and make-up. When she returns, wrapped in towels, I hold up the third dress, an emerald green halter-neck.

'Green was always good on you. It'll be perfect with these strappy sandals.'

'Fine. I'm in your hands.' She drops her towel, and puts on her dressing-gown. I'm half turned away, but I get a glimpse of a long taut body. Mine was like that once, long ago. She faces the dressing-table mirror while I straighten her hair, and I watch her as she relaxes, chatters about the party, the people she's looking forward to seeing after her year away. I should have been a beautician. People open up to me. I think of how she blushed yesterday when she said how excited she was about the party, and I take a punt, say, 'So are you going to tell me his name?'

Her head jerks up, and she stares at me in the mirror. 'Did Amy tell you?'

I smile, shake my head.

'Of course. I'd forgotten this was your speciality. *Boy* stuff.' She lets out a deep breath, or a sigh. 'Rob. Old college friend of Amy's.'

She's blushing again, her cheeks on fire. She used to do fabulous whole-body blushes, did little Miffy. So, not quite as grown-up and in control as she seems.

'He does development work, spends half the year

in Africa. Somalia. I, uh, met up with him while I was travelling.'

I raise my eyebrows, and she waves a hand at me.

'Nothing much happened.' She lights another cigarette. 'We'd both just separated from our partners. Bit raw. But, you know. We got on really well.'

'Oooh, this is so exciting!'

She grins. 'I'm nervous as hell. I haven't liked anyone this much since...'

'Since your ex-husband?'

'Ah, well, I'd known Jay for years. It wasn't quite as romantic.'

'How did you meet Jay?'

'We knew each other as children. You've met him too, Laura.'

'I *have*?' I can't think. 'When? Was he at our school?'

'No, he used to go to the *shul* in Edgware. Don't you remember?'

I don't remember all that much about her *shul*, apart from the plug-in heaters, and the excitement of seeing Danny.

'I don't think so. Hey, whatever happened to that blond rabbi, the one you liked?'

'Ah, Aron? He was so lovely. Very kind. I don't know; not long after my batmitzvah we changed *shuls* and I never saw him again.'

'That's a shame.'

'Tell me about you. How did you meet the dishy Huw?'

'*Dishy?*' I giggle.

'I know, I don't think I've used the word since we were kids. It seems appropriate somehow. He *is* rather dishy. Such blue eyes!'

I turn her round so I can do her make-up. She tilts her face obediently towards me and I smooth on silver eye-shadow. Why hasn't she got any lines?

'Have you had Botox?'

'Do I need it?'

'No, not at all.'

'Go on, tell me about Huw. Was it love at first sight?'

I've never told anyone the full story of how I got together with Huw. Ceri knows some of it, of course; she was a student with me at the time. But I've never felt close enough to her to discuss all the gory details.

'The official version is that Huw was my lecturer and I was his student, and we fell in love and got married.'

Without missing a beat, she says, 'And what's the un-official version?'

There's a knock at the door and Amy sticks her head in.

'Liss, some more of your relatives have turned up.'

Amy goes out, and I say, echoing Danny, 'It's a long story.'

'How intriguing. In that case, we must make sure we get together for a proper chat very soon.'

For the first time, I feel she's a little fascinated by me, the way she used to be. She gets up and dresses quickly. She looks fabulous. Glossy hair swishing down her back; shoulders and cleavage on display.

'I'm so jealous.' I watch her looking at herself in the mirror. 'I'd give anything for a flat stomach.'

'You'll get it back, though, won't you, once the baby's born?'

I make a non-committal noise. My stomach wasn't exactly flat before my pregnancy.

'You were always so good at doing hair and make-up and stuff.' Miffy tidies the clothes strewn over the bed. 'I wonder you didn't go into something artistic like that.'

'I do the window displays at the shop sometimes, when Ceri lets me.'

'It's not too late. You could go to college when the baby's older, do a design course.'

I nod, but know I never will. Nice idea. Maybe I would have, if someone like Miffy had been there at the right time, encouraging me.

We go into the corridor together. I'm about to head up to the top floor to find Evie, when Miffy puts her hand on my arm.

'Hey, Laura.' She gives me a thousand-volt smile. 'Thanks. Appreciate it.'

*

I can't find a soft drink. Every time I spot a bottle and thrust my arm through a group of people to reach it, it's wine or vodka. I haven't been to a party this rammed since I was a student, and I've certainly never been to one with such a weird mix. Miffy and Amy's friends in designer clothes mingle with Heifer's dark-tented relatives. Ordinary children run about with Orthodox girls in ankle-length skirts, boys with long curls round their ears. Whenever someone new arrives you hear a cry of 'Lissa!' and there's a flash of emerald green, a swish of golden hair, as they fling their arms round each other.

My mobile rings in my bag, and I edge into a utility room that leads off the kitchen.

'Hey, *cariad*.'

'Huw! I've been trying to get you all day.'

'Didn't get a sec to call. Devolution shit's hit the fan. Half the faculty aren't speaking to the other half. How's the party?'

A fat man in a loud orange shirt comes in. 'Sorry!' he booms, pushing past me. 'Just looking for the Chablis Melissa hid in the cupboard.'

I turn my back and mutter into the phone, 'Okay. Don't know anyone. Evie's off with the other kids the whole time. And Heifer keeps patting my hand like I'm a fucking widow.'

'She just wants to make sure you won't swear at her. You'll be okay; you love parties.'

'Ah ha!' Orange Shirt says, pulling out a bottle. 'Oh good, screw-lid.' He takes a swig and lurches over, fills up the empty glass in my hand, and says, 'Nice dress.' Then he puts his hand on my stomach – I'm too slow to stop him – and says, 'Hello, baby. Your mummy is a well fit MILF.'

I shove him away. 'Get off!'

'Find me when you're off the phone, okay?' He weaves out, leaving the door open, letting in a blast of party noise.

'Christ on a bike! Some fat wanker just touched my tummy and called me a MILF!'

Huw laughs. 'Sounds like a wild party. Sorry I'm not there.'

'He was horrible.' I sit down on a folding chair next to the tumble drier.

'Rotten, *cariad*. You keep away from nasty fat men, you hear? Okay, better go, professors can't be kept waiting.'

I'm not exactly psychologically ready, but I jump straight in; if only so I can tell Miffy I asked him. 'Huw, is it the same professor from the other week?'

'The what? I can't hear you. Is that the noise from the party? Sounds like a complete rave.'

'The important one who'll put you on the map. Professor Hartfield?'

'That's right.'

'I was just wondering if there are ever any, you know, women professors?'

'Well, sure.' He sounds very far away, as if he is at the bottom of the ocean.

I gulp my wine. 'Blonde ones?'

'I can't hear you, Laura. Did you say blonde? Fuck's sake, what is this? I don't fancy them! They're all your classic blue stockings. Most of them are about ninety.'

'I didn't say anything about you fancying them.'

'You didn't have to. I know you. Go, have a good time. Bye.'

I click the phone off and go back into the kitchen, squeezing past crowds of people, clutching the glass of wine as a kind of prop, keeping an eye out for the fat orange pervert. I move into the hall and an oddly familiar voice says flatly, 'Why Laura, how utterly delightful.'

To my horror I am face to face with Andrea Cline. She looks much as I remember her, apart from a lot more wrinkles. Same sour face, hair the exact vibrant auburn as before. Still keeping her colourist busy.

'You're looking very, uh, striking,' she says, with a brittle smile.

'You too. Your hair looks amazing.' I try to give the word ironic emphasis, but she pats her hair in a self-satisfied manner.

'I was *so* surprised when Melissa told me she'd invited you.' She sways abruptly, catching hold of my arm to steady herself. I realise she's completely drunk.

'Yes, I was surprised too. But very pleased.'

'Did you know I've remarried? He's over there, my lovely new husband.' She waves vaguely. 'One husband door closes, another opens, you know.'

'Good. Well, nice to see you.' I turn, but she holds on tight, her fingers digging into my flesh, a terrifying skeleton come to life.

'Have you seen my engagement ring?' She holds up her bony hand to show off a Liz Taylor-size diamond. 'Bit nicer than the last one, everyone says.'

'Amazing what they can do with cubic zirconia these days.' Zing! Feels good to get my mojo back a little.

She lets out a humourless laugh. 'Oh, yes, same old Laura Morente with her hilarious observations.' She brings her face close to mine. 'I can't believe you'd have the sheer brass front to come here.'

'Melissa and Daniel specifically invited me. Could you let go of me, please?'

'*Melissa and Daniel* had such a guilt trip laid on them by their sentimental old fart of a father, they felt they had no option but to invite you to their *family* party. Can you imagine he'd be so silly? Though, of course, he does have previous on being silly.'

'Don't we all.' I try to shake her off but she is a leech, a limpet.

'Well, you'd certainly know about that. By the way' – she

mimes an enormous stomach – 'is that a baby, or have you put on a ton of weight?'

'I need to go, Andrea. I need the loo.'

'I always felt sorry for poor old Michael, God rest his soul. Suspect his last years weren't very happy. Still, that's what comes from following your dick.'

I grit my teeth and raise my voice. 'Andrea, let me go; I have to piss!'

Taking advantage of her slight surprise, I pull my arm away and move quickly to the door. She calls after me, 'You will give my very best to your mother, won't you? Do tell her I'm so pleased that everything's worked out.'

I do a massive wee in the downstairs toilet and then creep along to the kitchen, which is full of strangers talking and talking with big red mouths. I still can't see any non-alcoholic drinks. Fuck it. I'm so thirsty. I drink half my wine in one go. I can see the indentation of Andrea's fingers on my arm. I go into another room, keeping an eye out for her and Orange Pervert. They're not there but I also can't see anyone I know, so I turn to go out and – thank you, God – there's Danny.

I stumble, spilling some wine on the carpet, and he steadies me.

'You okay?'

'Not really. I just had an encounter with your mother.'

'Oh dear.' He laughs, but kindly. 'You look shell-shocked. What did she say?'

His laughing makes me feel better.

'Nothing, really. Do you know if there's somewhere quiet to sit? I feel a bit strange.' This isn't a fib.

'Sure. There's a room here. Let me help you.' He holds his favourite part of my body, my elbow, and guides me along the corridor.

It's a small room compared to the others – meaning it's as big as the ground floor of my house – and less crowded, just one or two couples, and a group of people standing chatting. I sink into a sofa, leaving a hinting space next to me, but Danny takes a hard-backed chair to the side. Still, the bright side is he's at a good height for staring into my cleavage.

'Are you having a nice time?' I ask, so softly he has to lean forward to hear, making him look you know where. When he sits back up, he looks a little flustered. I shouldn't think he's ever seen such a sexy dress, not with Heifer single-handedly keeping Millets in business. My mind races. This weekend's already been so weird, I'm just going to say it. This might be my only chance. Come on now, Laura. Be assertive. Say what you want, Miffy said. She meant to Huw, but still.

I take a deep breath. 'Shall we talk about what happened yesterday?'

'Laura,' Danny says, glancing round the room. 'Maybe there are things best left unsaid.'

'You were the one who said it was good to get things out in the open.' I smile. 'Did your rabbi change his mind?'

An old bag in a British Homes Stores outfit sits down next to me and starts talking to her friends about her episiotomy. Can't she see we're in a conversation? She's worse than that woman in *Brief Encounter* who spoils their last meeting. I close my eyes for a moment, and the silence between Danny and me stretches on and on.

'Listen,' he says at last, 'I need to find Micah. Get the speeches going. Last I saw the kids they were watching films upstairs. Shall I check on Evie while I'm there?'

I struggle to my feet. 'I'll go, you can start rounding people up.'

'You sure? Are you feeling all right?' I can't read the look on his face.

'I'm fine now.'

At the top of the first flight I drink the remainder of my wine. Courage, *mon brave*! Then I slog up the second staircase, which leads to the kids' rooms. The music and laughter from the party become fainter. I round the corner and see a couple kissing in a doorway. The boy is Micah Cline. His arm is snaked round the girl's waist, one hand tilting her head back. The girl has her back to me. She seems a grown woman in a short black skirt and it takes my brain a moment to register that it's Evie.

They're so focused on each other they don't see me dart back down the stairs. I stumble in my high shoes and grab the banister so hard I nearly dislocate my arm. I stay on the first floor landing for a while, smiling absently at people who pass, pointing them to the bathroom. When my legs have stopped shaking, I go back up. Micah and Evie have disappeared. I knock anxiously on the only closed door, but there's a chorus of 'Come in!' All the children are there, lounging on the floor watching television. Micah's sitting with his arm round Evie, but he moves it when he sees me. When I tell them it's time for the speeches, he gets up obediently, and the others troop after him. Evie turns off the film and gives me a shy smile before following.

Downstairs, I look in at the quiet room. Danny's not there any more, but Miffy is sitting in a corner, talking intently to a beautiful fair man in a grey shirt. For a confused moment I think it's that rabbi from when we were kids, Rabbi Aron, then I realise it must be Rob.

Danny is gathering everyone in the main living room. I go in hesitantly, keeping an eye out for enemies. Evie sidles up to me and takes my hand. I am so grateful, I give her a massive kiss on the cheek, which she wipes off.

'Mum, you smell of drink.'

'Someone spilled their wine on me, the idiot.'

Andrea pushes past without noticing me. She's dragging along a thin silver-haired man who must be the saintly Morris. Evie waves to Micah, who is at the front of the room. He waves back, and Andrea turns to see who he's signalling to. The look of horror on her face when she realises it's my daughter makes the rest of this terrible evening worthwhile.

Amy and two of her friends squeeze round with trays of the champagne Danny and I bought yesterday. I grab two glasses and give one to Evie. The excitement of this stops her noticing how quickly I drink mine. Oops, forgot to wait for the toasts.

The room fills up, and Evie and I are trapped in the middle of the room. I look towards the door to work out an escape route, and at that moment Miffy comes in. Danny and Heifer call her to the front and she has to start making her way through the crowd. When she passes near us I see her face is shuttered and say, 'You okay, Miff?'

She shakes her head: no. For a moment she looks very young, like her childhood self. Then she is moving forward to take her place as chief aunt and party organiser at the front of the room.

Danny, commanding and handsome, makes a sweet speech about his oldest son being barmitzvahed. Everyone says, 'Ahhh!' Heifer, surrounded by children, grins smugly and is the first to start clapping. Then Micah says a few words, some of which I imagine give Evie a thrill, as he describes the party as 'the best night of my life'.

Miffy thanks everyone for coming and for welcoming her home so fulsomely. Finally, brother and sister stand together and link hands. Miffy says, 'It's also a sad occasion tonight as we remember our father, Michael, who died less than a month ago.'

Evie strokes my arm, which makes me feel teary. I concentrate on staring at Andrea Cline, who is fumbling ostentatiously with a tissue.

'He would have loved this party so much. He felt it would be a chance to bring us all together, and it is. We're so glad Michael's grandchildren are all here.' Miffy names all Danny's kids. Then she looks across at me and adds, 'And his granddaughter Evie.' A sea of faces turn to smile in our direction. 'With Laura, his stepdaughter.'

Andrea gives me such a filthy look I almost miss the next thing Miffy says. 'Michael, wherever you are, I hope you're glad we're all here tonight, finally together in one room, to celebrate your oldest grandchild becoming a man.'

It feels odd that Mama is absent from the speeches, her long marriage to Michael airbrushed out. But now people are clapping, and Miffy is enjoining us to keep drinking and make merry; people are moving, talking, laughing, refreshing glasses. Evie walks towards Micah, who I now see is tall and strong. He easily sweeps her up off the floor into a hug. Is that allowed? I glance at Heifer but she's not looking, so I scan the room for Danny, who's almost disappeared in a press of people, and he follows my gaze, shakes his head very slightly.

Miffy goes past, her face pale and drawn. Before I can reach out to her, she is swept into an embrace by her old school-friend Sasha, a slim woman in a sparkly dress too young for her. When I get to the hall I see them going upstairs, Sasha's face bent towards Miffy. I feel a pang of something like homesickness.

This isn't a good moment for Orange Pervert to sway over to me. Before he can say anything I snap, 'Touch me again and I'm calling the cops.' I don't know why I go all American; it just comes out.

'Jesus! You'd have to pay me, you fat bitch.' He turns and disappears into the crowds. What a night I'm having.

Danny appears, wearing his coat. He smiles at me and says, 'Just taking some of the older relatives back to their hotel.'

A voice bangs in my head, saying, *Leave him alone, for God's sake, just leave him alone.*

I always ignore those sorts of voices.

'I'll come along. I could use a change of scene.'

'I'm not sure that's a good idea.'

'Maybe not. But I'm coming anyway.'

Three elderly people arrive in the hall. 'Ready, Danny-boy?' one asks, and we go outside. When we reach the car, a woman says, 'Who's this?'

'Oh, hello. I'm Laura. Danny kindly said he'd give me a lift too.'

'To Eastbourne?' an old guy says, and I improvise hastily, 'Oh, just a bit further.'

Danny leaves me floundering as they question me. Is it Pevensey? Bexhill? Hastings? I choose Bexhill as it sounds quite nice. We climb into Danny's huge Volvo, me in the back with two old ladies who introduce themselves as Aunt Faye and Aunt Shirley. Uncle Kenny sits in the front with Danny. Soon as we set off I remember what Miffy said about Danny's terrible driving. I seem to be the only one who notices. For most of the journey I cling to my seat in terror, occasionally closing my eyes, feeling like I'm going to be sick, as he mounts the kerb, runs red lights, goes through 30-mph zones at what feels like 60 mph. Meanwhile the old people chatter on about the trouble Melissa went to with the party, the lovely cooking, the beautiful house, how handsome Micah looked.

Aunt Faye says, 'Fascinating to see Andrea welling up during the speeches. Obviously still has a soft spot for your father, no matter what she says.'

Danny says, 'Naturally she was upset.'

195

Faye says, 'Thank God Melissa didn't go completely doo-lally and invite that *shiksa* he married. Bad enough asking that woman's daughter.'

I sit very still.

'Um, Aunt Faye,' Danny says. 'Laura, sitting next to you, is Olivia's daughter.'

'The *shiksa's* daughter,' I confirm, turning towards Faye. Luckily it's dark. I'd hate to see her face.

Aunt Faye gives a little laugh. 'Oh dearie me, I had no idea.'

No one says anything for the rest of the journey. Danny puts on a CD of Yiddish songs, which seems to make his driving a little slower, thank Christ. We all listen to the music. It's awful.

At last we pull up in front of a huge hotel on the sea-front. There are coaches out front and grey-haired people milling about. The two women get out of the car with muttered goodbyes, but Uncle Kenny leans his head into the back and says to me, 'Congratulations: you're the first person who's ever shut Faye up.'

Danny sees them into the lobby, and I climb into the front passenger seat. He's gone quite a while.

Danny: Sorry I took so long. Faye couldn't stop apologising.
Laura: That was kind of awkward.

Danny: I'm so sorry.

Laura: She didn't say anything untrue. Mama is a *shiksa*, and I *am* her daughter.

Danny (*leaning over to kiss her*): A *shiksa* I've never stopped thinking about.

I jump as Danny slides into his seat, slamming the door.

'Hi. It took a while to see them all in,' he says, almost exactly like the dialogue in my head.

I say, 'That was kind of awkward.'

'I'm really sorry. Thanks for not being rude back.'

'She didn't say anything untrue. Mama *is* a *shiksa*, and I *am* her daughter.' It's like being in a film.

'*Shiksa* is not a nice word. I feel bad about it. I'm so sorry.'

He turns the key in the ignition. Then, unexpectedly, he giggles. It makes me jump; it's such a strange sound, so at odds with his usual demeanour.

'What's funny?'

'I don't know. Just, Aunt Faye. She's such a motor-mouth. You being so dignified. And something about how naughty a word *shiksa* was when I was young. It symbolised everything we weren't allowed to have.'

He eases the car into the traffic, and I just go for it. Blame it on the wine, or on Danny's sympathy towards me over Aunt Faye.

Blame it on Heifer saying, 'I just want you to know that I trust Dan-Dan completely.'

Blame it on Huw doing who knows what with blonde professors.

Blame it on Miffy telling me, 'Say what you want.'

Blame it on the boogie.

I say, 'But you did have it, for a little while.'

'Oh, Laura.' My name is one long sigh.

'You could have it again, too, if you wanted.'

'I'm going to pretend you didn't say that.'

'When we kissed, you did want it. Pointless to deny it.'

'Laura. You're pushing me to say something I'd rather not say.'

'Oh, why don't you just say it, Danny?' I try to make it sexy.

He stares straight ahead at the road, looking gorgeous and determined.

'Just because I have, ah, a certain response, if you know what I mean...' A hand gestures at his crotch. 'It doesn't mean what you think.'

'Uh huh?'

'I admit it, I am really turned on' – he stops and then continues in a deeper voice – 'really turned on by the thought of what we did when we were kids. But it doesn't mean I want to do anything now.'

I don't say anything.

'I shouldn't have to point this out, but not only are we both married, you're also my stepsister. Had you forgotten that?'

'No.' Yes. Sort of. Who cares?

He almost runs into the back of a blue Fiat, swerves to overtake it only at the last minute. Christ, we're going to crash and be together for ever in eternity. I look at him, rather than the road. Better I don't know what's going on out there.

'Laura, forgiveness is a *mitzvah*. I really have done my best to forgive you for everything that happened when we were kids. I'm sorry Lissa and I kept away from you for so long.' His voice drops. 'You seemed so sure of yourself, but I realise now that, of course, you were just a kid yourself.'

We're now on the fast road that takes us back to the party. At least, it's fast when Danny drives on it.

'It's good to get it said. I've hated having these bad feelings. I hope we can start afresh, move forward as brother and sister. Evie and my kids as cousins. Dad so wanted that to happen. Do you think we can?'

I want to grab him. Slap him. Kiss him. 'I don't know, Danny. I think you still have feelings for me. You even admit I turn you on. All this brother and sister stuff: I think it's bullshit.'

Danny pulls over abruptly, screeching to a halt in a bus lane. He leaves the engine running, and stares ahead, hands on the steering wheel, his arms straight and taut. He says slowly, not looking at me, 'Do you want to leave Huw?'

'I think he's having an affair with a blonde professor, a very clever PhD-type of person.'

'That's terrible, Laura. I'm so sorry to hear that. But it doesn't change how I feel.'

'It changes how I feel, though.'

'Do you want me to leave Hella?'

Well, yes, obviously. The only puzzle is why he hasn't already. I say nothing.

'Or do you just want to have an affair? Like Huw?'

Yes, of course I want to have an affair. Perfect scenario. Huw gets it out of his system with Bardot; I get it out of mine with Danny. Then Huw and I come back together, stronger than before. Us and Evie and the baby. So, yes, Danny, I want to fuck your brains out. I want to see if it's as brilliant as I remember. But the way he says, 'Do you just want to have an affair?' makes it sound as if he's saying, 'Do you just want to have a bath in shit?'

The silence goes on and on. I can hear my own breathing. Then he laughs. I can hardly believe I'm hearing that sound again.

'Chip off the old block, aren't you?'

'What do you mean?'

'Laura. You're having Huw's baby in a few months. You've got Evie. I've got six children...'

Is it really only six?

'. . . and we want to have more.'

I touch his arm, but he pushes me away. Turns, and almost shouts in my face. 'Do you really want to fuck everything up for all those kids? Like things were fucked up for Miffy and me?'

He whacks the steering wheel with his palm, then takes a deep breath, moves into first gear, and we drive back to the party without another word.

16 MARCH 2003

If there's a better hangover cure than singing along to 'Wouldn't It Be Nice,' I've yet to find it. If only Evie felt the same way. 'Mum! Will you please. Just. Turn. It. Off!'

I raise my voice a bit louder, and put my foot down harder, as we reach the chorus and a clear stretch of road at the same time. 'Mum, you're doing my head in.'

'So, Evie,' Miffy says. She switches off my compilation tape and dangles her cigarette out of the window. 'You had a good time last night, honey?'

'It was brilliant, Auntie Lissa.'

Auntie Lissa now, is it?

'You seemed to be getting on well with Micah,' Miffy says, and Evie giggles soppily.

I overtake some slow bastard in a Vauxhall Cavalier and

glance at my daughter in the mirror. 'Well, Evie, think about the girls he's seen till now. Covered head-to-toe in polo necks and woolly tights. You must have seemed a mirage.'

'Shut up, Mum.'

'Actually, now I come to think of it, you're sort of related to Micah. Isn't she, Miffy? Some kind of step-cousin.'

'I'm listening to my music now.' Evie plugs herself into her new iPod.

Miffy expels a blast of smoke out of the window. 'Not feeling too great today, Laura?'

'Just a bit.' I ache all over. My head throbs, my back hurts, and my stomach's not feeling too clever, either.

'Me too. God, I'm wrecked.' She gives a massive yawn. 'I barely slept last night.' She settles down into her seat and closes her eyes.

Maybe you're wondering why she's in my car? It was her idea. She knocked on my door at nine this morning, looking like hell: eyes red, hair wild. 'Laura, feel free to say no, but any chance I could come to Wales with you and Evie? I could really do with getting away for a few days.'

'Oh, that'd be lovely!' I was surprised, but thrilled.

'I can't face going back to my mum's, and I don't have my own place yet.'

'You're a homeless hobo. You're going to have to start selling the *Big Issue*.'

She laughed. 'Thanks so much, Laura, I really appreciate it. Danny offered but they're so crowded. Amy's going back to her flat, and Sasha's got her sister staying.'

So I wasn't exactly first choice, then. But still, it's a brilliant chance to spend more time with her. Reconnect.

I managed to get Evie and myself out of the house without seeing Danny. Or Heifer. Or Andrea. Or Orange Shirt Man. Wow, I made so many friends last night. And so now, here we are – me, Evie and Miffy – on our way to North Wales. I put my foot down and stay in the outside lane, flashing past all the slowcoaches. I'm in a trance when Miffy says, 'Christ, you're driving like Danny,' making me jump.

'Thought you were asleep.' I cross into the middle lane and slow to 80 mph.

'Power nap. So,' Miffy says, 'how was your evening?'

'You first. I'm desperate to know what happened with the gorgeous Rob.'

She lights another cigarette and winds down the window. 'Nothing. He got back together with his wife, and she's pregnant.'

I glance across at her. She's wearing a little flowery skirt, her long brown legs stretched out, perfect other than the faded scar on the calf, her bare feet with their painted silver nails resting on the dash. It's hard to feel too sorry for her.

'Right guy, wrong time. Fucking babies. Sorry. So. What about your night, Laura?'

'Your mum was pretty weird with me.'

'Oh dear, she'd had too much to drink. She's not used to it at all.'

'And I had a horrible encounter with some fat bloke. Orange shirt?'

'Oh no, not Simon! He's a total creep, married to my cousin Alisa, the poor woman. I'm sorry, my family have given you a rotten time.'

'Also, I think Danny kind of hates me.'

'He was saying after the *shiva* how nice it was to see you again. I'm sure he doesn't hate you any more.'

Any more? I brake as the car in front slows down.

'Seeing you again was quite a milestone for him. You were such a significant person in our lives. He was probably just anxious.'

I look in the mirror. I can't hear any music coming from Evie's iPod, but her eyes are closed. I think she's asleep. She went to bed very late last night. 'I was wondering,' I say, lightly, 'if I broke Danny's heart back then.'

'Ach.' Miffy lapses into Irish brogue. 'But didn't we all get our hearts broken at that age, to be sure?' She takes a deep sunken-cheeks drag on her cigarette.

As we're doing accents, I put on my Greta Garbo, which Miffy used to like. 'You know, *darlink*, sometimes

I seenk my heart it stay broken all zese years.'

There's a catch in my voice that's not put on, and I feel Miffy staring at me.

'Oh my God. You still fancy him!'

'This traffic's bloody appalling. Look at that twat.'

'It's so romantic. You saw Danny for the first time in a million years and fell in love with him all over again – him all *frum* and untouchable.' She starts singing the theme to *Love Story*.

'Don't, please. It wasn't funny last night at all.'

'Sorry. So, go on. You told him you loved him, and said, "How about it?"'

I don't reply, and she starts laughing again. 'Oh God. You didn't! I can just about imagine how that might have gone. My poor Laura-sister.'

It's the first time she's used my childhood nickname. Despite her teasing, it makes me feel warm. Closer to her.

'He did maybe act a bit surprised.'

'Well, honey.' She sounds like she's going to laugh. 'Didn't you notice that he's sort of married, and, well, so are you?'

'You should remind Huw of that.'

'Shouldn't *you* remind him?'

The traffic speeds up again and I move the car into fourth gear.

'Danny's clearly still very attracted to me.'

'You're so much how I remember you, Laura. Go on.'

'He kept getting angry whenever we talked about the past, then had to apologise. Very emotional. His rabbi had told him it would be painful.'

'Love those crazy kosher shrinks!'

'Ha! Yes. Anyway. I kind of implied, uh, that I had, well, feelings for him.'

God, I hope Evie really is asleep.

'You did, huh? And how did that go down?'

I wince, thinking of Danny's face as he slammed the steering wheel. 'Not great.'

'No wonder he looked like the wrath of God this morning.'

'He seemed so happy to see me when we arrived at the house.'

'I'm sure he was. He really wanted to mend bridges.'

'But it was more than that, Miff. I kissed him the day before the party and he practically came in his pants.'

I'm trying to shock her, just a little bit, but she says, 'He can't help it. He's probably just thinking about what you got up to when we were kids.'

This is irritatingly close to Danny's explanation. Maybe they've discussed it.

'Danny and Hella are the strongest couple I know,' Miffy says, more gently. 'He thinks she's the most amazing, beautiful person.'

'You're kidding, Miff! She's hideous!'

'Really, do you think so?' she says calmly. 'I think she's very pretty. And they really love each other. Despite some of the old-fashioned Jewish stuff, it's a proper, caring partnership. Jay and I certainly never had what they have.'

'If he loves his fucking wife so much, why would he get a hard-on just looking at me?' I try to keep my voice steady, but it wobbles into a higher register when I say, 'Fucking wife.'

'It's been strange for all of us, hasn't it, meeting up again after all this time?' Miffy stretches her arms above her head and the bracelets clang into each other. 'It's brought up a lot of feelings we thought were dead and buried.'

Fucking psychologists.

'I guess,' she continues, 'that both you and Danners had a funny reaction seeing each other again. Things were said in the heat of the moment. That's all.'

I get into lane for the M40 exit, and neither of us says anything for twenty minutes. I'm trying to think how to break the frost when Miffy says, 'It's a hell of a long way to North Wales, isn't it?'

'You got that right. Bloody long way to the back arse of beyond.'

She laughs. Then whispers, 'Is Evie deaf to us, do you think? You were going to tell me how you got together with Huw.'

I watch Evie for a moment in the mirror and say her name, but she doesn't look up. And then, relieved to be chatting again, I tell Miffy nearly everything.

Voice-over: When Laura was fourteen she had to move to a new town and school. It was a miserable few years. But all that changed when she went to university. A chance to reinvent herself. To talk, drink and flirt with people who knew nothing about her. And then one day she walked into Professor Ellis's lecture.

Huw's Beardy Colleague: Modern Welsh History. Pretty unpopular course it was then. Still is, in fact. Got to wonder why we've stuck with it so long.

Laura: Huw was gorgeous. I used to sit in the front row of the lecture hall, gazing at him.

Beardy Colleague: As do little girls even now for Huw Ellis, in their tiny skirts and crop-tops. Lucky swine.

Voice-over: There weren't crop-tops back then. Laura wore her tightest jeans, her reddest lipstick.

Laura: I was so flattered he chose me. He could have had anyone.

Voice-over: He took her for drinks in romantic out-of-the-way places. He told her his wife didn't understand him. Original.

Huw: I married Carmen too young, *cariad*, and she's crazy. I work late every night to avoid going home.

Voice-over: Huw would sneak into Laura's Halls and they'd make love in her narrow single bed. Or they'd meet in his office with the blinds down, the framed photos of his wife and child on his desk.

Huw: Meeting you, Laura, was the best thing that ever happened to me.

My eyes fill up as I talk. Has he been fucking that Bardot woman in his office? In front of photos of me and Evie? I am suddenly quite, quite certain that I don't want to lose Huw. What lovers we were, before domestic life ground us down.

Miffy says, 'Wasn't it a problem that he was your lecturer? Didn't the college object?'

I blink the tears away. 'No one cared back then.'

It's all different now. Last year another lecturer at the college, someone in Biological Sciences, had to resign after shagging a postgraduate, and she was twenty-five! Disciplinary hearings, abuse of trust, blah blah. But in 1985, who gave a shit? His colleagues all said, 'Go on, my son,' and my friends thought I was the business to be having it off with a glamorous older man.

Miffy says, 'What happened to his wife?'

Voice-over: Everyone knew it was a dead marriage. Carmen was a nutter.

Carmen: Still am!

Voice-over: She was depressive, on medication, in and out of hospital.

Carmen: I cut up Huw's clothes, sprayed paint on his books. I wrote poison-pen letters to his friends and colleagues. I have no imagination.

Voice-over: When Huw moved in with Laura, there were phone calls in the middle of the night.

Carmen: Oh, the names I called Laura, the things I told Glynn to say.

Voice-over: And then Laura got pregnant. And then Laura lost the baby.

The words are pouring out. God, it's good to remember how much Huw used to love me!

'Bloody hell,' Miffy says. Out of the corner of my eye, I can see her watching me.

'Eventually, Huw divorced Carmen and married me. I didn't get pregnant again for a few years, but finally, along came our pride and joy, the Charming Miss Evie.'

'Well!' Miffy sits back and blows out her cheeks. 'It's like a soap opera.'

'Look, we're not too far now.' Trundling along the winding A5, we have at last reached the outskirts of Gwynedd.

Miffy goes into rhapsodies about the scenery. 'If I'd

known there were mountains like this here, I wouldn't have bothered travelling halfway round the world.'

'I guess it is beautiful. I've stopped seeing it, I guess. The scenery doesn't really substitute for a cultural life.'

'So, that's how you got together with Huw. But why did you choose to be a student here in the first place? Rather far from Norfolk.'

'God, I didn't *choose* to come here. My A Levels were so bad, Bangor was the only place that would take me. History was the only course I could get on. And sleeping with my professor was the only way I could get decent grades.'

'Mum!'

'Sorry, Evie. Didn't know you were awake. Let that be a lesson to you: work hard for your exams. Only joking.'

Miffy says, 'Did you have "God Only Knows" as your wedding music?'

'I don't think so. It was a register office do; bit of a rush job. Was that what I said I would have? I think I'm getting Alzheimer's. I can't seem to remember anything.'

There's a lot I can't recall about life in Edgware. Mind you, Miffy remembers too much to be healthy, if you ask me.

She laughs. 'Pregnancy hormones rather than Alzheimer's, I'd have thought.' Then she says, 'Go back a step. How come your A Levels were bad? You were always so smart.'

We pass through Capel Curig, my marker for being nearly home. I look longingly at the Byrn Tyrch, where Huw and I had many illicit drinks in our secret courting days. That little bar where we drank wine and held hands, ready to drop them the minute anyone we knew came in.

Laura: I arrived in Great Yarmouth at a new school in the middle of the term. Two weeks later, I had to take time off to have an abortion.

Voice-over: Laura never settled back into school. She failed her O Levels and spent her A Level years smoking dope and screwing around.

Laura: Well, if you're known as the English tart, you may as well live up to it.

Voice-over: And there you have it: why Laura didn't get very good A Levels.

I don't say this bit. I've already told Miffy way too much. And Evie's listening. When I think about some of the things I went through – at not much older than she is now... Well, I can't bear to think about them. I just say, 'I didn't fit in too well at my new school.'

Miffy says, 'You were always the cool one at our school.'

'It might be different now; all the kids in Evie's class try to sound like they come from Brixton, rather than Menai Bridge.'

'I love Evie's accent.'

'She thinks she sounds like a Cockney, don't you, darling?'

I pull off the main road and on to the winding lane that leads up, up, into Aber, our tiny village. To our cottage, built into the side of a hill. Huw hears the car coming along the road and stands in the doorway to meet us. Too late, I realise I haven't rung to tell him Miffy's with us. Nonetheless, he is courteous and welcoming. He hugs Evie, and says, 'I'm sure you ladies would like a cup of tea after your journey. Or perhaps Melissa would prefer a glass of wine?'

Miffy smiles up at Huw and says, flirtatiously, 'Think I'm going to like it here.'

Miffy

1979

Lucky Day

Dad dropped me off at *shul* for my historic first batmitzvah lesson with Rabbi Aron. All week I'd been planning to wear my belt-skirt, but Mum made me throw it away. She wouldn't even let me give it to Oxfam. 'The last thing the poor Cambodians need is clothes that don't cover their bottoms,' she said. So I was just wearing my usual jeans.

It was odd being in the *shul* on my own. There were funny noises, and I was just starting to get scared when the door opened and there he was, looking gorgeous in casual slacks and a jumper. 'Melissa!' Good start – right name. 'Right, let's get started.'

He pulled up a chair and sat opposite me, and asked me to start reading. I injected lots of feeling into it, and moved quickly over the difficult bits. I could feel him watching me. When I finished, I smiled, but he looked very serious, like a strict teacher.

'I think, Melissa, as time's getting on, we had better meet twice a week now. Don't be upset – it isn't your fault. Max hasn't moved you on quickly enough.'

I just stared at him. Upset? I couldn't believe it. It really was my lucky day.

Blooms

Brilliant, amazing, fantastic news! Mum and Dad told us that we're going on holiday with Laura and her mum at half-term! We're going to Spain for five days, to stay with Laura's grandparents, who live in a villa with a swimming pool. I'm so excited!

Dad said to me, 'I know you had your heart set on Pontins.'

'I don't mind.'

'We'll go there next time. A weekend in autumn, before your batmitvah.'

'Will we, Michael?' said Mum, and she walked out of the

room. I really don't know what she has against Pontins. It looks lovely in the brochure.

In the afternoon, Mum, Danners and I visited Booba Preston in hospital. She was sleepy and her head was hanging down onto her chest. Mum held her hand and chatted about what we'd been doing. She didn't seem to mind that Booba stayed silent. Danners and I went to the canteen. It had one of those brilliant machines you put money in and the chocolate falls down, but we didn't have change so Dan sent me back to get some. Mum was still chatting to Booba. I heard her say, 'He said *she* made a pass at *him*.'

Booba didn't say anything.

'Leila says I'm mad, Mum, but the holiday will be make or break and I'll be able to see exactly . . .' Then she saw me. 'Hello, darling. Are you all right?'

Afterwards, Mum took us to a kosher restaurant called Blooms. It was very busy and the waiters were rude, but Mum said they were always like that: it was part of the tradition. When one of them crashed down our plates so the soup spilled onto the tablecloth, she just started laughing. I couldn't believe it. Normally she would be furious. She could barely eat her meal for giggling. Danners and I started laughing too, because Mum was, and in the end all three of us were in hysterics. But Mum carried on laughing after we left the restaurant. She couldn't seem to stop, and it was a bit embarrassing on the tube home.

When we got home, I looked up 'pass' in the dictionary, but I still didn't understand what Mum had meant.

Sarong

I took my packing list to Laura's, but she was in a really bad mood. She scrunched the list into a ball and threw it across the room.

'What's the matter?'

'I'm fine,' she said, in a nasty voice. 'I wanted to go to the church disco with Fiona, not be stuck here with you, but it's fine, fine, *fine.*'

'Why did you ask me to come over, then?'

'My bloody mother, that's why.'

I burst into tears and ran to the door. But she grabbed me into a big hug and said, 'Sorry, sorry, little Miffy-sister. I didn't mean to hurt your little rabbity feelings,' and lots of other nice things.

She told me she was mean because she was pre-menstrual, which always made her ratty with those she loved the best. We did 'make up, make up, never, never break up'. When I was sure she wasn't cross any more, I asked what she'd meant about me coming over because of her mother.

She said, 'It's embarrassing. Mama thinks you're a good influence. Can we shut up about it now?'

I felt very proud. I'd never realised Mrs Morente

thought anything about me at all. She never talks to me unless Dad's there. Even when she taught me piano, which is how I first met Laura, she often called me the wrong name. It felt amazing to think I was an influence on Laura. I jumped up and autographed one of her Beach Boys posters in red felt-tip pen, pretending it had been signed by Brian. Laura fell about laughing when she read the message. Then she carefully smoothed out my packing list. 'This is good, but you'll need a sarong as well. You can buy one in Spain.'

She showed me her sarong, which was gold and red. I think a sarong would be perfect for my transformation. I drew a picture of myself with straight hair, no glasses and a sarong, and Laura said it was very realistic. She'd saved a cigarette to share with me, and we sat on the window ledge smoking. She said it was easy to buy cigarettes in Spain, so hopefully we can get some more. Then we talked again about whether she should sleep with Danners. Laura said that at confession the priest had told her it was a mortal sin as well as being illegal.

When I went to throw away a tissue, I saw the gold pipe-cleaner jewellery tree I'd given for her birthday, all bent and shoved into the bottom of the bin. I decided to give her the benefit of the doubt, as Dad always says I should do when I don't know the facts. Probably it got broken and she didn't want to tell me.

Gorilla Man

Laura and I became friends six years ago. When I was six, in fact. Half my lifetime. Mum wanted me to have piano lessons, because she wished she had learned the piano when she was little but couldn't because it was the war. I've never really understood why the war stopped her. Maybe pianos were rationed? She found Mrs Morente, a piano teacher who lived a few miles away. When I first met her she shook my hand. No one had ever done that before. Her nails were red and sharp on my wrist. She had big black hair and wore tight dresses. I didn't think someone like her could be a mother.

I used to go to her house for my lessons, which was scary because Mr Morente still lived there then. He was huge, with a bushy beard and dark hair covering his arms like a gorilla. His accent was so thick I couldn't understand him, and I dreaded him opening the door. Mrs Morente's accent was easier to follow, but I didn't always understand what she meant. When I was playing she would say things like, 'Imagine you are in love with a wonderful man. Let the love play through your fingers.' I don't remember being very interested in wonderful men when I was six.

Then there was the day Mum dropped me off early for my lesson. I was waiting in the living room when an older girl came in, wearing a red velvet party dress with a frilly petticoat. She had long straight black hair and brown eyes, and I thought she was the most beautiful person I'd ever seen. 'That's my mama in there,' she said, pointing to the piano room. I thought it was funny someone so grown-up should use such a babyish word, though later I found out it was Spanish for 'mum'. Laura didn't hear me properly when I said my name. Back then I called myself Missy, which I don't like any more. She thought I said Miffy, and I didn't correct her.

The front door banged and Laura jumped up quick as a fairy, and ran behind the sofa. Then the big gorilla man – her dad – came in, and asked me if I'd seen a little girl. I shook my head and he went out. His footsteps banged upstairs. Laura crept out and sat next to me, put an arm around me. I stroked her hair and it was just as silky as it looked. We smiled at each other and I said, 'Will you be my best friend?'

Secrets

Laura's grandparents had a pool but no telly. Laura said everyone here has a pool because it's so hot. It was the hottest I'd been in my whole life.

The best thing about the holiday was sharing a room with Laura. We talked for hours after we'd gone to bed, just like sisters. Last night she said she had a big secret. She got into my bed and snuggled down next to me, under the covers. I could smell her soap. She squashed my arm but I didn't say anything because it was so nice to be cuddled up together. She was wearing a short T-shirt and I could feel the heat from her legs right down the bed.

Her breath fluttered against my ear. She whispered, 'You'll never guess. Danny and I did it today.'

I practically fell out of bed. 'What?'

'Danny and me. Today. Together. Making sweet lurrve.'

I turned to face her, though I couldn't go onto my side properly because of her lying on my arm. She looked so happy.

'Tell me!'

Laura said they hadn't planned it. They'd gone for a walk into town and they'd seen a little hut at the side of the road. The door was open and there was a mattress on the floor.

'Someone must be staying there at night,' Laura said, 'because there were ashes where a fire had been lit.'

'Oh, Jesus, didn't you worry they'd come back and find you?'

'I didn't even think about it, *darlink*, because Danny kissed me and pulled me down onto the mattress.'

This made me feel warm down below. It made me think of Towse.

Laura told me she kept her top and skirt on, and only took off her knickers, which is something I have always wondered: whether you have to be completely naked to have sex. The answer is a most definite no. *Patches* always says the first time can be painful. But Laura said it only hurt a tiny bit when he pushed his willy in.

'And then it didn't hurt any more – it felt wonderful.'

She stopped talking, all of a sudden.

'So, go on!' I yelled. 'I'm in suspenders here!'

'Time for sleep now, girls,' Laura's mum said, walking past the door. Laura put her finger on my lips. Her hand smelled of oranges. We waited, holding our breath, till the footsteps went past and her mum went into the room next door to us. When the door clicked shut, Laura snuggled in closer and whispered in her foreign film-star voice, 'Listen, Meefy, *darlink*, I'm not telling you ze gory details.'

'Oh, please, Laura, please. I really need to know.'

'*Nein, nein.* I like to keep zese sings private. But I'll tell you one thing,' she added in her normal voice. 'You know when you wank?' She looked right at me, so I just nodded.

'Well, all I can say is that with sex, it's a different kind of orgasm all together.'

'Oh.' I had no idea what she was talking about, and the only dictionary I had with me was my English-Spanish one, so I couldn't look it up.

'I'm going to sleep now.' Laura got out of my bed and padded across the room. My arm felt numb at first, then went into excruciating pins and needles. I heard the creak as she got into her own bed.

'Oh my God,' I whispered, the realisation hitting me. 'You're not a virgin any more!'

We started giggling, and Laura whispered, 'I'm a prossie,' which made us laugh even more.

My mum called up the stairs to my dad, 'Michael! Are you up there?'

The door next to us opened and I heard Dad come out onto the landing and call down, 'Coming!' He'd been next door the whole time. I hoped he hadn't heard what we were saying.

Laura whispered, 'Who do you want to lose your virginity to?'

I went bright red, even though it was dark. 'I don't want to for ages, not till I'm sixteen.'

'But when you're older, who do you want to give it to? Aron?'

'No, I'd prefer Towse.'

'Good choice,' she said sleepily. 'He's got a cute bum.'

It took me about two hours to get to sleep after all that.

Today everyone except Laura's grandmother went out to a market. I slid under the sheet with nothing on except the silver heart-shaped necklace Laura gave me yesterday. Her grandmother bought it for her years ago, but Laura only wears gold.

The house was really quiet. I touched my breasts but they just felt like my breasts. I thought of Towse touching them and that felt better. Then I touched myself down below. There was a sort of nobbly bit at the front and I touched that really gently. Nothing much happened but I carried on for a while. I sort of guessed that an orgasm was what happened in the end, but I didn't know how long it would take. My hand started to get tired and my mind wandered. I realised I was thinking about what to wear with my new pink sarong.

Then I discovered that if I pressed on my thigh with my other hand, it felt much better. All at once I was really excited; I became breathless and knew I wouldn't be able to stop touching myself even if someone came in. My thighs got really sweaty, I went warm all over, then lots of muscles all closed up inside me. It felt wonderful, and I could see why people go on about sex.

Sheets

At lunch, Laura's grandpa said in his funny accent, 'Are you an adventurer, Melissa?'

My stomach crashed down into my shoes. I thought he'd somehow found out what I'd been doing in my room yesterday, and was going to say he'd heard I like to explore 'down under' or something. Then I realised that he was talking about an ancient well in the back garden. Thank God! My heart slowly went back to normal as he droned on about it.

'I thought it might be fun for you children to see if you can find it under the vegetable patch.'

I liked him better than Laura's grandmother, who was bent over like a hunchback and never smiled. She disapproved of Laura's mum – her daughter – Laura said, because of her divorce. Even though it was years ago.

After lunch, the grandparents went to church. They went every day. Bloody hell, imagine if I had to go to *shul* every day. Danners was out with the boys from the next villa on their mopeds, and no one was around apart from Mum sunbathing by the pool, so Laura and I found spades in the summer house and started digging into the soft mud of the vegetable patch. I didn't really know what I was looking for. The only well I'd ever seen was in a garden near Booba Preston's. It had a wooden bucket and a red roof, and a plastic cat on the edge waving its paw. Laura knelt on one side, and I crouched on the other, our heads bent close together, sometimes chatting, sometimes quiet. When we'd had enough of digging, we started making mud pies. I examined Laura's face to see if she looked any different after losing her virginity, but she looked the same as usual.

It was hot and windy and the big sheets on the washing line kept flapping just above our heads.

'We could have a swim in a while,' I said. 'And then maybe another cigarette upstairs.' I felt completely happy.

She nodded. 'This is the best holiday ever. I hope Mama doesn't want to leave early. She always gets fed up with Nana being so grumpy about the divorce.'

'What did happen with your dad?' I remembered the big man with hairy arms. I'd sometimes seen him when I went for my piano lessons.

'He was always angry, and sometimes,' Laura said, 'he even hit Mama.'

I once saw a TV programme where the husband punched the wife. Sometimes Mum was so cross with Dad, she looked like she might hit him. She hadn't yet, though.

'One time he whacked her right across the face and I called the police.' She laughed. 'I was only seven. I hid in the living room and dialled 999.'

A gust of wind blew one of the sheets into my face, and I pushed it aside so I could see Laura properly. She was so brave!

'The police came but they didn't do anything. They said it was a Domestic.'

I could only think of Domestic Science at school, but that didn't seem relevant.

'There were more fights, and finally Mama said, "I've had enough," and she threw him out.'

I sat back on my heels and pulled the silver heart necklace away from my neck. It felt hot.

'Were you sad when he left?'

'Mama said I should be glad.' She pushed a sheet aside impatiently with a muddy hand. 'The only good thing was he left his Beach Boys records behind.'

To cheer her up, I pointed at the small amount of earth we'd dug and said, 'We're not doing very well with this well, are we?'

We both had hysterics at this pathetic joke, and she toppled backwards onto her bottom.

'Oh, no! Look at my shorts.'

This made me laugh even more. 'I wondered if white *broderie anglaise* was the best outfit for digging, but didn't like to say.'

Laura grabbed me round the waist and hissed, 'No one likes a smart-arse.' Then she pulled me onto the ground and we went rolling down the grass slope, our faces and bodies stuck together, out of breath, laughing. At the bottom of the hill we came to a stop, Laura on top of me. I wondered if this was how she had lain with Danners. Her ear was right next to my mouth. I whispered in it, 'Are you going to have sex again?'

She turned, her hair swirling across my face, and kissed my mouth. I tasted warm strawberries. She said, 'I bloody hope so!'

Then she jumped up and started running round me, yelling like a mad thing, 'I bloody hope so! I bloody hope so!' I lay on the grass watching her. Then a shadow went across me and I looked up into Mum's face.

'What are you two doing?'

Laura stopped jumping. 'Just playing, Mrs Cline.'

'Look at the state of you!' Mum pulled me to my feet. 'That dress'll have to be soaked right away.' She marched me back up the slope, then stopped when she saw the sheets. Mud was spattered all along their edges.

'For heaven's sake, what a mess, girls!' She turned to Laura, trailing slowly behind us. 'Do you have any idea where your mother is?'

Laura shook her head.

Mum ran me a deep bubble bath. I was amazed to see that the water was brown after I got out, and there were dark ring-marks round the side of the bath. I was wrapped in a towel and brushing my hair when I heard Mum talking next door. I couldn't hear what she was saying, so I put a glass against the wall and pressed my ear to it. I'd seen someone do that on telly.

Dad: 'Mumble mumble.'

Mum: 'Making a mockery of the entire thing.'

I wondered if it was a Domestic, and whether I'd have to call the police.

Mum: 'Sick and tired of it.'

Dad: 'Mumble mumble.'

Mum: 'Three hours, totally embarrassing me.'

Dad (*yelling*): 'You're becoming a paranoid old nag, do you know that?'

I put the glass back on the shelf and crawled under the covers in my towel. What did 'paranoid' mean? I wished I'd got my dictionary. I'd needed it more in these few days than in a month at home.

Laura

I'm loving Miffy being here. I've been starved of grown-up company since Huw started working every evening. After Evie's in bed and Glynn's God knows where, Miffy and I sit and talk for hours. I'd forgotten how lovely it is to have a close friend.

We curl up in front of the fire, her with a glass of wine and a cigarette, me with a boring decaf tea, and talk. Often it's about the baby. I'm keen to know more about her own situation, why she hasn't got kids, but she's quite hard to approach about personal things. She seems very happy discussing my baby, though. In fact, she often brings it up.

'Any more girls' names?' she'll say.

We both love the baby names discussion.

'I'm still torn between Chloe, Grace and Amber. What do you think?'

'Oh, they're all lovely. You have to try them with your surname, of course.'

'Amber Ellis. Hmm. Sounds like a lager.'

So we consider the merits of Chloe versus Grace, and whether a boy or girl would be easier, disposable nappies versus washable, the differences between baby-rearing now and when Evie was little. We often talk about Evie, too. *I* think she's special, but Miffy always finds endless little things to praise. 'Evie said such a sweet thing today,' or 'Didn't she look cute in that top?'

Sometimes Miffy gets me to teach her some Welsh. Not that I know much, as Huw never speaks it and Evie goes to an English school. But I've picked up a bit and it's fun passing it on.

'Um. *Diok in veer*?' Miffy tries.

'Not bad. *Diolch yn fawr*. Means "thank you very much".'

'*Diolch yn fawr* for having me to stay.'

'*Dim problem!*'

'Meaning "no problem"?'

'Impressive, Miff.'

'All right, Mrs Sarky.'

It's like we're thirteen again and hanging out in my bedroom.

Miffy's not completely reticent. Topics about her own life she's happy to discuss include:

Her travels; her various jobs; her friends; Danny's children, which I thought might be good for some gossip about Danny's weird life, but turns out to be mostly yawnsome anecdotes about what a great mum Heifer is.

Topics she isn't keen on discussing:

Her marriage; her divorce; why she doesn't have children; Rob.

Topics neither of us are keen on discussing:

Our childhoods in Edgware, particularly the weeks leading up to me moving away; and the year or so after that.

Then yesterday, after we'd been watching Evie dancing to something on the telly, Miffy suddenly mentioned the dances we used to choreograph. 'I'd jump up and you'd catch me and swing me from side to side.'

'You were such a tiny thing,' I said.

'That *Grease* album – we almost wore it out.'

'I used to love those songs!'

'And your *Pet Sounds* record,' she said. 'We did a rather experimental dance to "God Only Knows".'

'We did?'

'I wonder why you...' She stops.

'Why what?'

'Oh, nothing. Hey, let's play Evie "Greased Lightning" and see if she thinks it's hilarious.'

She's so good with kids. It really is a shame she hasn't got any. She manages to get proper conversation out of Glynn, and Evie reverts to her child-self, all enthusiasm and affection. Without it being a big deal, Miffy's taken over making Evie's packed lunches, finding her sports kit, making sure her hair is brushed. Miffy calls it 'making myself useful' but it's made me realise how stressed I've been, how absent Huw is, how accustomed I've got to doing everything myself.

Her first weekend with us and unfortunately it's our turn to host the Jenny-and-Paul dinner. I try to imagine Miffy and Jenny in the same room. Then Miffy and Ceri. Oh God. Trial by North-Welsh fire. The phone rings just when I'm wondering who is the least offensive person to seat next to Miffy. Huw, I suppose. When I hear Jenny's voice, I hope she's going to say they're cancelling owing to an isolated outbreak of bubonic plague.

'Sorry for the short notice, Laura, but could Nick tag along? He's staying with us after the, you know' – and she whispers loudly – 'messy divorce.'

Nick, her younger brother, is rather dishy, to use Miffy's word.

'No problem. Maybe he'll hit it off with my stepsister.'

'He's only just getting over that gold-digging bitch he married, so please don't start your matchmaking, Laura.'

Miffy's pleased when I tell her about Nick. 'I knew I could rely on you for a blind date.'

Huw comes in with the shopping and I have to listen while Miffy goes on about what good a job he's done at the supermarket, how she always forgets to get half her list. God, why doesn't she just call him a sexy great hunter-gatherer and be done with it?

'What's on tonight's menu?' she asks.

Huw picks up two ducks, displaying them like a magician revealing rabbits from a hat. Miffy claps her hands. 'I know an amazing sauce, shall I make it?'

'Oh, you star,' Huw says, beaming.

'Let's get started,' Miffy says, 'then we'll have time to make my special chocolate brownies too.'

I'll fuck off, then, shall I, even though this is my dinner party? I go upstairs for a long-overdue session of chin-plucking. I really need to do it three times a week; bit tricky, though, as I'm trying to have a life as well.

When I go back down, Miffy is washing herbs under the tap, Huw is whistling and chopping vegetables, Glynn is stirring flour and eggs, and Evie is polishing the cutlery. They're all singing along to 'I Saw Her Standing There' on the radio. In the twenty minutes I've been gone, they've turned into a family from an advert.

'Wow, Miffy, you've done well to get Huw cooking.'

'He's a natural.'

He is not.

I prop the back door open and let the watery sun stream in. Miffy patters about bare-foot on the quarry tiles in her little flowery skirt. She's wearing a halter-top, much too young for her, and no bra.

'What shall I do?'

'It's all in hand,' Miffy says. 'Sweetie, you're six months pregnant! My superb team of chefs and I will sort it. Least I can do after you've put up with me all week.'

Huw says, 'Go on, *cariad*, we'll be fine.'

I *am* really tired. I lie on the sofa and watch Evie try to make napkins into swans. They look like shit. Still, it's nice she's helping.

I wake with a start, head thudding, face scrunched damply against the sofa cushions. My arm's soaked in sweat where I've been lying on it. I throw off the heavy blanket some arse has put on top of me. No wonder I'm so bloody boiling! My mouth is furry and in the mirror I see sofa imprinted on my face. Beautiful.

It's just after five and still sunny. The kitchen is spotlessly clean and completely empty. The only sign of life anywhere is Evie, reading in her room. She shoves something under her pillow when I come in. Her diary, I suppose. If she's stupid enough to leave it there, I'll have a look when she's at school.

'You look rough, Mum.'

'Thanks, darling. I fell asleep. Where is everyone?'

'Glynn's in the garden.'

Like I give a shit where Glynn is. But I make a show of going over to the window to look. He's lying on the grass, smoking a cigarette. I hope it's a cigarette.

'Where's Daddy and Lissa?'

'Dunno. Think they went for a walk.'

Okay. That's good. They're getting on well. That's great. *Fuck.*

I shower and wash my hair. Squirt Rhianna's red maternity dress with Possession to freshen it up. My tits feel unbelievably heavy; they've each gained a stone while I slept, making my bra so tight that, like Miffy, I leave it off altogether. Unlike Miffy, it doesn't look perky. I catch a horrible glimpse of my naked body as I'm pulling the dress over my head. Might have to take a beauty tip from Heifer and start putting towels over the mirrors.

Six o'clock. I put the ducks into the oven, praying Huw and Miffy will return before the guests arrive.

Where are they?

For something to do, I tidy the drinks cupboard. Evie comes in as I'm kneeling on the floor holding a gin bottle. 'Mum, you're not supposed to drink.'

'I know, sweetheart. I'm just sorting these.'

She gives me a sceptical look. Somehow she knows that I would kill for a gin and tonic. I put the bottles back and firmly close the door.

It's almost quarter to seven when there's a commotion at the back door. Miffy's first in, laughing, flushed, her hair half out of its clip, smudge of mud on her forehead.

'Oh my God Laura. Sorry, sorry, sorry, but blame your so-called local-boy husband! He got us completely lost!'

'Can you believe it?' Huw is laughing too. He has a matching smear on his cheek. 'I had to reconnaissance up a mud bank! Look at me!'

I do look at him. He is ten years younger. His eyes are sparkling. Such a beautiful blue. I remember the first time I saw those eyes. He was leaning against a table at the front of the lecture theatre. Jeans and a dove-grey T-shirt. Dark hair flopping onto his forehead. Wife and child at home.

'I wanted to show Lissa the Carneddi, and we walked round that lake at the bottom, but then we took a path I didn't know...'

'Huw, you've lived here all your sodding life. How could you not know it?'

'That's what I said!' cries Miffy, washing her hands. 'I thought the big advantage of being a stick-in-the-mud' – she wrinkles her nose at Huw, and he laughs – 'and living in the same place your whole life, is that you know every blade of grass like the back of your hand.'

'Well,' I say, watching Huw, 'despite being a Welshy, he's not really an outdoors man. It's all a front. I have to read the map if we go for a walk.'

'Hell, I was convinced,' Miffy says, bustling about with oven gloves. 'Mmm. This smells great. You had me out there under false pretences, Dr Huw.'

Huw giggles – a proper giggle, I'm not kidding – and starts mixing stupidly strong drinks for me and Miffy. I'm about to remind him I'm not drinking, then I just take it and swoosh down half in one go. It's not like I asked for a drink; I was just given it.

I'm a little unsteady by the time everyone arrives, and I make the introductions in a haze. Ceri thrusts her coat, hat and wine bottle into my hands as though I were the Hindu god Shiva with seventeen arms. Rees kisses me lingeringly near my mouth and, worryingly, I don't mind. Jenny whispers, 'How *are* you, dear?' implying that I must be doing rather badly. Paul kisses me on both cheeks, and Jenny's brother Nick, handsome in the same silver fox style as Huw, shakes my hand and thanks me warmly for inviting him.

Miffy comes into the hall wearing a silky blue dress the colour of Huw's eyes. Ceri looks her up and down in that dreadful Bangor way and says a flat 'Hello'. Rees whistles, because he knows Ceri will just love that, and says, 'Wow, Laura, so there *are* more like you at home, yeah?'

'They're nothing alike, Rees,' Ceri says. 'They're not even blood relations.'

The atmosphere round the table is very odd, and I don't think it's just because I'm slightly drunk. It's highly strung and somehow sexually tense. These dinners have never been remotely like that before. I think it's partly me. I can't stop thinking about sex and how long it is since I've had any. I mean proper sex; I'm not counting that weird bathroom thing with Huw a couple of weeks ago. Even the thought of Rees kissing me is making me feel horny rather than grossed out. Must get a grip. I've let Glynn take the head of the table opposite me, and Evie's on his left; it's the first of these dinners she's ever wanted to come to, though what with all the randiness in the air it's probably not all that suitable. Ceri's next to Huw, and Rees is on my right (we all have to make sacrifices). Miffy is sandwiched between Huw and Nick. I have inadvertently devised an edgy Alan Ayckbourn-type table arrangement.

Miffy and Huw keep sniggering, clearly still finding their lost afternoon utterly hilarious. Nick twists in his seat to face Miffy. He's very attractive, despite a faint resemblance to Jenny. He has cute dimples. I certainly would. Jenny-and-Paul watch Miffy as though she were a cabaret act. Rees keeps glancing at me – I can see him out of the corner of my eye – and although it's just him, it does feel nice to be fancied. Poor Ceri is wearing the most hideous top in the history of clothes. Pillar-box red, it shows every bulge, and it has an appliquéd poodle on it, for some fucking reason. Perhaps I should sit her in the kitchen, for all our sakes.

I pass a bowl of roasted carrots across to Nick, and knock over his wine glass – mostly empty, luckily. This makes me giggle, attracting Jenny's disapproval.

'Oh, Laura! Have you been drinking? I know that crazy laugh of yours.'

I show her my water glass. I just had that one vodka before dinner.

'I think I've had five, Jenny,' I say, to annoy her, and Miffy, grinning at me, says, 'Oh, now, it was only four.'

'I know it's all so funny,' Jenny says, 'but you must think of that little baby in there. He really doesn't need any booze.'

We all go quiet: teacher's telling us off. Jenny puts her hand on Paul's, but he moves it away and picks up his glass.

'Delicious food, Laura,' says Nick, to break the silence.

'It's no thanks to me. Huw and Lissa did most of it.'

Huw and Miffy high-five each other. I feel Ceri's eyes on me and focus on my plate, circle my fork round a carrot.

Eventually everyone is scuttered, which is unfortunate in Ceri's case as she's a depressed drunk. As she drones on about her failed marriage, I see her as Miffy must: a grouchy middle-aged woman in an appalling top. Miffy catches my eye and does a great job of changing the subject, making everyone laugh with an account of a job interview she had a couple of weeks ago. The panel had the wrong CV in front of them, which caused great confusion, and was only resolved at the end when an interviewer said, 'Do you have any questions, Dr Patel?'

'How was your fancy party in England?' Rees asks Miffy. 'Put me on the guest list next time, yeah?'

'It was a great night, wasn't it?' Miffy says to me. She sits back in her chair and lights up a cigarette. Ceri raises her eyebrows, because she's never been allowed to smoke in our house, then smiles as Miffy stretches across Huw to offer her the packet.

Glynn, who's been as polite as I've ever seen him, asks if he can be excused to meet some friends. Evie stays in her seat, fiddling with a bracelet Miffy has given her: a silver string of blue and green stones which glint in the light.

Miffy says, 'It was wonderful having people there from all different parts of my life. Like Laura, and her beautiful daughter.' She smiles at Evie.

'Bloody long way to go, though, just for a party,' Ceri says, blowing smoke defiantly in Huw's face.

When we move to the comfortable chairs for coffee, Nick quickly sits next to Miffy on the sofa. Annoyingly, I miss what happens between them, because Huw's too smashed to care about Evie going to bed and I have to practically drag her up there like she's a toddler. Evie is over-tired and I have to insist in my strictest voice – okay, by yelling – that she gets into her pyjamas. When I kiss her goodnight and go out, firmly closing her door, Rees is standing in the hall. He makes me jump.

'Oh, Rees! Are you looking for the loo?'

'No, I'm looking for you.' He laughs at the rhyme. He's really plastered; he staggers and grabs my arm.

'Are you okay?'

'I am now.' He puts his face right up close, and then his mouth is on mine, his boozy tongue pushing inside, his hand on my breast. His eyes are closed, and I close mine too before I realise what I'm doing and push him away.

'C'mon Mrs Ellis, you liked it when we were students.'

'That was a long time ago, thanks very much,' I say primly. 'You need to be in bed.'

'Good idea.' He tries to pull me towards my bedroom, just as Miffy appears at the top of the stairs.

'Am I interrupting something?'

'No, you're bloody not! Let *go*, Rees.'

'Ah, Mrs Ellis,' he says, letting me go. 'I'm very flattered you remember our night of passion, but we'd better not. I'm spoken for, yeah?'

Miffy and I stare at him as he goes downstairs. When he's gone she says, 'You all right? You look a bit shook up.'

I start laughing, and after a moment so does she.

'Come in here,' she says, opening the door to her room. We sit on the bed. 'So...your night of passion with Rees?!'

'Oh, don't. It was, like, 1985 or something. I was a crazy mixed-up kid.'

'Bless, he's never stopped burning that torch, yeah?'

'Cruel impression, but something like that, perhaps. So, what do you think of Nick? *Dishy*?'

She pushes a frond of hair behind her ear and says, 'Very cute. Lovely smile.'

'Don't get excited, they're not all like that in North Wales. Most of them are like Rees.'

'But I think it's all a bit soon for him. Nick keeps mentioning his ex-wife. I know all about the fight for the wide-screen TV.'

Jenny calls up the stairs, 'Yoo-hoo, Laura, are you all right? I'm just going to make coffee.'

'Shit, we'd better go down. I don't want her rifling through my cupboards. Thanks for saving me from a Rees worse than death.'

In the kitchen, Ceri and Jenny are washing up and right in the middle of a lovely bitch. Ceri is saying, 'Always has an eye for the ladies,' as I come into the room, at which point they stop abruptly. I whisk them back into the living room. I hate people washing up; that's why we have a dishwasher. At work Ceri doesn't even rinse the suds off our mugs. I have to do it, if I don't want soapy tea. Miffy leans against the fridge and lights a cigarette, gazes up at the ceiling and says quietly, 'I guess at our age all men are going to come with a bit of baggage.'

I fill the kettle. 'But not necessarily the full carousel.'

Miffy exhales with a laugh. 'You were a bit of a match-maker, back in the day,' she says.

'Okay, Miffy-sister.' I heap coffee into the cafetière, press my hand against my tired back. 'What is it you're looking for?'

When her smile fades she looks older. 'I'm not *that* fussy. I just want someone kind, intelligent and solvent.'

'I'll do my best.'

'If they want kids, that'd be just fine.' She runs her half-smoked cigarette under the tap. 'Talking of kids, did you see what Evie was wearing at dinner?'

'What?' I pour boiling water. 'Her eensy-weensy T-shirt that barely covers her eensy-weensy boobs?'

'I think maybe Glynn noticed that too.' Miffy grins. 'She's going to be stunning in a couple of years. Like you. No, I meant her necklace.'

'What about it?' I can't understand why Miffy's interested in Evie's beads from New Look.

'It was the silver heart-shaped pendant you once gave me.'

'Was it? Bloody hell!' I push the filter down too fast and splash boiling water on my hand. 'Ow. I don't know where she got it from. I didn't give it to her, anyway.' I feel a blush coming on, as if I've been caught out in a lie.

'It honestly doesn't matter. It was just funny to see it again after all these years.'

We go back in with the coffee, and Ceri asks if we went to Colombia to get it. God, the wit. The rest of the evening passes off uneventfully. Miffy talks to Nick, I avoid Rees by listening to Jenny bang on about her annoying cleaning lady, and at last everyone fucks off. Miffy helps me bring the dirty cups and things into the kitchen.

'Lovely evening, Laura, thank you. Ceri seems nice.'

I look at Miffy to check she's being serious. God, you know what, she is. I don't want Miffy to think this is the sort of person I hang out with. Even if it is.

'Good to see another of her dreadful tops,' I say, scraping

leftovers into the bin. 'Christ. She must get them second-hand off Gyles Brandreth.'

Miffy laughs. 'How come you ended up working together?'

'Oh, we briefly shared a student flat. Few years later when she set up her shop, she emailed her entire address book to see if anyone fancied helping out part-time.'

'What's it sell?'

'Interiors. Pretty things. You know, cushions, candles, lights. It's not a brilliant career. She's still paying the same crappy wage as when I started seven years ago. But it's easy. And I'm good at selling things.'

'I bet you are! So, do you think Ceri will last long with Rees?'

'What, since he's dying for love of me? Nah. Ceri isn't exactly lucky in love.'

'Which of us are, though? Talking of which' – she drops her voice – 'what's the latest with Huw and the mystery blonde? You've not said anything about it.'

I hesitate. I'd love to tell her how I really feel.

Laura: I think it's still going on.

Miffy: That bastard! How can he even think of anyone else when he has you?

Laura (*crying*): Oh, Miff, I don't know what to do.

Miffy: I tell you what we do. We take the initiative. Tell him you're thinking about a trial separation. When he realises he could lose you, he'll stop mucking about.

You're not alone, Laura-sister. I'm with you every step of the way.

But I'm too knackered for the conversation. And I feel a bit weird about the way Miffy was with Huw today.

'Did she turn out to be just a professor after all?' Miffy says.

'Yeah, storm in a teacup.'

'Oh, I knew it! I'm so glad.'

'Why don't you go up, Miff? You must be quite done in.'

'I am. I'm beat. That stupid walk took it out of me! We must have gone miles.'

Huw comes in and says, 'You both go up. I'll load the dishwasher.'

'Marvellous man,' sighs Miffy, the silly moo.

'Then I've got to go out for a bit.'

'What, now?' How embarrassing, after what I just told Miffy. 'It's one in the morning.'

'I've got to get this book from my office, *cariad,* else I'll be out of the loop for my meeting. In fact, I'll probably just stay in the office and read the bits I need.'

'Aren't you way over the limit?'

'I've ordered a cab.'

Miffy catches my eye and I shrug. She comes over

and hugs me goodnight. I draw in a breath of her scent, musky and expensive, not quite covering up the smell of cigarettes.

When she's gone up I look at Huw, busily stacking plates. I open my mouth to say something, but at the last minute all that comes out is, 'Well, goodnight, then.'

He flashes his falsest smile. 'See you in the morning.'

24 MARCH 2003

As we leave the house my eye is caught by something glinting against Evie's collar. I see it without properly seeing it. Then I remember what Miffy said the other night. The silver heart-shaped necklace.

In the car I turn to Evie and gently cup my hand round the pendant.

'Where did you find it, baby?'

'Drawer in your dressing table at Grandma's. You can have it back, if you want.'

'No, you keep it.' I turn the ignition. 'It looks nice on you.'

We smile at each other. She's starting to get pretty at last, with her cute snub nose, her smooth lips that know how to kiss. Before she gets out of the car she gives me a hug. Rare these days. 'Happy birthday, Mummy.'

I almost cry when she's disappeared through the school

gates. My little girl. How long is it since she called me Mummy?

When I get home Glynn is up and dressed: a morning miracle. He and Miffy are at the kitchen table, heads close together. She looks up. 'Happy birthday, Laura! What did Huw get you, anything nice?'

'Um. A scarf.' I pull it out of the Christmas paper he'd wrapped it in, and hold it up.

'Not really you, is it?'

'My mother would reject it as too elderly.'

'Well, to make up, I'll take you out for a birthday lunch. You choose where.'

'Really?' No one usually pays much attention to my birthday. Including me. Thirty-eight. How did that happen? Two years till the end of everything. Thirty-fucking-eight. No wonder everything's sagging.

'Definitely. You deserve a treat. We're nearly done here. Can you think of an example of Glynn's organisational skills?'

Christ, he can barely organise getting out from under the duvet each morning.

Glynn says, 'What about when I was stage manager for our school play, Miffy?'

Who said he could call her that?

'Brilliant! That'll do perfectly.'

She's so good with him, so encouraging. Behaving like I

should, if I were a proper stepmother. Miffy's mobile rings. She glances at it and says, 'Oh Lord, it's Hella. I love her to bits, but a phone conversation with her will be at least forty-five minutes.'

'I'll talk to her, say you're in the bath.'

She laughs. 'That's so naughty! If you're sure?'

I take Miffy's phone and saunter upstairs. 'Hi, Hella, how are you?'

She expresses surprise and I explain about the bath, but she says, 'I'm glad it's you actually, Laura.'

Oh God, I'll die if she wants to ask me again if I trust my husband. But no, she says, 'Do you think Melissa is all right? I'm worried about her.'

'She'll come to no harm here among the heathens, Hella.'

'Oh, ha ha! No, I meant – she's more vulnerable than you think. She can't hear, can she?'

With your foghorn voice, nearly.

'Remember, Laura, she's not that long divorced. She and Jay were together for such a long time, I worry how she's coping.'

'She's fine. She's just been helping my stepson with a job application.'

'She's so amazing with children. It was so devastating that she and Jay couldn't have them.'

Oh *really*? I say something non-committal like 'Uh-huh?' willing her to go on.

'I was always worried it would cause a breakdown between them, and sadly, I was right. Children are so bonding in a relationship, don't you think?'

Not always, love. 'Mmm. They tried for a baby for years, didn't they?' It's a guess, but these not-able-to-have-kids stories only have one plot. I should know.

'Yes, we lost count of all the IVF treatments. The expense! Poor Jay. You know it was his fault, they finally discovered.'

All I have to do is make encouraging noises and she just keeps going.

'I always wished I could give her a baby, you know, Laura. It seems so sad, doesn't it, that some like me are so blessed, and others so unlucky? God's will, of course, but terribly sad.'

Heifer continues prattling, but I barely pay attention. *I always wished I could give her a baby*, says the woman with a hundred kids. Why didn't you then, bat-brain?

When she at last hangs up I go into Evie's room to change her bed. I pull back her duvet and a sweet musty smell reaches my nostrils. Thank God Mama doesn't know how long these have been on. When I take off the pillowcase, some papers fall out, and I remember Evie shoving something in there when I came into her room the other day. It's a letter, three pages of small, unfamiliar handwriting. 'Dear Evie, Told you I would write, and I really hope you write back...'

I flick to the end.

'…the most interesting and unusual girl I have ever met. Love, Micah.'

Dear God. Micah. I laugh out loud. She's a total chip off the old block with that Judaeo-Christian romance thing. I sit on the bed, intending to read the letter in full, but my conscience kicks in. My eyes close almost against my will, stopping me from reading. I carefully fold up the pages, put a new case on the pillow, and put the letter back where I found it. I'm clearly going mad.

I head downstairs to the kitchen and find Miffy wiping the table. I hand back her phone and she says, 'Thanks for that. Glynn's gone off to finish his application.'

'It's so kind of you to help him. You've got the patience of a saint.'

'Oh, he's a nice kid. Easy to talk to.'

She's a loony. He's as easy to talk to as a sandwich.

'Can I give you this now?' she says, all excited, and hands me a small package in dark-green paper, tied with a flamboyant purple bow. It's a very expensive lipstick. Gold case, tasteful little diamante for decoration. I twist off the cap to reveal a beautiful glimmering red.

Cock-sucker red.

'You always used to love make-up. Do you still?'

'Yes. I need even more of it these days. This is perfect. Thank you.' I peer into the mirror over the sink and smooth the deep rich red onto my lips, then pout at her.

'Beautiful. I'm a lot better at presents than I used to be. Do you remember that jewellery tree I once made you, out of pipe cleaners? It was terrible! I got the idea off *Blue Peter.*'

She looks so eager that I say, 'Oh, yes, that's right,' but she can see that I don't remember. I run a bowl of soapy water to wash last night's wine glasses. Miffy sweeps the floor, puts cereal packets away.

'I'm really enjoying it here,' she says. 'Hope I'm not out-staying my welcome. I'll leave soon, I promise.'

'Oh, don't, we're loving you being around.'

'It's nice to get to know Evie and Glynn. And Huw, of course.'

She turns away and bends down, her back to me, to open a cupboard. Jesus, her tiny bum in those jeans.

I say, 'That working late thing he did the other night.' A glass almost slips out of my soapy hand, and I catch it by its spindly stem. 'It's an academic thing. They all do it. Some of them sleep in their offices!'

'Sure.' She doesn't look at me. I don't know if she believes me. I don't know if I believe it myself. But I very much want this to either be nothing, or to blow over quickly – a last hurrah before he settles back down with me and Evie and the new baby. I've decided that if I don't make a big fuss about it, it'll be okay.

'I'm just delighted you're having a good time with us. Though it's got to be pretty dull after your travelling.'

'Not at all. It's good to stop moving. Be somewhere I speak the language. Well, *dim Cymraeg.*'

Oh, she's remembered the 'no Welsh' phrase I taught her.

'Anyway,' she says, wiping glasses, 'I need to work out what I'm going to do next. Make plans. Find a job, somewhere to live.'

'Stay as long as you like.' I mean it. 'You could look for jobs near us.'

'Ooh, I'm vibrating.' She pulls her phone out of her pocket again. 'Text from Danners. Says Jay's been to visit – calls him "your lovely ex-husband". Ah, that's why Hella was phoning. She and Dan would *so* love it if Jay and I got back together.'

'I guess they're not very pro-divorce.' I rinse the cloth under the tap.

'You could say that.' She giggles. 'Well, you probably realised that about Danners when you made a pass at him.'

'Thanks, Miffy. Do you have to bring that up?' I pout, half joking, but she stops smiling, grabs my damp hand and holds it tight.

'I think you're great. I wish I was more like you.'

'Christ, why?'

'You just always go for what you want. Take risks. I

never have. Except for travelling. Suppose that was better late than never.'

She lets go my hand and sits down at the kitchen table. In a fluid, elegant movement she picks up her cigarette box, taps one out, puts it between her lips. 'Yeah,' she continues, talking round the cigarette like Humphrey Bogart, 'lived at home while I was at university. Married a boy I'd known for years, because he was safe. Took the first job I was offered.' She ticks off her decisions on her fingers. 'It's time to be more adventurous.'

'Is that how you see me? *Adventurous*?'

She shakes a box of matches, lowers her lashes, strikes a match with a whoosh and a flare. How I used to love the paraphernalia of smoking. 'When we were kids, I always wanted to be you,' she says. She blows out a long stream of smoke. 'I love your sassiness. Listen, over the years, a lot of women have fallen for our Danny-boy, but far as I know not one of them has had the balls to put the moves on him.' She smiles hugely, her cats' eyes creasing with amusement like they used to when we were young.

'What, just cos he's a married Orthodox Jew?' I say, playing up to the image she has of me. 'What wussies they are to be put off by little things like that!'

She cracks up, and so do I, and we sit there giggling like teenagers.

25 MARCH 2003

Because I can't sleep, I hear Huw come in very late, after three. I roll onto my side but can't get comfortable because there's a dull pain in my back. I wish I could take a paracetamol. Huw doesn't come up. I suppose he'll crash on the sofa again.

I think about Miffy saying I'm someone who goes all out for what I want. My mind flashes an image of Huw, that first time I saw him, leaning against the table; and me, deciding there and then that I was going to have him. The first man I'd wanted since I was fourteen.

Since Danny.

I know Miffy thought I was sophisticated when we were teenagers. But when I found out I was pregnant, just weeks after we'd left London, it transpired I was really naïve. About everything.

I drift, the past playing in my head like the afternoon drama on Radio 4.

Mama and Michael, they promised nothing would change.

'It's only Norfolk. Not the other side of the world.'

'Of course you'll still see Danny.'

'Cheer up, Laura! Let's see a smile!'

It couldn't happen to me. It only happened to stupid girls, ugly girls grateful to be screwed, girls who wanted someone to love.

The magazines say don't worry about irregular.

Except mine were always Bang. On. Time.

'Don't you need more Tampax? How long has it been?'

When Mama slapped my mouth I tasted metal.

'You little slut, you stupid girl.'

What a mess on her shiny new life.

'He's your brother now, it's sick, it's wrong, you're just children.'

First time since we left I dialled the familiar number.

'Hello?' Shit, it's Miffy.

Dial again.

'Hello?' Fuck off, will you, Miffy?

Dial again.

His voice at last. 'Having a lovely time by the seaside are you? With my dad?'

'Danny, I am . . . I have got . . . It's yours . . . It's ours . . . I'm . . .'

Big breath.

'When you make love and you get something . . . Not crabs, nicer.'

He says, 'I don't believe you.'

He says, 'You slut, you shiksa slut.'

Mama says, 'We'll have to deal with it. You know what I mean.'

But we are Catholics!

Mama says, 'It's all arranged a week tomorrow.'

No one hugs me.

Shiksa slut.

*

I get to work late, my back one big dull ache. Ceri's in the shop window arranging the velvet cushions she's optimistically over-ordered, and she mimes drinking tea. I go out back and put the kettle on, and a few minutes later she joins me.

'Thought maybe you'd decided not to bother today.'

'God, Ceri, sorry I'm a bit late. I slept badly.' I hand her some tea, and put the telly on as a peace offering. It's *Jeremy Kyle*, her favourite. She lights a cigarette and there's an awkward silence, into which some first-class moron on the TV says, 'She can do a BEEP lie-detector test and put my BEEP mind at rest or she can BEEP off.'

I say, 'So, did you and Rees have a good time at ours the other night?'

She wrinkles her nose, meaning no. 'Yes, thank you.'

'Miffy said she liked meeting you.'

'Did she.'

Oh my God, I'm pulling teeth here. 'Yes, she said you were very interesting.' White lie.

'She's certainly, uh, *vivacious*.'

'She is, isn't she? Nice to see a bit of London glamour. Hard to believe she was so geeky when we were kids.'

'Yes. Well.' She blows out smoke. 'No easy way to say this, Laura. So I'm just going to come out with it.'

'Oh God, what?'

She turns off the telly. So it's something big.

'I'm going to have to let you go.'

'You're what?'

She taps ash into the sink. 'The shop's not doing so well. Going to have to make cuts. You can have a week's wages.' She doesn't look at me.

Rees flashes across my mind. What has he told her? 'It's been slow for years! I thought we liked working together.'

I'm being fired by a woman wearing a jumper decorated with a dancing penguin. He's got a top hat on. She fucking well ought to have worn a fucking suit. Tears come into my eyes.

'Listen, Ceri, you can't just sack me. I've been here a long time. I have rights, you know!' I put my hand on my stomach, and add, 'I'm pregnant. It's not very PC of you to sack me in my condition.'

'It's not very cool of you to make a pass at my man in your condition, either, but that didn't stop you.'

'Excuse me?'

'I know all about it, so don't worry. That tart from London been giving you ideas, has she?' She starts crying now. 'How's it work? She shags Huw and you shag whoever's around? Swapsies, is it?'

This framing of my life like something off one of her crappy TV shows dries up my tears nicely. I stand up.

'Ceri, I've no idea what you're on about. I'm sorry to

have to tell you that Rees lunged at me the other night, but I made it very clear that I wasn't interested.'

'That's exactly what he said you'd say! You're so predictable.'

'Go on, then. I'm fascinated. What's his version of events?'

'That you tried to drag him into your bedroom, tried to kiss him.'

I laugh. 'Well, Ceri, be honest, how likely does that seem?'

'Pretty likely, Laura. After all, I hear you snogged your stepbrother at that fancy fucking party down south.'

'Jesus Christ, Ceri, where d'you get that from?'

'And as you were happy to snog your stepbrother – you know, your *brother*, your *religious married brother* – I'm sure Rees being my boyfriend wouldn't bother you in the slightest.'

'At least have the decency to tell me who's spreading these lies.'

She drinks her tea, the tea I made. I should have spat in it. 'Glynn told me.'

I think fast. Glynn knows... how? The only people who knew were Danny and Miffy. So Miffy must have told Glynn. But why would she? It feels as if my world has tilted. I don't know who my friends are; don't know who to trust.

'I love it that you believe *Glynn*. You know he's always hated me. You believe him and not me, who's been your friend all these years.'

'Have you, Laura?' She folds her arms across the penguin. 'All I hear about all day long is your lovely husband, your wonderful life. You set me up with the most godawful men and expect me to be grateful. And then when I finally get one who's halfway decent, you try to take him off me.'

'For the last time, I am not trying to take Rees off you! I wouldn't touch him with a bargepole! The one time we had sex he said my fanny was his "cuddly furry bear" and came in about three seconds! I DON'T WANT HIM, OKAY?'

Ceri's hands fly to her mouth, her face as red as the bow tie on her jumper. She says, 'Could you please just go now?' Then she turns her back and starts washing up her cup. As usual, fails to rinse the suds off, for fuck's sake.

I become aware of the clock ticking on the wall. I've never noticed it before, which is odd because it's really loud. Then the bell on the shop door pings, making us both jump. While Ceri goes out front, I take the things out of my cupboard. Not much to show for seven years. My mug and decaffeinated tea bags and a drawing Evie made for me to take to work, when she was little. Wish I'd got round to sticking it up.

I walk past Ceri but she says nothing, doesn't even acknowledge I'm there. Carries on chatting to the customer about rose-shaped fairy lights. I can't slam the door because it's got one of those slow hinges, but when I'm outside I stick two fingers up. And then I drive myself slowly home.

Miffy coos like all tourists do as we drive over the Menai Bridge. It does look beautiful this afternoon, the sun glinting off the iron chains, the gentle hills of Anglesey ahead of us, the Menai Straits to our side.

'How you feeling, pregnancy-wise?' Miffy asks.

'Fat.'

'Apart from your bump, you're slim as anything.'

'God, I'm not. My arse is the size of this car. I feel a bit depressed, to be honest.'

'Poor you. I suppose it's all the hormones zapping about.'

'It's not just that. This morning I got sacked.'

'Oh no, Laura!' She whips round to look at me.

'Ceri pretended it was because the shop wasn't making enough money, but really it was because Rees told her I made a move on him.'

'That's outrageous! She can't do that. You're pregnant! You should get a lawyer right away.'

Ah, it's so lovely having someone on my side. Even if she did tell Glynn about Danny.

'I know, but what would be the point? Aggro, bad feeling, spending money I haven't got, for what? We wouldn't want to work with each other again.'

'I'm a witness, that it was him not you.'

'That's true! I wonder if it would be worth you talking to Ceri?' I steer the car through the main street of Llanfair PG. Tourists are parked on both sides of the road so they can buy shitty memorabilia with the full name of the town printed on. Some people and their uncomplicated lives. Must be nice.

'Actually, though, you know what?' says Miffy. 'Now I come to think of it, I didn't really see who did what to whom.'

'Oh God, Miffy!'

'No, don't be silly. I know which way round it would have been. But I didn't actually *see* anything. It wouldn't stand up for five seconds in a court.'

'Ceri thought her case was made because she somehow knew about me kissing Danny. Glynn told her.'

'He did? Bloody hell, how did he know?'

I glance at her. She looks genuinely shocked. Is she just a good actress?

'Laura, this is just awful. I'm really sorry about your job, and about you being treated so appallingly. How are you feeling?'

I think about it. How *am* I feeling? 'A few weeks ago I banged my head against the wardrobe door.'

'Deliberately, do you mean?'

'Yes. I know that's weird, but I felt so pissed off and

frustrated. Then we went to one of those stupid dinners and I bet Jenny thought Huw had been walloping me.'

'So are you saying that equates to how you feel now?'

'Very Psychology doctor sort of question.'

'Sorry, didn't mean it to come out like that. But I'm worried about you.'

'Don't be. I'm saying that despite that bitch Ceri, I don't feel quite as bad as that right now.'

As we pull into the car park of the birthing centre, a young couple, brand-new parents, come out of the entrance, carefully holding a car seat between them. Tiny baby strapped in tight. Miffy says, 'Happy punters.'

'You sure you're okay to go round with me?'

'Of course. I love anything to do with babies.' We get out of the car and she says, 'Talking of which, I'm thinking of looking into sperm donors, did I tell you?'

Before I can reply, we're through the doors and a smiling nurse is coming forward to show us round. It's a nice place, modern but homelike. There are five rooms, decorated like bedrooms, and the midwives wear normal clothes. Miffy goes into raptures over the decor, the duvets, the birthing pool, asks me if I'd like to have the baby here, but I can't concentrate at all because an idea is bubbling in my head.

Miffy lights a cigarette as soon as we're outside. 'That was lovely!' she says as we return to the car. 'So much nicer than a hospital.'

'Mmm. So what were you saying? About a sperm donor?'

She blows a stream of smoke into the sky. 'Makes sense, Laura. I'm still pretty fertile, least I was according to some tests Jay and I had the year before last.'

'You might meet someone, though.'

She clicks her seatbelt into place, dangles her cigarette out of the window. 'Even if I meet someone tomorrow. Even if I say yes to your friend Nick, who keeps texting me. How long before we're ready to make that commitment? How long before we're ready to start trying? I haven't got that sort of time, Laura.'

'I'm older than you, and look at me!' I gesture at my belly.

'We can't all be as lucky as you.'

We're quiet on the drive home. I can't stop thinking about what Heifer said. What a crazy, lovely idea. A way to say sorry to Miffy. Sorry for everything I did to hurt her when we were young.

I think I can make everything all right.

26 MARCH 2003

Spaced out and weird this morning. My head's woolly and nothing quite connects. Things move more slowly than usual. Even the baby's calm – none of the usual flutters when I'm in the shower. When I put my hairbrush down on the shelf, it makes such a noise I jump. It's like being hung over without the fun of getting pissed the night before. I think I see a tiny bit of blood when I wipe myself. But my head's too muddled to decide if it *is* blood or just a mark on the bog roll, that stupid bamboo stuff with bits in that Huw buys.

I'm not really safe to drive, but Miffy's gone to the gym early so I can't get her to take Evie to school. Cars flash past us, leaving dancing streams of red and yellow in front of my eyes. I stop at a zebra crossing even though there's no one waiting, and the car behind me hoots, which is unheard of: usually everyone round here drives like an old lady. I'm the most old lady person on the road today.

'Why we going so slowly, Mum? God, you're really sweating. Gross.'

I wipe my arm across my soaking forehead. 'It's just very hot, isn't it?'

'Not particularly.'

Once I've dropped her at school, things are easier. Luckily I don't have to go to work. Every cloud. On the journey home I stick to side roads, go at 20 mph, though it still feels very fast. I'm so happy to get home. I drink three glasses of water, standing at the sink, then I lie down and sleep for an hour. A shrink would love this dream. Miffy is Marilyn Monroe and we're in a restaurant. Marilyn/Miffy keeps lighting matches then blowing them out just before they burn her fingers. The waitress is Ceri in a wedding dress.

When the food arrives, it's just plates full of flower petals.

Miffy's still not back when I wake up and make my way down to the kitchen. I wish she'd hurry. I want to tell her my idea. Maybe that's why I've been feeling weird: because of my idea. Because I don't know how she'll react. I can't work out any more if it's brilliant or stupid; I just know that I have to tell her. But she doesn't come. Glynn mooches in, looking for Miffy to read his application form.

'I can look at it, Glynn. I may not have a degree but I'm not entirely stupid.'

'Yeah. It's just Miffy knows more about the job.'

'Miffy is a nickname for her old friends. You should call her Melissa.'

'I'll leave it there for her.' He puts the form on the kitchen table and stomps upstairs.

I make a cup of tea, and put it down on Glynn's form. That'll teach the little shit. Then I take it off. I'm going to have to start filling in job applications myself soon; I don't want bad karma. After I've drunk the tea I decide that rather than wait here all unsettled, I'll go to confession. Father Davies talks a lot of sense. I scribble a note and drive sedately into Bangor, managing to get up to 30 mph on the main road. Wooh, Speedy Gonzales. I haven't been to church much in the last few months, but that doesn't matter: you can always confess.

Except you can't. As I climb the steps to the entrance,

Father Davies comes running out. We almost bump into each other.

'Oh, Laura! Did you want me? I'm so sorry, Mrs Mayfield just called. Her husband's been taken terribly ill.'

There's a taxi waiting for him, its engine running.

'It was just…I think I've found a way to make things right with my stepsister. I was hoping to talk it through in confession.'

'That's wonderful, Laura.' He clasps my hand. 'To repair the wounds of the past is a tremendous thing.'

'Shall I go for it, then, Father?'

'Yes, yes. Why don't you come back this afternoon and I'll hear your confession then?'

He gets into the taxi and waves as it drives off. Too late I realise I should have offered to drive him, then we could have talked on the way. I step into the cold dark church and the sweat evaporates from my face. There's no one else here so I go into the confessional box anyway. I love it in there, all tiny like a Wendy house. Just enough space for a chair. I sit down, do some pregnancy breathing, close my eyes. Unbidden, a montage of images flits across my mind. Images that have been playing more and more in my head lately. I annotate them, imagine it's a slideshow of the past.

A young face in a three-way mirror.
Lacy white shorts, smeared with dust.

A piece of paper ripped from a school book, black biro.

A flash of high-heeled orange sandal.

Two young naked bodies, flickering like a black-and-white movie.

A derelict shed at the side of the road.

Perching on a windowsill to smoke a cigarette.

Piano scales going up and down behind a closed door.

A sheet flapping in the hot Spanish sun.

Sitting in confession, tears soaking my shirt.

Miffy's mouth saying, 'I don't want this any more.'

I open my eyes and make it all disappear by summoning the present-day Miffy. The more I think about it, the more right it seems. Not everyone has the chance to offer something so special, so big, that it can make the past white.

At last! Miffy's back when I get home, sitting in the kitchen reading Glynn's application. 'Hi, Laura. Glynn's done well with his form.'

Bully for him. 'How was the gym?'

'Good. Knackering. I had a swim as well.' She points to my note. 'How was church?'

I sit down. 'Pretty quiet. Good for my mortal soul.'

'Would your mortal soul like some lunch?'

'Thanks, that'd be great.'

I watch her, bustling about, finding plates and cutlery.

I'm going to tell her my idea now. I'm just going to go for it. That's what Miffy says I'm like, doesn't she? I'm a risk taker.

'Miff, you know you asked me to do a spot of matchmaking?'

'Yes, indeed. Nick's a good start. Do you want cheese or chicken?'

'Cheese, thanks. What if I was to tell you I had your perfect match?'

'Really? Who is he?' She closes the fridge door with her hip.

'Not perfect as a partner, but the most perfect match for a sperm donor.'

'Ah. Not quite the sort of matchmaking I had in mind. Chutney?'

'No thanks.'

'I'm sure you know some lovely Welsh boyos, Laura, but I thought I'd go down the official route. Clinics and that.'

'Cost a bomb, though. Quite cold, too. Clinical.'

'That's the thing about clinics – their clinical-ness. I'll do a bit of salad, shall I?'

'You said you wanted to be more adventurous.' I smile.

'When I said that, I wasn't thinking of impregnation by a stranger, though.'

'I'm not talking about a stranger. What if I said I'd got someone who totally fits the bill? Nice-looking, fertile.'

'Fertile's such a funny word, isn't it? Can I use up this cucumber?'

'Someone who wouldn't try to get involved. Someone who's already got his own family.'

She stops what she's doing and looks at me. 'Oh my God, Laura. You surely don't mean...'

'Honestly, he only has to look at me and I'm pregnant. Those sperm are still going strong, Miffy-sister.'

'Have I got this right, Laura? Are you offering me your husband?'

'I think it's a brilliant solution.'

'Are you serious? You have got to be kidding me.' She starts to laugh. 'You really are a case. A total case. What's the plan, then? Will he wank into a tube or would it be better if he and I did it the old-fashioned way?'

'Miffy! I hadn't thought about that side of it.' I have, of course. I've thought about it a lot. I'm sure Huw would vote for the more traditional route, but of course we'd do it with a turkey baster. But I don't want to go into the mechanics right now.

'We could do it in your bed,' Miffy says, still laughing. 'That's the place that's always worked for you, isn't it? Or has his office floor been more productive?' She laughs harder and harder, till her whole body shakes so much that she knocks against the counter and a plate falls and shatters. The pieces skid across the quarry tiles like marbles, but she just carries on laughing manically. She looks out of control. She's still holding the knife, which worries me a bit.

'Sloppy seconds, don't they call it?' She gasps. 'It's like Towse all over again.'

'Towels? What have towels got to do with it?'

'I can't believe you don't remember. It was such a mean thing you did.' She's not laughing any more; tears pour down her face. I step across the shards of china and try to hug her, but her arms remain rigidly at her sides, hand still clutching the knife.

'Or why don't you just give me your baby?'

I step back. 'Don't be silly, Miffy.'

'It's no sillier than your suggestion. Why don't you? It's not like you or your husband want it.' She points at my stomach; she points with the hand holding the knife.

I say calmly, 'Give that to me, Miffy.'

The tears keep falling down her face. It's like a scene from a TV drama.

Laura: Give that to me, Miffy.

Miffy: Leave me alone!

Laura: You were always jealous of me: I was the cool one, the pretty one. Now I'm the one with the husband and kids. I've got it all, haven't I?

Miffy: Yes! And I hate you for it! I'm going to make sure you lose that baby. (*She lunges with the knife...*)

'You always just blunder in, barge across people, never mind what they want.'

'Miffy, give me the knife.'

'You never think about how anyone else might feel.' She drops the knife on the floor, thank God. I put my hand on her arm and she yells, 'Get away from me!' and pushes me, a hard shove, so abrupt and unexpected that I stumble and fall onto my knees on the hard quarry tiles.

'Fuck, Miffy!'

She stands over me as I kneel there, stares as if she's never seen me before. She makes a funny little gesture, like wiping her hands, and I put my arms over my head in case she's going to thump me or grab the knife and stab me. 'Christ,' she says. 'Christ, Christ, Christ,' and runs out, crunching bits of plate underfoot. The front door slams.

When I'm sure she's not coming back, I get up carefully and lower myself into a chair. One sharp piece of china is sticking to my knee, and when I brush it off I see it has pierced my jeans. I slowly roll up the trouser leg and dab at the cut with a tissue. Then I walk stiffly to the sink and get out the dustpan and brush. You can't leave broken china lying on the floor. It could be dangerous.

My knees ache as I drive slowly along. Things still look off-kilter. A man walking his dog appears from nowhere and I do an emergency stop before realising he's a lot further away than I thought. He doesn't even notice me. After this, my back spasms so painfully that I pull over onto someone's drive. There's nowhere else to stop. The old bag whose house it is comes out and says, 'Can I help you?' in an unfriendly tone. I explain I'm not feeling well and will move on in just a moment, and she says she's sorry to hear that but she's expecting a delivery. I tell her to go fuck herself and reverse noisily off her precious bastard drive and nearly bash into an SUV with bull-bars. I can hear her yelling abuse after me all the way up the road. It seems so mean that I start crying, and only just manage to stop when I reach the school.

Evie's leaning against the gate, trots over on her gangly legs when I pull up. How come kids are so thin? The girls Evie knows all look as if they've got nowhere to store their internal organs.

She whirls into her seat. 'You're late.'

'I know. Sorry. Not been feeling well.'

'Have you been crying? Your face is a state.'

'Not really. I had a bit of a row with Auntie Melissa.'

I look in the mirror before setting off: something I haven't done since I learned to drive.

'About Uncle Danny, was it?'

'What? No, not at all. Why would you think that?'

'You told her you loved him. You kissed him.'

Ah – there we have it. She *wasn't* asleep in the back of

the car, after all. So it was her who told Glynn, and he's probably told the whole of North fucking Wales.

'I wasn't serious, okay? Danny and I went out together for a while when we were kids, not much older than you and Micah. I was excited to see him again, is all.'

She doesn't say anything. I glance at her. She is staring straight ahead, fiddling with the heart-shaped pendant.

'Evie? You all right?'

'You told me you and Daddy weren't getting divorced.'

'We're not, baby, okay?'

'Glynn…'

'What's he said?'

'Nothing.'

'Listen, whatever crap Glynn's been putting in your head, ignore it. Everything is fine, all right?'

'All right.' Sulkily.

At home, I make peppermint tea and sip it slowly, stalling the moment that I have to go up and see if Miffy's in her room. My tummy feels a bit better; it's just a kind of dull, bearable ache now. I refresh my lipstick before knocking tentatively on Miffy's door. She's in there, thank the Lord, sitting up in bed and typing on her laptop. She pushes it aside when I come in.

'God, Laura, are you all right?'

'Miff, I'm so sorry.'

'No, *I'm* sorry. I feel terrible. I shoved a pregnant woman.

I don't exactly feel good about myself. Really, are you all right? Did I hurt you?'

'My knees are a bit sore, but I'll live.' I sit down on the bed.

'Laura, I am so, so sorry. I don't know what got into me.'

'I didn't think it through, Miff, didn't think how you might react.' Actually, I did think it through but assumed she'd be pleased.

'I over-reacted. You caught me off guard. Babies are kind of an emotional topic for me.' She reaches for a cigarette. 'Slight understatement.'

'I was shit and you were right. I didn't consider your feelings. I do blunder in sometimes.' It feels like the confession I didn't make to Father Davies.

'It's my own fault. I said I loved your bull-in-a-china-shop quality.' She strikes a match to the cigarette and lets out a long breath. 'Laura, love, listen. I know your head must be in an awful state. You're pregnant, you've lost your job. I really don't mean to upset you. But from where I'm sitting, things don't look too great between you and Huw. Spin it how you like, it's obvious to me that he *is* having an affair, and you're just trying to pretend it isn't happening.'

Miffy's become such a bitch. Wish with all my heart I'd never told her about that stupid blonde. I should never tell anyone anything. I'm sure it was nothing. I check his pockets, sniff his shirts, look at his credit card bill. Clean as a whistle. Apart from the working late, there's no hint of anything. The more I think about seeing him that night in the pub, the more I think she could just have been a colleague. They weren't *doing* anything, after all.

'You know nothing about Huw and me, *Melissa*. You only just met us. We got together against all advert-isy.' I always have trouble saying 'adversity' and it makes Miffy smile. Which makes me furious. 'Everyone was against us but we made it through. All long-term relationships have wobbly patches. *You* should know that. But we don't all split up at the drop of a hat.'

She raises her eyebrows. 'That's me told, then.'

'Anyway. I'm sorry I suggested it. I haven't even asked Huw yet.'

'I kind of guessed that. I wouldn't mention it to him, if I were you.'

'Thanks for the Relate advice.' I stand up. 'I'm making chilli. Want some?'

'Yes, please. Be good to have something before I go.'

My anger drains away. 'You're leaving? Now? Because of this?'

'Not just that, Laura-sister.' She smiles. 'I need to get on with my life. Whatever it's going to be.'

'Where will you go?' I'm embarrassed to feel tears starting again. I don't normally cry from one week to the next. Today, it's every other minute.

'For now, back to Mum's. After that, who knows?'

The tears come, and she pulls me into an awkward embrace. We sit like that for some time, my face against her shoulder, smoke from her cigarette coiling into my face.

It's gone ten by the time Huw gets home. He eats a bowl of chilli, standing up like a starving man.

'Why don't you sit down, Huw?'

'I'm going to head back again in a minute to finish this paper.'

'Do you have to? I'm feeling a bit low.' I haven't told him about the job yet. There hasn't really been time. And it's complicated, explaining why I got sacked. So I just say, 'Miffy's leaving later tonight and I'll miss her...'

'That's unfortunate timing.' He clatters his bowl down onto the counter. 'Why's she going so suddenly?'

I try to think how to phrase it, and a laugh spurts out of my mouth. 'I, um, made her an offer she wanted to refuse.'

'Oh, Laura, for fuck's sake. What does that even mean?'

I don't know why he's so exasperated. Maybe he's in love with her. Maybe that's how she can be so sure he's having an affair.

'What did you do, Laura?'

Why should I lie? Is it really so bad, to try to help someone get what they want? 'I, you know, just offered her some of your sperm.'

Huw stares at me. There's a big space between us, and I can't reach his hand without moving. Which is a shame, because I'd like to touch his hand. Then he laughs, a proper, barking laugh, which startles me into laughing too. He opens the drinks cupboard, still laughing. He's not hysterical, like Miffy was. He puts a bottle of whisky in the middle of the table and sets down two glasses, as he has done so many times over the years. One for me, one for him.

'You silly cow,' he says, but it is affectionate.

'Are you cross?'

'No.' He smiles. 'It's funny. So, finish the story. Did Melissa want some of my freshly minted spermatozoa?'

'Freshly minted's going a bit far. No, she didn't. In fact, she got a bit upset. But it wasn't that bonkers an idea, honestly. She's wanting to find a sperm donor.'

He opens the whisky and sniffs it – 'Ah, Laphroaig. Nothing like it' – and pours me a large dram. I point to my bump and he says, 'Just in case you fancy a little bit.'

'So go on, then. Why is it unfortunate timing?'

He sips his drink. 'Fact is, *cariad*.'

Something in his voice makes me feel cold. The hairs on my arms rise and prickle. Huw's face looks odd to me. A stranger's face. How long has he had that spot on his cheek? When did he last shave?

My stomach starts to churn. Not now, I need to

concentrate. I have two medicinal sips of my drink. The worst of the pain lasts only a moment, subsides quickly.

He swirls the whisky round its glass. Then he stands, says, 'Get some ice.'

I say, 'I suppose it's that blonde cunt I saw you with in the Ty-Nant.'

He turns around the freezer so fast that he spills some of his drink. 'Oh.'

My tummy needs more medicine. I drink my whisky and pour another.

'So where did you meet her? Who is she? Have you fucked her? Of course you've fucked her.' I take a nice big sip in between each question, and you know what? I definitely don't hurt quite so much. The downside is I can't concentrate on what Huw's saying. He's mumbling, something about meeting her last year, conference, Liverpool, research fellow, but who fucking cares anyway?

'I'm really, really sorry, Laura. I am truly sorry.'

Huw's hand falls onto mine, maybe to stop me raising my glass. His hand is a dead fish. I shake it off and drink some more. Wish Mama was still here. She could make all the nasty bits go away.

Now he's going on again about shitty timing. He's obsessed. Ought to buy him a new watch, a calendar, a desk diary, a clock. Carriage clock, cuckoo clock, grandfather clock.

My grandfather's clock was too tall for the shelf, so it stood ninety years on the floor.

Evie used to love that song.

'I wanted to leave it till the baby was born. But she won't wait any more. And I want to be with her.'

'Is that what you said to Carmen?' Did Carmen drink whisky, the night he left her for me? Hot tears spill onto my face. Mine, I imagine. They taste like whisky. A new world record for crying has today been set by Laura Ellis, née Morente, soon back to being Morente again.

'I don't want to talk about Carmen. God, *cariad*, we've got to try and discuss this like adults. Even if you are offering my sperm to your girlfriends.' He smiles. He's in grown-up mode. I hate that. I could punch him. Shall I just fucking punch him?

'I know you've not been happy lately, *cariad*. We haven't been too good for each other, have we?'

Will you stop calling me cariad? *You don't love me any more, so I'm not your fucking* cariad.

The front door opens then slams, and we hear Glynn go upstairs.

Huw says, 'Talking of Glynn, he told me that Evie said you're in love with Daniel Cline.'

It takes my brain a few moments to work this out. I can't quite remember who Daniel Cline is. Who am I in love with? Shouldn't I be able to think? Then I do, and I'm outraged. 'You're basing decisions on lies your fucking son tells you? On some crap our eleven-year-old daughter has completely misunderstood?'

'I didn't base any decisions on that. I want to be with Tania.'

I've never liked the name Tania. Hairdressers are called Tania, tarty girls with red fingernails, fat thighs in miniskirts. I hear him saying words. He says them so rhythmically, they are like a poem. Familiar as a poem I learned at school. All the fights we've had since New Year, turned into a funny little poem:

I just didn't want another child/ You knew that, and you/ Went ahead anyway. I know you/ Wanted another but I don't want to/ Face it all again.

'Does *she* have kids? Barbie?' My glass is empty. Shit, the bottle is empty too. I stand up, not sure what I'm going to do – find more whisky, go upstairs, run into the street, hit Huw – but then I have what feels like a contraction, the room tilts and I sit down on the floor. It's clear *that's* what I must do. Sit on the floor.

'The thing is, Huw, the important thing you've forgotten, how could you forget, is that I love you.'

Huw crouches next to me. From somewhere far away I see his face is very pale. 'Melissa!' he yells, and there's an answering call from upstairs. 'Can you come here a sec? Quickly?'

I feel giggly because the fridge looks much bigger than normal. I try to tell Huw that the fridge is funny. Wasn't it white before? Now it's grey. It must be a magic fridge. The magnets on it dance about. Another *Guinness Book of Records* right there; this day is full of them, full of them, to be sure, to be sure, begorrah. Wasn't Norris McWhirter Irish? I think he was. Roy Castle wasn't, though.

Miffy is carrying a suitcase. When she drops it on the floor I feel the vibrations. 'Oh my God. Laura.' She rushes, sits down next to me, other side from Huw.

Huw says, 'Phone.'

Miffy fumbles in her coat pocket and holds out her mobile. Huw grabs it.

'That was rude,' I say. 'You mustn't snatch.'

Huw jabs at numbers, says, 'Ambulance.'

Why do we need an ambulance? Because you're leaving me?

Miffy strokes my hair, says, 'It'll be all right. We'll get you to a doctor.'

'A doctor won't help, Miffy. Huw's leaving. He's met someone else. It's too late for therapy.'

I don't think the words come out; they are only in my head.

'It's all right, sweetie.'

'My tummy hurts.'

Huw gives our address, says, 'My wife. Laura. Yes.'

I am still his wife, then. That's nice.

'She's twenty-eight weeks, I think. Hang on.' Huw talks to Miffy across me. 'Melissa, do you know if that's right?'

'It's twenty-seven weeks.'

Ooh, she's good, isn't she? She didn't even have to think about it. The room is pink when it ought to be green. I chose green when I was pregnant with Evie – breakfast-room green. Am I going to pass out? I used to faint with heavy periods at school. Those funny long afternoons lying on sunny beds in the sick room, listening to everyone in the playground. Same hot feeling in my head.

Miffy is so close I can see tiny lines next to her eyes. I thought she didn't have any lines. I tell her, you are naughty, you haven't been using your moisturiser, but she just carries on stroking my hair. My lap is wet. I must have spilled whisky on my skirt; no wonder there was none left.

Huw's head bobs on my other side: bob, bob, bob. It's so funny, I start laughing. Huw puts his arm round me but I don't think it means we are back together; it is like he would put his arm round anyone.

Glynn's here now and he's shouting. 'Jesus fucking Christ.'

I look down, where he is looking, and see that the floor is covered in blood.

Miffy

1979

Lamb Chops

Big row tonight. My fault.

I asked Dad to test me on my batmitzvah portion. Mum is no good at Hebrew so it has to be him. But he said he was too tired. Mum was at the sink but whirled round so fast I thought she might get whiplash. 'Can I have a word, Michael? Now?' She stormed into the hall, dripping Fairy Liquid suds all over the floor. Dad followed.

'Spending enough bloody time round that tart's house

helping her daughter, but when your own flesh and blood...' Then it went muffled as the door slammed.

Danners looked up from his magazine. 'Well done.'

'You got loads of help off Dad for your barmitzvah, why shouldn't I?'

'Listen, Twat-Face. First, everyone said my barmitzvah was the greatest the universe has ever seen, and I got £150 in present money, which is £150 more than you'll get. And second, I don't know if you've noticed but Mum and Dad aren't getting on very well, so it might be a good idea to stop bloody annoying them.'

Dad came back in, whistling. 'Who wants lamb chops?' he said, and we both shouted, 'Me!'

He said Mum had gone for a lie-down. Dad does very pink lamb chops, a bit bloody on the inside. But I told him they were lovely. After supper he listened to my portion, and said it was really good.

The Postcard

Mum and Dad went to look at a Home for Booba Preston today. I watched them drive off, then went into their room and opened Mum's bedside cabinet. I put on her perfume and tried on a pale-pink lipstick. Then I pulled out the letters and cards that were squashed underneath, and lay down to read them on Mum's slippery grey eiderdown.

There were a few letters from Auntie Leila, which talked mostly about what she was up to in Brittany, but ended with things like, 'Keep your chin up, love' and 'Let me know if you need anything'.

In the middle of the pile was a postcard of the Alhambra. I recognised it straight away because it was near where we'd been in Spain. My first thought was that Mum must have brought it back from our holiday. But it was stamped and covered in Mrs Morente's spiky handwriting. The postmark was April 1979. It must have been sent at Easter, the last time Laura and her mum were in Spain before we all went at half-term. It was addressed to Dad and said, '*Mi querido* Michael. Feel brave as they are away, so daring to send this. Your last words touched my heart. *Te amo.* O.'

I stared at the card for a long time, trying to work it out. I remembered that at Easter, Mum, Danners and I were meant to be at Auntie Leila's. But we cancelled at the last minute because of Dan's flu. Mrs Morente would have sent the card thinking only Dad was at home. But Mum must have seen it first.

I wondered if Dad knew. Mrs Morente must have said, 'Did you like my postcard?' and he would have said, 'What postcard?' and she would have said, 'Oh no!'

Alarm

Danners and I were so excited about Auntie Leila coming, because her presents were famous. Last year for Dan's birthday she sent a packet of condoms and a card that had phone numbers of brothels in Paris!

Mum said before she arrived, 'I know Leila's a bit off-colour sometimes, but she'll help with Booba's move, and it would be good to get some support round here.'

Danners and I started protesting that we were lots of support but Mum said, 'I didn't mean you, darlings,' and went upstairs.

I asked Dad why Booba Preston couldn't live in our spare room, though I wasn't sure I really wanted her to, as she smelled. Dad said she needed nursing care and would be better off in a Home. Which was fair enough.

Auntie Leila arrived at teatime wearing an ankle-length purple coat. Her present to Danners was a smoking jacket! It was red pretend-silk and he looked a complete idiot in it. She clapped her hands when he put it on and said, 'Noel Coward, as I live and breathe!' She's the one who needs a smoking jacket, as she is always puffing away on her French *Gauloises* cigarettes. I might try to borrow a couple to share with Laura.

My present was in a small thin box. I hoped it was jewellery but the thing inside was more like a pen. When I tried to take the cap off, Auntie Leila yelled, 'No, Melissa!'

making me jump out of my skin. 'Only take the top off in emergencies. It's a rape alarm.'

'For heaven's sake, Leila,' said Mum.

'Better safe than sorry.' Auntie Leila showed me how it worked. 'You just pull the lid and it makes such a noise that any young man trying his luck will get the fright of his life, believe you me.'

'It's a sad world when a twelve-year-old needs a rape alarm,' Mum said.

'Surprised you haven't kitted her out yourself, Andrea, after what you told me about that pervert Max Kaplinsky.'

'Ssh! I told you, he doesn't teach Melissa now. The Rabbi's tutoring her.'

'Well, who knows what thoughts the Rabbi has in his head about our Melissa?'

I went bright red at the wonderful idea that Aron might have thoughts about me, but Danners laughed. 'Honestly, Aunt Leila, do you think all men are rapists?' Under his breath to me, he hissed, 'Like anyone would want to rape you!'

'I'm sorry to say, Danny,' said Auntie Leila, 'that when it comes to sex, you never know which men you need to worry about.'

Mum let out a sob.

Auntie Leila said, 'Oh, sweetheart, I'm meant to be here to help. I'm sorry.'

She put her arm round Mum, and motioned for Danners and me to leave the room. I got a good Chinese burn on him on the way upstairs, and also managed to tell him exactly what he looked like in his smoking jacket. Then I went to my room and looked up 'rape' in the dictionary.

Lark House

Today Mum, Auntie Leila and I visited Booba Preston in her new Home in East Finchley. It was called Lark House and it smelled like the dustbins at school. Booba was in a large living room with French windows and a loud telly on a high shelf. She was sitting in a chair with leather on the arms. There were other old ladies around but no one was talking to anyone else. Most of them were asleep. No idea how, with the noise of the telly. Booba smiled at me and held out her hand. Mum said, 'Thank God she still knows who you are, at least.'

Mum and Auntie Leila went to talk to the manager. Booba didn't smell as bad as usual. Or maybe she just smelled better than Lark House. It was weird talking to someone who didn't talk back. I told her I was studying hard at school, and for my batmitzvah. Booba kept smiling as if she wanted more, and I found myself blurting out a lot of other stuff. About Laura. How she wasn't always nice to me. How sometimes I felt her mum pushed her into being friends with me. I whispered, 'I'm really scared.'

Booba squeezed my hand tightly, and then Mum and Auntie Leila came back, so I said loudly, 'And in English we're doing *Macbeth*.'

To my surprise, Booba said, '*Hubble, bubble, toil and trouble*,' making us all laugh.

Auntie Leila took Booba outside for some air, and Mum sat back, looking round the room. 'It's not such a bad place, is it, Melissa?'

The worry crease between her eyes was very deep today. I told her it was lovely, even though it wasn't.

Under the Carpet

When I got home from school, something made me go in really quietly. I left the front door open, and crept along the hall. In the kitchen I could see the edge of Auntie Leila's leg and her purple high-wedge shoe.

'Not like you to be a wimp, Andrea. Why don't you just get it into the open?'

Mum sounded like she was crying. 'It's such a can of worms. There's Mum, and the batmitzvah , and everything.'

I'd taken the Alhambra postcard Mrs Morente sent to Dad. Ripped it into fifteen pieces. Put the bits in a bin on the way to school. I was hoping if I got rid of it, Mum might forget about it.

Auntie Leila said, 'So it's better this way, is it, everything pushed under the carpet, happy families?'

I must have made a noise because Mum called out, 'Melissa, is that you?'

I slammed the front door, said, 'Hi! I'm home!' and went into the living room as though I hadn't heard anything.

Chicken and Cashew Nuts

Auntie Leila took us all out for a meal at the Mandarin Palace. I'd wanted to go there for ages. We were allowed to order whatever we liked. I had chicken with cashew nuts, and Danners had sizzling beef in Szechuan sauce, and we shared noodles and egg-fried rice and spring rolls. It was completely delicious. The grown-ups had white wine and Auntie Leila gave me a sip when Mum went to the loo, though I didn't like it. It was lovely all sharing food. Dad gave me some of his pancake duck. I didn't try Auntie Leila's because she had king prawns – she doesn't keep kosher – but Mum didn't say anything. In fact, it was the most smiley I'd seen Mum for ages. She looked very pretty; she'd had her hair done and was wearing green eyeshadow to match her dress. Halfway through the meal she raised her glass and said, 'A toast!'

We all raised our glasses too. Mum said, 'To Leila, my wonderful, crazy sister.' And we all said, 'To Leila!'

I said, 'I want to do a toast,' so everyone had to raise their glasses again. I said, 'To my family, who are brilliant.' And everyone said 'To the family!'

Then Dad raised his glass and, looking at Mum, said, 'To my beautiful wife and children. And my sister-in-law, of course! Thank you for being so wonderful.'

Danners and I shouted, 'To my beautiful wife and children!' and everyone laughed.

Dad said, still looking at Mum, 'You do look very beautiful tonight, Andrea.'

Auntie Leila let me order lychees and coffee with cream on top, and I felt completely happy.

Helene's Paris Fashions

My heart sank when we pushed open the door to Helene's Paris Fashions and the bell pinged. It was always so messy in there. It looked like someone had grabbed armfuls of dresses and chucked them in the air. A headless mannequin stood in the middle of the room wearing socks and nothing else.

Mum told the owner, Mr Zucker, that we wanted something special for my batmitzvah. He nodded eagerly. 'Do wait a moment, ladies, while I peruse my most select collection.' He disappeared into the back room.

Auntie Leila said, 'Is this really the best we can do for Melissa?'

Mum said, 'We get Faye's discount, Leila. And they have some very nice traditional things. Melissa's pretty yellow blouse and skirt came from here.'

Mr Zucker put some clothes for me to try in the changing room. I got undressed and stared at myself in the mirror. I looked okay in my bra and knickers. Perhaps I should do my batmitzvah just in them?

Mum called, 'Show us, Melissa,' so I threw on a bright pink dress with a flared skirt, and opened the curtains.

'Oh, that's sweet,' Mum said, but Auntie Leila said, 'Are you kidding me?'

When I reappeared in a white sailor dress with a blue ribbon round the neck, Auntie Leila barked her husky laugh. 'Andrea, this is Melissa's special day. The day she turns from child to woman. The day she's been working towards for a year. She's a beautiful girl. So why do you want her to look like an *alter kocker*?'

She meant an 'old fart'. I nearly laughed out loud.

'Excuse me, madam,' butted in Mr Zucker. 'I dress half the *kinder* in North London for their barmitzvahs.'

'Is that so?' said Auntie Leila, pulling out her Zippo lighter. 'Well, half the *kinder* in North London are going to be mighty embarrassed looking at their barmitzvah photos a few years down the line.'

She lit a cigarette and said, 'Andrea, let me buy Melissa's outfit as her present. I'd soon as die as see the poor kid in these *shmattes*.' She swept out of the shop in a cloud of smoke, leaving Mum apologising to a furious Mr Zucker. I got back into my jeans in double-quick time and raced outside.

Auntie Leila was waiting in the car, her cigarette dangling out of the window. I couldn't believe she'd said I was beautiful. I jumped into the back and whispered, 'Thank you.'

'No problem, kid.'

After Mum had slammed into the front seat we drove to a West End shop called Maxine's. It was very posh, with scary, thin sales assistants, but they all smiled to see Auntie Leila. She ordered them about, flicking through rails and throwing dresses over her arm. The thin ladies gave Mum a cup of tea and she sat on a golden chair.

The best dress was short-sleeved, in dark-green velvet. Auntie Leila called it a shift dress. It stopped just above my knees and fitted my body perfectly. I looked different in it. Prettier. Older. All the thin ladies gasped and clapped their hands when I came out of the fitting room. One said, 'Oh, for a figure like that!'

It cost fifty pounds, but Auntie Leila paid without blinking. Then she took us to a shoe shop and bought me a pair of black grown-up pointy courts with a thin heel. I threw my arms round her. 'You're welcome, choochie-face,' she said, and even Mum had to smile at how happy I was. In fact, we were all in a great mood on the drive home. Mum and Auntie Leila sang tunes from *Cabaret* while I did backing vocals.

The house was empty when we got back. I said, 'Where's Daddy? I want to show him my dress.' Mum went upstairs without saying anything. Auntie Leila muttered something in French that I didn't understand. Then she put her arms out, and I cried in them like a baby.

Melissa

Just for a second, when I first see Laura at the hospital, I think: *She's died and no one told me.* Just for a second, before I register the tubes and monitors, the blip-blip of the heartbeat machine, I feel so bereft, so utterly and abruptly hollowed out by the shock of it, the shock of her not existing any more, that my knees give way. Huw grabs my arm and leads me to a chair. 'She's going to be fine. She's lost a lot of blood, but they spent all night filling her up again.'

What an odd turn of phrase the man has. I already

know about the baby so I don't ask any more questions. Now I can see Laura is breathing. Tiny shallow breaths, but undoubtedly alive. Asleep, nothing worse, in a high metal bed, lying on her back like the princess and the pea. As I stare at her I stop noticing the noises in the ward, the nurses, the other patients. I stop noticing Huw sitting next to me, his arm resting on the bed, a metal watch on his brown forearm.

Laura would be pleased to know how beautiful she looks lying there, face pale as the sheets, hair spread out black against the stark white pillow. I am miles away in my thoughts when she says, 'Miffy, what shall we do now?'

Huw and I jump up. She looks straight at me, doesn't seem to see Huw at all.

'Whoops, we messed the sheets,' she says, and falls asleep.

We wait, holding our breaths, but that's it, that's her waking up for the day. Huw and I sit back down and after a few minutes he starts to fidget. Clears his throat. Jiggles his knee up and down. Looks at his phone. When a nurse checks Laura's pulse, Huw questions her about any changes, developments, deterioration. Clearly her non-committal answers satisfy him, because after she moves away, he coughs and says, 'Uh, Melissa. Work have been texting. There's a difficult situation come up. Slightly urgent.'

'Oh yes?' Who knew that History departments could have urgent situations?

'Would you mind dreadfully if I went into the office for a bit, sorted some of this stuff out?'

'Don't work know what's happened? Surely they can manage.'

'The nurse doesn't think Laura will stir again today. Would you stay till Olivia arrives?'

'Okay, Huw. If you want to go, I'm happy to stay.'

So he heads off, saying, 'If you're quite sure,' though not waiting for an answer, and adding, 'Many thanks, you're a star.' Not very impressed. Certainly *not* the sort of man I'd want sperm from, thanks very much. Ha ha.

I sit for hours, leaving the bed just once, to get coffee and a sandwich. Nurses come by now and then to check Laura's monitors, but outside of their visits I fall into the sort of meditative trance Rob tried to teach me, that night in Hargeysa. I told him I couldn't empty my mind and he asked what I was thinking about. My big chance to say I was in love with him, but I bottled it. Said I was thinking about what we were going to have for dinner. He laughed. I'm sure he guessed that food was the last thing on my mind. My thoughts were all about him. Delicious, naughty thoughts.

There's such an ache in my heart. A proper, physical ache that hurts when I breathe too deeply. I shallow my breath till it's barely there at all, like Laura's breaths. I feel like Superman grieving, pushing the world backwards so that Lois Lane was no longer dead. Wish I could do that. Wish I could have back that moment. What the hell was going on with me? I behaved like a lunatic. Knocked down a pregnant woman. Put her in hospital. Put two lives in danger.

It's amazing to me that Laura is just the same as when we were children. Still impulsive. Still totally hopeless at guessing how other people feel. But her craziness, her spontaneity, are things I once loved about her. Things I've missed. Of course, I hated her, too. For a very long time. All those difficult years looking after my mother, bearing the brunt of her bitterness and pain. All those doors that closed for Danners and me when Dad fell in love with Olivia.

But when hate finally fades, what is left? I missed her, is all. Missed her intensity, her unpredictability. Once, years ago, when I was in my twenties, I saw a girl who looked like her. She was with her mother, in front of me in the supermarket queue. I didn't realise I was crying till the checkout lady asked if I was all right.

Every time Laura says 'Miffy', my old nickname, I feel the past more strongly, feel my old self, the little girl who was Miffy. Names are powerful, I always tell the students working on placement with me. It's important to get children's names right; names are so bound up with identity.

I've been saying these things glibly for years, and now I'm experiencing it myself. Miffy. A girl from long ago I'd half-forgotten, assumed I'd never see again.

I've been noticing childhood smells a lot lately too. Smells that take me back to school, to the streets near our house, to Laura's bedroom. Here on the ward, when a woman walks past carrying freesias, the scent conjures up the room where I had piano lessons with Olivia, the heavy floor-length curtains of dark-red velvet. Dust glittered off them in lazy clouds when you touched them.

Time passes. I watch Laura. Count her breaths. Follow the line on the monitor.

Her latest mad scheme: to try and give me a baby. Why did I react so badly? I, who pride myself on taking my time, not rushing into a response, all my years of training and practice. None of it stopped me lashing out. How many times have I explained to a client how the baggage from their past is holding them back, weighing them down? Yet I let my own baggage get in the way, so that it stopped me seeing things from Laura's point of view. By her lights it was actually quite a logical suggestion. And generous. Why did I cry? Why did I wish her far away? Why did I push her? Why didn't I just say, no thanks?

Or even, yes please.

I'm glad to have found you again, you crazy kid. I touch her arm. Don't die.

My dramatics are nothing next to Olivia's. She bursts into the room in her horrible fur coat, shrieking, '*Ay dios mio*,' and waking up another woman in the ward. 'It is unbearable,' she cries, throwing herself into a chair and clutching Laura's limp hand to her heart. 'I am the unluckiest woman in the world. First Michael, now my daughter and her baby. What have I done to God, to deserve such punishment?'

My mind reels with answers, but I just say, 'She's doing really well, Olivia. She's out of danger.'

'She lies there like a corpse.'

'She's just heavily asleep. They've given her a sedative so her body can heal.'

'And as for the *bebé*...' Olivia buries her face in her hands.

Whenever I think about the baby, my mind slips away. It can't stay with it; it darts off to settle on something less painful. A defence mechanism.

'Laura and I have not spoken, Melissa, you know, since a silly, silly argument.'

Oh, you too?

'*Querido dios*, I pray it is not too late for me.'

I don't think I can stand a grief-stricken Olivia any more than I can bear her smug and selfish incarnation. She clutches my hand and says, 'I had a terrible relationship with my own *madre*, you know.'

'I remember.'

'How can you? You never met her.'

I gently extricate my hand. 'I did, that time we all went to Spain . . .'

'I always said I would not have that coldness with my own daughter. I prided myself on our friendship. And now she is dying and we are *separada*.' She dabs her eyes with a tissue.

'Really, Olivia, she's going to be fine.'

She looks at me as if seeing me for the first time. 'Why are you here? Where is Huw?'

For some reason I protect him. I don't honestly know why. 'He's, uh, he'll come when I get back to the cottage. He wants one of us to stay with Evie.'

'Well, you can go. I'm here now,' Olivia says, her lips thin. She puts her handbag on her lap and waits for me to leave.

28 MARCH 2003

Olivia and I are keeping vigil again. Though we have a few breaks – she regularly goes upstairs, while at other times I go for a smoke in the grounds – there are still long periods when we're stuck with each other. A typical conversation:

Me: 'It's quite stuffy today, isn't it?'

Olivia: 'I hadn't noticed. Laura is so terribly pale.'

One of my psychiatrists back in the 1980s said I couldn't move on till I lost my anger towards Olivia. Got me to whack a cushion and pretend it was her. It didn't work. Olivia always put me on edge when I was a child, and it's the same now. If you don't like someone, well, you just don't like them. You can't fake it for ever. It works the other way round too. I spent so many years telling myself I hated Laura. I can still find many things to dislike about her. But you can't help who you like. I just like her.

Hospitals are Jay's *milieu*, and I miss him. He'd know how to get proper information out of the staff, keep things cheerful with flowers and treats. For the first time since I left, I wonder if I have made a mistake. I was so sure that a baby was more important than our marriage. So absolutely sure. But now I don't feel quite so certain.

Olivia says, 'Melissa, I have been thinking, ought I contact Laura's father?'

'I didn't know you were still in touch with him.'

'I'm not. I have hardly heard from him since he left.' Her eyes are brimming with tears. 'But I know how to reach him.'

'Would Laura want to see him, after all these years?'

'I don't know. They never got on. He was so *ardiente*. Fiery. When he left us I told Laura a little white lie. I said I had sent him away.' She smiles. 'She was proud of me. But it was terrible to lose him. He was the love of my life.'

I want to say, *I thought* my *father was the love of your life.* But I can't bear to get into a conversation about Dad.

At twenty past three Laura opens her eyes. In a rare moment of accord, Olivia and I both gasp, and smile at her encouragingly. Laura seems bewildered. She looks from Olivia to me, back to Olivia, her eyes great dark question marks.

'It's okay, *bebita*,' Olivia says loudly. 'You're in the hospital.'

Laura frowns, as if that is irrelevant information. She smoothes her hands over her stomach, then turns to me.

'Where's the baby?' Her voice is tiny, cracked.

I lean across the tangle of wires so she can see my face properly. 'It's a boy. He's in the Special Care Baby Unit.'

'He's beautiful, *bebita*,' Olivia says. 'So tiny. I have seen him several times. He only weighs one pound nine ounces.'

For heaven's sake, Olivia. That's way too much for her to take in.

Laura struggles, looks like she is going to try and sit up. We both gently soothe her down again.

'Is he going to be all right?'

Olivia and I glance at each other. She says, 'I'm sure he is,' at the same moment I say, 'They don't know yet, sweetie.'

Laura looks past us. 'Huw. Not here? Gone already?'

'He had to pop to work, *bebita*. He'll be back soon.'

'No, he won't,' she says. She grabs my arm, her touch surprisingly strong, and pulls my wrist up to her face.

She inhales, and whispers, 'Can I have some of your perfume, please?'

'What's she saying?' Olivia says.

I find my perfume in my bag and spritz it onto her wrists. It sprays onto the needles holding the wires into her body, but I don't suppose that matters.

Laura says, 'That's better,' and goes back to sleep, her scented arm across her face.

30 MARCH 2003

Ten-thirty in the morning and I've already smoked nine fags. It'll be Olivia's fault when I die of emphysema. She's on top form, dishing out a stream of consciousness about Laura, Michael, the baby, how everyone she loves is very ill or dies.

Nurse Canton, who trips over English because Welsh is her first language, takes Olivia up to the SCBU to watch the baby having his nappy changed. I like Nurse Canton: she's usually the person who removes Olivia. Laura's been asleep all morning, or so I thought, but once Olivia's clicking heels have disappeared down the ward, Laura's eyes open. She is far more focused than the previous times she's woken.

'Thought she'd never stop talking,' she says.

I laugh. 'Have you been awake long?'

'About ten minutes. Have you seen the baby yet?'

'No. They said only family.'

'Miffy, you *are* family.'

Well, of course I am. She's more lucid than me. I never think of Laura as my stepsister, but that's what she is. Laura-sister.

She watches the realisation dawn across my face. 'Miffy, I want you to go and see him. I need you to tell me what he's like.'

'Haven't Huw and Olivia told you everything? And here are the photos, look.'

She clings to me, pulling herself higher up the pillow. 'I don't trust them. I want you to tell me the truth. About how ill he is. If he's really alive.'

What doesn't she trust? The photos, or her mother and husband?

I already know how ill the baby might be. Dr Massi says possible problems with lungs, heart, eyes, brain. They don't know yet; he's still too little for them to do more than try to keep him alive.

I've never felt such dragging guilt in my life, never felt like such a shit. I wonder if Laura remembers who put her here in the first place. I promise to arrange to see the baby right away, though it takes a little explaining to Nurse Probyn, the not-so-nice nurse. She makes me go into way too much back-story about why I've suddenly decided that Laura is family, having previously told the nurses she was just a good friend. Presumably she's hoping to extract some nice gossip about our families to take to the nurses' station, but finally she escorts me up to the SCBU.

'You can look through the window, Mrs Jacobs. Only Mummy and Daddy can go in.'

The windows are crowded with the relatives of other babies peeping in. Olivia frowns when she sees me. 'What are you doing here? Is Laura all right?'

'She's fine. She asked me to . . .'

'She's awake?' She pushes past the parents and jabs impatiently at the lift button, muttering, 'Come on, come on.'

The nurse points out Laura's baby. He's asleep in his plastic incubator, lying on his back, covered in wires. A tiny scrap, not much bigger than my hand. His body, naked but for a miniature nappy, is red and mottled. His little arms and legs are splayed across his mattress. He is beautiful.

I don't want to cry in front of these parents.

I don't know how long I stand there, looking through the window. Other people come and go, but I just stand, feeling the great ache in my womb.

Fucking babies.

Miffy

1979

Fiona's Party

Laura had somehow managed to get me an invite to her friend Fiona's end-of-term party. I asked Mum if I could wear my new black shoes. I was sure she'd say no, but she said, 'Yeah, what the hell.' She sounded just like Auntie Leila. Then she added, 'But for heaven's sake, Melissa, try not to scuff them.' That was more her usual self. The shoes looked amazing with my jeans. My hair was finally long enough to pull into a ponytail, and I put on some of Mum's new lipstick.

There were loads of people at Fiona's. I saw Towse, wearing a tight black T-shirt. He smiled at me and I took off my glasses and put them in my back pocket. The room went all blurry with the coloured lights reflecting off the windows.

Dad and Mrs Morente helped Fiona's mother, Mrs Bryan, put out the food and drink. Then the grown-ups left us to it. Laura switched off the main lights and turned up the music. She played the Boomtown Rats just for me. Everyone was in a fantastic mood. Laura kept hugging me. We did a bit of our 'Greased Lightning' routine, though without my glasses I nearly missed her when I jumped up, but everyone cheered.

As a thank-you for getting me invited, I gave Laura one of Auntie Leila's cigarettes wrapped neatly in a tissue. She said, 'I was already feeling fantastic and this has made my day, Miffy-sister.' We smoked it in the bathroom with the window open, sitting on top of the toilet cistern. The *Gauloises* was strong and made us feel a bit dizzy. We pretended it was dope and giggled so much we nearly fell out of the window.

When we came downstairs I sat down and blurrily watched everyone. I didn't notice Towse come over, and nearly had a heart attack when I looked up and saw him smiling at me. He sat down and handed me a plastic cup of wine.

'You look pretty tonight, Missy.'

I grinned like a loon and took a big gulp of wine, which tasted like vinegar. He told me about what he wanted to do after his O Levels, and the conversation went along really easily, and I didn't need any of the tips in *Patches* to get a boy to talk. When I finished my wine he got me another glass. This one tasted better and I drank it quickly while we chatted. Laura danced past us and winked, and a minute later a slow tune came on.

Towse pulled me to my feet and said, 'Shall we?'

My first slow dance. He put his arms round me and I leaned my head on his shoulder, which I could just about reach thanks to my stiletto heels. He smelled really nice, sort of coconutty. I couldn't quite believe I was suddenly allowed to touch him. Out of the corner of my eye I could see others slow-dancing, though I couldn't see faces properly, and the lamps in the room left long streaks across everything, like slow-exposure photos of cars at night. I saw Laura dancing with Danners. At last I was like all the others, looking nice, dancing with a boy. Towse pulled me closer against him. I went into a dreamy state, feeling that I could stay like this for ever. Then he started fiddling with his zip. I guessed he was adjusting himself, like Danners was always doing, but he gently took my hand down and pushed it between us, into the gap between our bodies. Something warm, shaped like a big

311

Vienna sausage, flopped into my hand. I nearly jumped up to the ceiling. He closed my palm round it and moaned in my ear, whispering, 'Just move your hand up and down it, nice and slow.'

I did as he asked, while we both carried on turning in a slow circle, his hot breath in my ear. Then he whispered, 'Do you want to come upstairs and play with it?'

Before I knew it we were out in the hall. With the sudden bright light and my lack of glasses, I stumbled on nearly every step. At the top of the stairs Towse pulled me into a dark room which I guessed was Fiona's. I just had time to see a blur of posters before Towse closed the door and pushed me against it and started kissing me really hard. The glasses in my back pocket made a cracking sound. After just a few seconds his hand went right under my top, pushed up my bra and started squeezing my breast. He was so close he was standing on my foot, scuffing my new shoes. Mum was going to kill me. He pushed his other hand down the top of my jeans, and tried to put his fingers up inside me. I wriggled away as it didn't feel very nice, and he breathed, 'Will you suck me?'

I wasn't sure what this meant but guessed it might stop him putting his hands all over me, so I nodded. He pushed my shoulders so I was kneeling on the floor, and too late I realised he wanted me to suck his penis! His penis, that he pees out of!

I said, 'Won't I hurt you?' and he said, 'Just keep your teeth out of the way.'

Then he pushed his willy in my mouth. I didn't know what I was supposed to do but it didn't seem to matter, he was pushing my head up and down and groaning. It tasted salty, but not in a nice way. I couldn't stop thinking about him peeing, and the smell was horrible. I could smell his pubic hair and everything.

Suddenly he pushed it in much further than before and I practically choked. I stood up quickly before he could try it again, and said, 'That was miles too much!'

He put his arm round me. 'Sorry, Missy. You got me so excited.' He lifted the heart-shaped pendant from around my neck and said, 'That's pretty.' I started to tell him that Laura had given it to me, but he interrupted to say, 'Shall we lie on the bed?'

I suppose this was exactly the kind of situation for which Auntie Leila had given me the rape alarm, but of course I hadn't got it with me. Anyway, I could easily have said no and run out of the room. Although it was dark, I knew where the door was. But I'd fancied Towse for so long. He was so handsome. He had such nice eyes.

So we lay on the bed and I let him take off my jeans. Thank God I had put on my best knickers – not that we could see them in the dark, but it made me feel better. He climbed on top of me. I was amazed at how heavy he was.

He had somehow taken off his jeans and pants. He kissed me gently, and it was nice.

Then I heard a weird sound from the room next door. 'What's that?' I said.

Towse lifted up his head to listen. We heard it again: someone moaning. He laughed. 'It's only someone else shagging, like us.' His foot pushed my pants down to my ankles.

'Listen, Towse.'

'I told you, it's just some other people making love.'

'No,' I said. 'I mean, do you even know who I am?'

It was a line from a programme I saw a few weeks ago. It was after nine o'clock on ITV, but Dad was out and Mum was lying down. The woman told the man he made her feel like a piece of meat.

'Yes, of course I know who you are.' He kissed my cheek. 'You're Missy. You're Dan's little sister.'

'I don't like to be called Missy.'

He sighed. 'What do you like to be called, then?'

'Melissa. Or Mel. Or Lissa.'

'Okay. Lissa.' He leaned up on an elbow and said, 'Can we carry on? My balls are blue with frustration.'

'You know I'm not even thirteen yet.'

'Yes. But you're quite, you know, big for your age.' He made a rude bosoms gesture. 'And Laura said you wanted to lose your virginity with me.'

I pushed him off me and sat up, found my glasses and put them on. The frames were a bit bent but the glass was okay. 'When did she tell you that?' I turned on the bedside lamp and looked at him.

He blinked at me in the light. 'Was she lying?'

'No, I did say it.' I blushed. 'But I didn't mean now. I meant when I was sixteen, or older.'

'Oh. I'm sorry. She kind of made me think that you meant right now.'

I felt bad. I put my arms round his neck and kissed his cheek. He whispered, 'Lissa, could you at least give me a hand-job?'

I didn't know what he meant, but I nodded. I felt I ought to give him something. He lay cuddled next to me, which was nice. Then he put my hand round his penis. How weird for boys to carry these round with them all the time. He put his hand on top of mine and showed me how to move it up and down. His willy got harder and his breathing became more like gasps. My hand was getting quite tired, when he cried out and gloopy stuff went all over my hand and tummy. I was prepared for this because Laura had told me about the mess boys made when they were excited. I quickly wiped it off with the edge of the sheet so that nothing could climb in my vagina and make me pregnant.

We lay side-by-side for a while without talking, then he

said, 'Let's have a fag.' He lit a cigarette from a gold pack of Benson & Hedges and we took turns to smoke it, like in a French film. That was the best bit.

'You know what?' he said. 'That was really good.'

Downstairs the music was still playing. I left my glasses on so I could see properly. Danners and Laura were talking in a corner. It looked like they were arguing. I looked for Dad but couldn't find him. A couple I had never seen before were snogging in the kitchen, and Fiona was lying on the living-room floor, her skirt round her waist, laughing hysterically.

I found the phone in the hall and dialled our home number. Mum answered on the first ring. 'Darling, what's the matter? Is everything okay?'

I said in a happy voice, 'Oh yes, I'm fine, only I can't find Daddy. I think he's gone out and I want to come home now. I'm a bit tired.'

'Where is Fiona's mother?'

'I'm not sure.'

'I'll be right there, darling. Just stay where you are.'

We hung up, and I sat on the bottom stair. Some people brushed past me, then Towse appeared and said, 'Are you okay?' His eyes were bloodshot and I noticed dandruff on the shoulders of his black T-shirt. I nodded, and he went back into the living room. I thought that if I hadn't stopped him, I would be a non-virgin right now. It would be a great story for Sasha. Actually, even the truth would be a great story. She would love my 'Do you even know who I am?' line.

Then Laura was there, squashing next to me on the step. 'What you doing out here, little Miffy-sister?'

'I'm waiting for Mum.'

'Your mum?' Laura almost shouted. 'Why's she coming? That's stupid. Your dad's here! Phone her, tell her not to come.'

Laura's eyes were glittering and her mouth was very red.

'Why did you tell Towse I wanted to sleep with him?'

'Fuck, Miffy.' She handed me the phone. 'You told me so yourself, on holiday.'

'But I didn't mean now.'

She grabbed my arm, hard. 'I mean it, Miff. Ring your mum. You don't want to cause trouble, do you?'

I realised what she was trying to tell me and dialled the number, fast as I could. But the phone at home just rang and rang, and I was still listening to it when there was a banging at the door. Laura and I looked at each other, and she froze.

I opened the door and Mum pulled me into a hug. Then I felt her look up, and I turned towards the stairs, to where Dad and Mrs Morente were coming down, holding hands and laughing. Dad saw Mum and stopped dead, dropping Mrs Morente's hand like it was a grenade. Mrs Morente's eyes opened wide. Laura stood still, looking from one person to the other.

Dad said, 'Andrea! Hi! I was just looking at the mould in Mrs Bryan's bathroom.'

Mum laughed, a funny little yelp. 'Always helpful, aren't you, Michael? Olivia. I didn't realise you were here. But of course you are. I'm taking Melissa home now, Michael. Make sure Danny gets back safely.'

Mum led me out of the door and into the waiting taxi. We sat in the back and she cuddled me all the way home. I cried into her blue coat. I had drunk too much wine. Mum stroked my hair and said, 'Soon be home, darling, soon be home.'

Iron Tablets

I couldn't sleep, because my mind was crowded with people: Laura and Mum and Dad and Mrs Morente and Towse. I thought about Towse kissing me gently, lying beside me on the bed. I didn't want to think about the rest. Especially not that sucking thing. Did Laura do that with Danners? Did my parents? Did everyone?

I must have gone to sleep finally, but something woke me up. My clock radio said 3.35 a.m. I lay still, trying to work out if I'd heard a noise. Then I heard it again. I crept downstairs and pushed open the kitchen door. Mum was sitting at the breakfast bar in the dark, her back to me, crying her eyes out. In her hand was a bottle of pills.

I snatched the pill bottle from her and she jumped a mile. 'Oh, Melissa! You scared me.'

I shook the bottle. There were still some pills in there.

'How many have you taken?'

She let out a snort of laughter, mixed up with sobs. 'Only one, darling, I promise. They're my iron tablets.'

I looked at the label. It did say 'Iron tablets'.

'You can't overdose on them?' I asked.

'I don't think so. But I really have only taken one. They're for building up my strength.'

I sat next to her. 'What's the matter, Mummy?'

She wiped her eyes. 'What the hell. Why not tell you. Basically, your father's trying to decide whether he wants to stay with us. Or go and live somewhere else.'

Despite me sort of knowing this, it was still a huge shock. I felt very cold, like I had been dropped into an ice bath.

She hugged me. 'Darling, nothing is going to happen straight away. We're talking about it. I don't want you or Danny to worry.'

'Where's Daddy now?'

'Upstairs, asleep. And I'm going up now. So should you. It's very late.'

She kissed me and I went back to my room. I sat up in

bed for the rest of the night, looking out of the window. There wasn't much to see, just the street lamp and an occasional car trailing past. I thought about how empty it would be in the house without Dad. I thought about Mrs Morente. I thought about Laura trying to stop Mum from coming to the party. I thought about the people making love in Mrs Bryan's bedroom.

It began to get light at about ten past six, so I got dressed, went downstairs, got a bowl of cereal and watched *The Open University* till everyone else got up.

Pontins

Today Mum and I went through the batmitzvah file. She showed me the caterer's menu. Poached salmon mayonnaise, fried gefilte fish, herring salad, cheese flan, potato salad, coleslaw and cheesecake or profiteroles (I'm having them). Plus tea, coffee and pastries. It was £8.50 per person and fifty-six people were coming so far.

Then we tidied my room and put away all my clothes. When Mum hung up my school blazer we heard something crinkle in the pocket. It was pages I'd torn out from a travel brochure weeks ago. When she asked what they were, I told her we were going to Pontins on holiday.

She sat on my bed. 'This is the first I've heard of it, Melissa.'

'Daddy said! For a weekend before my batmitzvah. He said!'

'Oh, darling. I don't think it's going to happen.'

I'd read every single word of the pages, imagined exactly how it would be. I lay next to her on the bed and cried, great ploppy tears that landed on the shiny pictures of people laughing round the pool at Camber Sands.

Mum said, 'Well, let me look at them anyway.' She smoothed out the pages and read them properly. 'The Lowestoft one looks nice.'

'I think so too, Mum! The chalets are bigger and there's more entertainment.'

'Well, darling, there's such a lot going on right now. But how about a post-batmitzvah trip to celebrate? Maybe we could even manage a whole week?'

I threw my arms round her and pressed my face against hers, kissing her all over. When I pulled away it looked like she'd been crying too.

Dad in the Bathroom

For the first time in ages, Danners walked home with me from the school bus. We didn't say anything for most of the way. Then he mumbled, 'Sorry about Towse.'

I felt my face go hot. 'That's okay.' Oh my God, how much did he know?

'I told him and Laura you were too young.'

'It was all right. Nothing happened.'

'Good. By the way, is your friend Sasha coming to your batmitzvah?'

'Don't even think about it. If Towse is too old for me, you're too old for her!'

'You're just a kid, though, whereas she's a sexy woman.'

I hit him with my school bag and we chased each other all the way home, laughing. It was good.

Mum was out and Dad was upstairs. Danners and I were starving, so we grabbed some snacks and watched telly. Dad was a really long time and I went to find him. He was in the bathroom. I was frightened he might have killed himself. But when I knocked he called out, 'Who is it?' He sounded like he was crying. At least he was alive, but I needed to get him out so I could make the room safe.

'I'm busting for the loo, Daddy.'

'Give me five minutes.'

I sat on the floor to wait. Eventually he opened the door, looking sad and tired. 'Think I'll do lamb chops,' he said.

'Brilliant!' I rushed into the bathroom and locked the door. I went through the medicine cupboard and wrapped all the razors, nail scissors and pills in a towel, and sneaked it under my bed.

After eating our pink lamb chops, Dad drove me to

shul for my last lesson. On the way I chatted non-stop about my batmitzvah, because I felt he would like to start talking and I didn't want him to. I'd almost run out of conversation when we arrived, and I jumped out of the car before he'd pulled over, and nearly twisted my ankle.

I don't know if it was because it was my last lesson, but Rabbi Aron was very kind and gentle. He ran his finger along the page as I read, nodding all the way through, saying 'That's right', or 'Good', in a pleased voice. His baby-blond hair was really clean, and he smelled like Imperial Leather soap. I couldn't stop thinking about what his penis was like, whether it was the same as Towse's, and whether it would taste nicer. I must know my portion inside-out now, because I could think all these distracting thoughts whilst chanting the whole thing word-perfectly. Aron said I had never done it better, and that I'd be fantastic on Saturday.

'Will your dad do some last-minute practice with you, Melissa, or shall I come over on Thursday evening?'

There was a time when I'd have jumped at the chance of another evening with Aron, but everything seemed a bit complicated. So I said Dad would practise with me.

We stood up and shook hands. '*B'hatzlacha*,' he said. 'Good luck, Melissa.'

Then he kissed me on my forehead. His lips were so soft

that it was like being kissed by a butterfly. I took in a great deep breath of shampoo and soap and was so muddled that I found myself outside in the car park waiting for Dad, without really knowing how I got there.

Melissa

Whenever I go outside, I'm astonished all over again by the backdrop of mountains. It's so beautiful here. And so welcoming. I thought the Welsh would be unfriendly when they heard my English accent, but they've been lovely. I feel like I'm still travelling: the same pleasurable sense of displacement, the unfamiliar language, the new discoveries. It's a good place to be when the rest of the world is imploding. You can almost forget about Iraq, war, people dying. I am far from the centre of things, detached from reality, living a quiet existence centred round Laura, Evie and the baby.

One traveller's discovery I've made is a small café in a village called Llandegai, which serves homemade 'Jewish' chicken soup, not quite like Mum used to make but not bad. I consider myself a regular now, having been in for the last three days. Today I sit at my usual table, and leaf through my diary while I wait for my soup. How full my diary used to be! Often there wasn't enough space to note down every meeting, every client. Now, this week, next week, the week after: totally blank. When should I go home? Where even *is* home, now? For the first time in my life I'm not tied to anywhere. Mum's fine. Fine as she'll ever be, anyway, thanks to Morris. Work's long since replaced me. Jay's already seeing someone, Sasha tells me – a woman he met at the tennis club. I'm glad for him, feel only a tiny pang. I can go anywhere. Do anything.

I look at Sasha's latest text – *When you coming back, hon?* – and don't know how to reply. I don't realise I'm sighing till a businessman at a nearby table says, 'Cheer up!'

Laura smiles broadly when I come into the ward. They've been letting her get up for the last couple of days, so they can take her in a wheelchair to see the baby. This has clearly made her feel much stronger.

I give her some of the cards and gifts that have been arriving at the cottage. Hella and Danners have sent flowers, and Laura studies the accompanying card intently. It's in the florist's handwriting but I can see from the phrasing that the words are Hella's. I don't tell Laura; why spoil her fun? Then she opens a card from Ceri, reads it and tosses it to the floor.

'She phones every day, you know.'

'She feels guilty,' Laura says. 'Good.'

She *is* getting better.

I give her some things I bought this morning. Glossy magazines, a box of Maltesers because I remember she used to love them, and a small spritzer of my perfume, the one she likes.

'Oh, Miffy, you shouldn't spend money on me, you're doing enough. You've already stayed miles longer than you meant to.'

'I want to be here.'

I've tried several times to talk about what happened the day she went into labour. But I haven't known how to begin. I don't think she remembers our argument. She hasn't mentioned any of it: not offering me Huw, not the things I said, not me pushing her. None of it.

Olivia bursts onto the ward, back from the SCBU. '*Dios mio*, Laura! He opened his eyes! He looked straight at me. He is so adorable!'

Another thing I haven't told Laura is the pull that tiny baby exerts on me. It's almost physical, my need to see him. At night, when I can't sleep, I imagine how he would feel in my arms, his tiny warm body nestling into mine. Sometimes I dream I'm walking along the corridor from the lift to the Special Care Baby Unit. In real life the green floor sparkles, the same kind of flooring as in the hospital where Jay works. Maybe it's non-slip or something. And in my dreams it's the same, an endless glittery corridor, and I feel so happy as I walk along it. I never actually see the baby in my dream but I know he's there, waiting for me.

'He's put on another ounce,' Olivia says to me, 'and the nurses think Huw will be able to hold him in a couple more days.'

'If he's here,' Laura says.

'Of course he'll be here!' Olivia says. 'Don't talk that way. Tempting fate. Didn't I just tell you he's getting stronger?' She gathers her things, kisses Laura, puts her hand on my shoulder briefly. When she's gone Laura and I look at each other.

'I didn't mean the baby,' Laura says. 'Huw's leaving me. Did I mention that?' She laughs, a hollow sound.

'Oh, Laura, I'm so sorry.'

'Shitty, isn't it? It's that blonde bitch I saw him with in the pub. Knew it all along.'

'But I can't believe he'd go now. What sort of man leaves his wife when she's just had a baby?'

'I'm sorry to say, the same man I fell in love with, Miff.

When he left Carmen for me, she was pregnant with their second child.'

This shuts me up. I didn't know that. Laura managed to miss that out of her romantic telling of their affair.

'He didn't want to have another child with Carmen, not with their marriage in such a mess. Yes, I know, the irony's not lost on me.' She presses the call button next to her bed.

'Laura, this isn't the same situation at all! He can't leave you with a premature baby.'

She looks suddenly much younger. 'Always knew it could happen, Miff. I messed up. I deserve it.'

'No one deserves this.'

'I do. I don't believe in abortion, but I went and had one anyway. This is my punishment. Another dead baby.'

'Your baby isn't dead, love. He's doing fine. Poor you. I didn't know you'd had an abortion?'

She rolls the perfume bottle I gave her round in her hands, not looking at me.

'Sorry, Laura. Don't talk about it if you don't want to.'

'I do want to. Really, you have a right to know.'

'Me? Why do I?'

She looks up at me. 'It was my baby with Danny.'

Someone's jaw dropping is such a silly cliché. But mine really drops. I feel it go, my mouth sliding open in a big round 'O'.

'I always assumed he'd have told you,' Laura says.

Nurse Canton comes over. 'You want to see your baby, honey? I'll just get the chair.' She heads back out of the ward.

'When was it?' I manage to say. My thoughts are whizzing about. It can't have happened since seeing him last month; she was already pregnant. Before that, she hadn't seen him since we were children. So she must mean...

'Found out I was knocked up a few weeks after we left Edgware.'

'Oh my God. Oh, Christ, Laura. You were only fourteen.' I put my hand on hers.

'You're shocked. I've upset you, Miff. I'm sorry.'

I *am* shocked. And yet... things are slotting into place. 'Did Danners know?'

She nods.

And he never told me. 'Who else knew?'

'Mama. Michael. That's all.'

'Not my mum?'

'Not unless Danny told her.'

No way would he have told Mum, not at that time, and in the state she was in. So he carried that secret all by himself. He was just a teenager himself, fifteen or sixteen. His dad has left, his mother's having a nervous breakdown, his girlfriend's betrayed him, his sister's had an accident, then he gets a phone call or a letter... *This* is the missing part of a puzzle about Danners that I had long since given up looking for.

'Did you want to keep it?'

She uncurls her hand from mine. 'I was just a child myself. Long, long time ago.' She breaks briefly into song – the beginning of 'American Pie'. Then says, 'Yes. *Yes*. Not at the time, not properly. But when I was older, oh yes. When I realised you can't always have the children you want when you want them. God yes.'

That's a feeling I understand.

She gives me a tired smile. 'What goes around comes around, Miff. I don't just mean the abortion. Huw leaving as well. I took him off Carmen, now this Tania has taken him off me. He makes you feel so special. I remember how amazing it was when he chose me. *Me*, out of all the girls he could have chosen.'

Since I met Laura again, I've often wondered why I thought her so sophisticated when we were young. And I've never wondered it more than now. 'He shouldn't have been choosing anyone, Laura. He was married then. And he's married now.'

'Men just follow their dicks, don't they?'

Nurse Canton arrives with the wheelchair. 'Ooh, talking about dicks are we, you must be feeling better.'

Laura laughs. The nurse helps her into the chair, arranges the drip, says, 'We'll be getting you off this tomorrow.'

'Thank fuck for that,' Laura says. 'Okay, ready.'

The nurse pushes Laura's chair and I keep pace along-side. The corridor from the lift isn't nearly as long as in my dreams, but the floor does sparkle. I point it out to Laura and she says, 'Oh yes. I'd never noticed it before.'

Laura can't go into the SCBU because of the wheelchair and the drip, so she sits outside, presses her face to the window. I stand next to her and we are silent for a while, gazing at the tiny baby. He's awake but he doesn't look in our direction – he's too busy scanning the ceiling. What a strange world he must think it is, all wires and lights and hardness.

'Beautiful,' Laura breathes. 'I can't wait to get in there. Touch him.'

Nor can I.

'I couldn't have got through this without you,' she says. 'It's been so wonderful having you around.'

I feel such a terrible fraud, hearing this.

'I feel so worried for you, Laura.'

'I'll manage, Miff. I'll take the fucking bastard for every penny, don't worry.'

'What about emotionally, Laura?' I want to shout: *Who cares about money? What about Evie? The baby? What about another broken marriage?* But I hold myself back. It's not any of my business. I take a breath, pretend she's a client. Move the abortion into a compartment, to be dealt with later.

Then just when I think I know how she's feeling, she throws her arms round my waist, and sobs, 'Christ, Miffy-sister, I love him. My heart stopped when he told me about that woman. He went through so much to be with me, I thought he'd never leave.' Her sobbing is more like gasping. 'It was just meant to be a rough patch.'

The toughness of just a minute ago has quite disappeared. She is so much more vulnerable than she pretends. I stroke her hair, make soothing noises, and after a while she wipes her eyes and sits up straight. The baby has gone to sleep.

'Let's go back down. Can you push me?'

What, like I did in your kitchen? I must, must talk to her about this today. The therapists I've seen would have absolutely loved that I pushed Laura. I can hear them, triumphantly making patterns out of the misery in my life. 'She pushed you, so, years later, you pushed her. It is appropriate, natural. A child pushing a child.' But I wasn't a child when I pushed her. I remember one therapist I saw during my clinical psychology training almost yelled, 'Your father couldn't have abandoned you in a more damaging way if he had tried! Don't be so hard on yourself.' But I can't help it.

Back we go, across the green sparkles. Laura says, 'When I saw the baby for the first time, it felt like being hit, it was so powerful. Hit by love. But I'm frightened.'

When we reach the ward, I ask a nurse for help and she gently eases Laura into bed. I smooth her covers. She looks absolutely exhausted, pale as the sheets.

I say, 'Tell me what's frightening you.'

'I guess we never know what's coming our way. If the baby makes it…'

'He will!'

'*If* he makes it, the doctor said he might be brain-damaged. Blind, maybe. Never been very good with stuff like that. How will I cope with it on my own?'

I'm going to have to tell her. Now.

Deep breath.

'Laura, do you remember what happened before you went into labour?'

'Huw told me he was leaving, and I had too much whisky.' She opens the Maltesers and offers the box to me. I shake my head.

'Before that. Do you remember our argument?'

'Oh no, I can't bear to talk about that. I embarrassed myself. And you.'

'Laura, listen. Me pushing you caused the baby to come early.' It's such a relief to say it that my eyes fill with tears.

'I don't think so, Miff.'

'I know so. You didn't have any symptoms of labour before, did you? And I shoved you and you fell, and then a few hours later the baby came. Oh Jesus, Laura, I wasn't thinking straight, I have never ever hurt anyone in my life before, I don't know what came over me. Thank God that little boy is fighting to stay here; if he didn't make it, I don't know what I would do.'

She is shaking her head but I keep going. It's so important to speak up.

'And I promise – I swear – that I will make it up to you. If the baby's disabled, or if he isn't, it doesn't matter to me. And now I know about Huw, it's even more important you have someone here, to help and support you. I will gladly do that. I'll stay with you for as long as you want, and help you look after him. That's the best way I can make it up to you.'

Laura stares at me. She starts to say something several times:

'I'm not sure that's what...'

'But I was already having...'

'Your work and your life...'

I wave my hand at the last one. 'It's providence that I'm a free agent. I can move here. Get a job. Look after us all. I don't want you to have to get another crummy shop job. I mean it, Laura. I feel this is what I am meant to do. What I must do. To try and make it up to you.'

There is a long silence. Laura looks at her hands. Finally she says, 'Thank you.'

By the time Huw arrives we've made lots of plans. He

saunters over, addresses Laura in his usual cocky tone. How could I ever have found him attractive? How could I have let him kiss me, on that crazy sunlit walk when we got lost? He fancies himself way too much, and behaves like he's still an irresponsible young man. But the buttons on his shirt are straining. The lines on his face are deep.

'Feeling fit enough to put on make-up, that's a good sign, *cariad.*'

'Need to start attracting potential new husbands, don't I?' She's brassy again, protective shell firmly back in place.

I pick up my bag. I feel such anger. Towards Huw. Towards all men who leave their kids as though it was such a little thing. Such an easy thing. Such a nothing.

Most of all, I feel anger towards myself.

'Oh, by the way, Huw, I'll stay around after you've gone. Help Laura and the baby.' I look straight at him, as I pull on my coat. 'It should be your job. But if you're not man enough for it, I'll step in.'

I turn on my heel and go out, leaving a gratifying silence behind me.

Miffy

1979

Batmitzvah Girl

Saturday, 1 September 1979. The day I officially become a woman.

I put on my new pants and bra, then stepped carefully into my green dress. I didn't feel scared. More weird, really. In the mirror I looked sad. Laura once said that the best cure for a tired face was sparkly eyeshadow. I chose the silvery-green one from my new make-up kit, which was a batmitzvah present from Mum's friend Bernice. Laura's heart-shaped pendant didn't go with the dress, so I took it off and put on my gold Star of David instead. Then I went carefully downstairs in my high shoes.

Everyone was waiting for me: Mum, Dad, Danners and Auntie Leila. Dad made special breakfast pancakes. Auntie Leila put my hair into a French plait and tied it with a green ribbon. She looked amazing in a red and white polka-dot dress. Mum was in a lovely new cream dress with pleats.

Dad and Auntie Leila started the car shifts to get all our relatives to *shul*, and Mum and I waited in the living room. I sat with my knees together and hands by my sides so I wouldn't get crumpled. Dad had polished my shoes so there was no sign of the scuff marks Towse had made.

'You look beautiful, angel,' she said. 'How you feeling?'

'A bit strange.'

'Nerves, I suppose. I never had a batmitzvah, of course; girls didn't in my day. I'm so proud of you.' She gave me a gentle, non-crumpling hug. She was wearing her new perfume, which Auntie Leila had brought from France.

'You smell really nice, Mummy.'

'Listen, Melissa. I just want to say, I love you. We'll always be together and we'll look after each other. Whatever happens.'

Dad beeped his car horn and we stood up and smoothed down our skirts. Mum held my hand as we went out to the car, but I didn't mind.

The *shul* was packed with my aunties and grandparents and cousins. My cousin Linda was wearing the sailor dress I'd seen in Helene's Paris Fashions, poor thing. Aunt Faye came gushing over. She flicked back the neck of my dress to read the label. 'Hmph,' she said. 'Leila always did go right over the top and into orbit.'

But everyone else was nice. Booba and Zaida Cline came over, pushing Booba Preston in her wheelchair. Booba Cline fussed over me, picking invisible threads off my dress. Zaida Cline gave me a big kiss. I bent down to say hello to Booba Preston and she said, '*Hubble, bubble toil and trouble.*'

I laughed, and said, 'Well, exactly.'

She took my hand and pulled me towards her. 'Whatever your silly parents do, you'll be all right, Melissa,' she whispered. 'Sound head on those pretty shoulders.'

Danners was leaning against the back wall with Towse, who looked cute in a dark suit. He shook my hand and winked at me. I thought of what he looked like in just his T-shirt, gloppy sperm all over his belly, and gave him a huge wink back.

'Good luck, Miff,' Danners said, and ruffled my hair. Then he straightened up as Sasha came in with her parents and rushed to hug me. She looked amazing in a blue sleeveless dress, but brushed aside all my compliments.

'No one looks nicer than you today, Mel!'

As I made my way to the front row, Jay met me in the aisle. 'Good luck,' he whispered. In front of the whole congregation he kissed my cheek and his face went pink. I sat down in my seat with a thud and tried to replace the smile on my face with a properly serious expression.

Bernice sat behind me and tapped me on the shoulder. 'Lissa, when do we pin the money on your dress? I've got a tenner and a pin all ready.' She showed me.

Danners started laughing. 'You're thinking of Greek weddings!'

'I thought it was batmitzvahs.' Bernice looked disappointed. 'Are you sure?'

Mum was laughing too. 'Oh, Bernice, you sweet confused Catholic girl.'

We were still giggling when the organ struck up. I turned quickly but it wasn't Mrs Morente playing; it was Rosa Spiegel. I caught Mum's eye but she shook her head very slightly. Dad sat down on my other side, Rabbi Aron came up to the pulpit in his bright white *tallis*, and the service began.

There were a lot of prayers and songs to get through and it was agony waiting to be called up, but finally, through a haze, I heard Aron say, '... and so to celebrate her passage into adulthood, we now call Melissa Cline to read from the *Torah*.'

A wave of calm blew over me as I walked up to the pulpit, where the scroll was waiting, unrolled to the correct place, right at the start. Aron smiled, touched my shoulder and moved away. Then I was up there all alone. I gazed out across the dozens of faces looking expectantly at me. Laura wasn't there but I could see everyone else, all my best people in the world, watching and smiling. My eyes filled with tears. They were all here for me. I bent my head, blinked away the tears, took a deep breath as Max had taught me, picked up the silver *yad*, the pointer, and began slowly to run it across the Hebrew so I wouldn't lose my place.

'*Barayshis borah Elohim*,' I began, loud and clear, as I had practised it a thousand times. '*Et Ha-shamayim vaetz ha-aretz*. In the beginning God created the Heavens and the Earth...'

I don't know what it was like, but I know I didn't make any mistakes. When I'd finished I stood quietly while Rabbi Aron whispered a special blessing, just for me. You could hear a pin drop in the *shul*, but I was the only one who could hear what he said. 'Melissa, it has been a privilege to get to know you. You will make a worthwhile contribution in whatever you choose to do as an adult. There will be hardships and difficulties ahead, but I'm sure you will overcome these. Melissa, you are a special young woman with a great future.'

He didn't tell me he loved me and wanted to marry me, but hey, you can't have everything.

He took both my hands in his and said the final blessing out loud. 'May the Lord lift up his countenance upon you, and give you peace.'

He let go of my hands and I turned to face the congregation, ready to go back to my seat, but everyone burst into applause. I didn't know you were allowed to do that in *shul*. Uncle Kenny stood up and started cheering. I waited a moment, taking it in, then I climbed down the steps and sat down between Mum and Dad. They both put their arms round me. Mum was crying, and Danners leaned across Dad to slap my back, and Dad kissed the top of my head, and the clapping died away, and Rabbi Aron delivered his usual boring sermon, and Nat Samuels fell asleep with his mouth open, and I felt for once that I was the right person in the right place at the right time.

The Last Dance

My batmitzvah party was held in the *shul* hall straight after the service. There were hundreds of cards and presents. Danners said I'd got even more than him.

Sasha told me I'd looked poised and beautiful, and Shelley from the youth club said she would never live up to me when she did hers next month. Max, leaning on a stick, came up with his wife, who was quite pretty for an old lady. Max said he was very proud of me. As soon as I turned away from them, there was someone else wanting to tell me how great I'd been. It was lovely.

I was allowed three helpings of profiteroles. After the toasts – to me, my parents, my grandparents, the Chief Rabbi and the Queen – the tables were cleared away and a proper disco was set up, with flashing coloured lights. All the younger people started dancing and I was right in the middle. Sasha and Shelley grabbed my hands and we whirled round till we were dizzy. I didn't even think about what my dancing looked like, it just felt so great. 'Good Vibrations' came on, which I'd put on the list weeks ago because it was one of Laura's favourites. I felt funny for a moment, then Danners and Towse came over to dance with us girls. It was all very mature. No one flopped their Vienna sausage willies into anyone else's hands; we all just kept dancing and laughing, swapping all the time so that one minute Sasha and I would be jiving, then Danners would be whirling me about, then I'd be swinging round with Towse. Cousin Alisa and Simon were dancing madly near us, and Auntie Leila was happily doing some kind of hippy moon-dance by herself in a corner. I caught a glimpse of Mum and Dad sitting by themselves, talking and looking very serious. I wasn't sure if that was a good sign or not.

We were all exhausted by the time the slower songs came on. Many of the older couples got up on the dance floor, even Booba and Zaida Cline. Jay asked me to dance, and as I stood up to take his hand I saw Towse sitting a few tables away, watching us. Jay and I danced as though we'd been together all our lives. It felt so comfortable and natural, and he didn't ask me upstairs to play with his penis. We smiled at each other as we moved slowly round the room.

When the song finished, Dad came over. 'Sorry to butt in, young man, but may I have this next dance with my daughter?'

Jay handed me over with a little bow, and Dad began to guide me round the floor. 'Do you remember when you were little and used to dance on my feet?'

'Oh, groan, Dad, so sentimental.' But I did remember. 'Shall we do it now?'

'I think you might do me a mischief in those stilettos. Anyway, you're too tall now to need the extra boost.'

I really must have grown. I was up to his shoulder, over which I could see Cousin Linda. She was watching Jay hopefully, but he sat drinking a glass of juice and looking across at me. Towse was hippy-dancing with Auntie Leila. I have no idea how that happened. Danners danced past with Sasha. She looked cool and in control.

Dad said, 'You were amazing today, Lissa.'

'Thank you.'

'And so that makes it even harder to say this.'

I stopped dancing, my heart pounding. 'What?'

He carried on moving me round so that we were still dancing. 'Everyone's having a great time. Let's not attract any attention.' When I started moving again he said, 'In a few minutes, I'll be leaving the party. I've arranged for taxis to take you all home later.'

'Where are you going?'

'I'm moving away, darling.'

There was a rushing sound in my ears, covering up the music.

'It's nothing you or Danny have done, do you understand? It's not anything Mummy's done, either. We just don't love each other any more.'

'But Mummy's got new perfume.'

'I know she has, darling.'

I started to cry, silent tears that I hid by putting my head on Dad's shoulder. He held me tight and hummed quietly as he whirled me round.

'You won't get to see my presents.'

'You can write and tell me every single thing you get, and soon, before you know it, you'll come to my new house and you can bring all your favourite presents.'

'Where is your new house?'

'As soon as I've found somewhere, you'll be the first to know.'

'Why do you have to go tonight?'

'Darling, I've waited months. Staying is just making lots of people very unhappy. I promised I'd wait till your bat-mitzvah, but I must go straight away.'

'Does Mum know?'

'Yes. But Danny doesn't. I'm going to tell him after I've spoken to you.'

I grabbed his arm. 'Does this mean you won't be coming to Pontins?'

'Oh, darling!' He half-laughed. 'I think maybe Mummy and Auntie Leila will take you very soon.'

I wanted to say it wouldn't be the same without him, but the song had ended and he was already moving away.

'Will you go and sit with Mummy?'

I nodded, and he pulled me towards him in such a tight hug I thought I'd be crushed. He kissed me on the forehead, and then he was walking away from me, towards Danners. Dad led him over to the front entrance. Before they went through the door, Dad turned and gave me a little wave. Then he was gone.

I went over to Mum. Bernice was sitting on one side of her, Auntie Leila on the other. The disco lights were flashing on and off their faces. Red, green, yellow. Bernice shifted down a chair for me and I sat next to Mum. She clutched my hand, and we all sat there, saying nothing, staring straight ahead at the happy dancing crowd.

After a few minutes, Danners reappeared alone, looking bewildered. Auntie Leila moved down a chair and he took her place. Mum in the middle, Danners and I on either side of her, we waited for my party to end.

Melissa

Sixteen days ago the baby was born.

Six days ago Laura came out of hospital.

Five days ago Huw moved out.

Despite living in a house where the marriage has just fallen apart, I'm happy. That's shocking. I'm happier than I've been for years.

Only when I think about Evie does my mood crash. She's a bit younger than I was when my dad left, but she seems much more mature. She knows more than I did. She knows her parents weren't getting on, that her dad didn't want another baby, and that her mum went a bit mad over Danners. She even knew, before Laura did, that Huw was seeing someone, because she saw messages on his phone. None of this awareness makes it any easier, of course. In fact, some of the things I didn't know when my parents split were good things not to know. Evie looks like she's carrying a physical burden on her slim shoulders.

There is one positive thing. 'At least the shouting's stopped.'

When she says that, the ground tips slightly; I am transported back to my teenage bedroom, playing loud music to cover up the sound of my parents arguing.

Olivia is taking Evie to Spain tomorrow for the Easter holiday, to the ancestral home I once visited as a child. Some cousins live there now. It'll be good for Evie to have a change of scene, but I'll miss her. I do the school drops and pick-ups, and I love that time with her, when she opens her heart and tells me how she feels about her parents, or her friends, or boys. She talks about Micah a lot, presses me for a level of detail about him that I don't possess. I don't discourage her, though I know Danners and Hella will forbid the friendship when they're older. For now, they're just kids, and I'm not going to tell anyone about their innocent correspondence.

Today's the last day of term. When I pull up at the school Evie turns to me.

'You know I'm going away tomorrow, Auntie Lissa?'

'I do. See if you can find the well in the back garden for me!'

'You'll still be here when I get back.'

It's a statement, not a question.

'Of course I will, sweetheart. I can't wait to hear all about it.'

She leans across and kisses me before getting out of the car. Oh, the feel of her lips against my cheek. Her face is almost the size of a grown woman's, yet so child-like, the skin impossibly soft. Dear God, what it is to have a child. To watch them grow. She goes into school and I sit in the car with misty eyes till someone hoots. Sentimental old fart.

Back at the house I collect Laura and drive us to hospital, our daily routine. In the lift we go, along the sparkly corridor to the Special Care Baby Unit, where Laura scrubs up and goes in, feeds the baby with a tiny bottle. I watch through the window. There was a heart-stopping scare last week when they thought he'd got an infection, but he is back on track now. Laura's face as she bends over him is something to see. She is radiant.

Later we go for lunch, often to my favourite café. Laura likes the chicken soup too. If we're feeling adventurous, we go further afield, one time to a café near Penmon Point, and once as far as a pub on the Llyn Peninsula. I am getting to know the area, the well-known places and the secret treasures.

Back home, Laura has a rest, as she's still rather weak, and I collect Evie from school. Then all three of us visit the baby together. This is my favourite part of the day. Evie and I stand together outside the unit and watch Laura with the baby. After that it's home, supper, telly, bed. It's not exciting, but it is extraordinarily fulfilling. I am needed, useful, at the centre of my own little universe.

I really ought to think about finding work soon. My savings won't last for ever. Occasionally when I'm drifting off to sleep I wonder what I'm doing here, what happened to my own life. But mostly I'm in limbo, agreeably disconnected from the rest of the world. Some days I feel as if the baby we're going to see is mine. Other days I feel so close to Laura I wonder if the staff think we've become a couple.

I've only left Wales once since I got here nearly a month ago; it was last week to meet Danners. He was at a conference in Chester and we met for lunch. It took me nearly the whole hour to get up the courage to ask about the abortion, but as soon as I said, 'Laura's been telling me some things I didn't know about, from when we were younger,' he knew what I meant.

I've seen him cry plenty – he is an emotional man – but the expression on his face was so sad, so lost, I almost cried myself. We held each other for a few minutes in that dingy town pub, with its brown walls and violently patterned carpet, the barman wiping glasses in a trance, the barmaid flirting wearily with the lunchtime punters, on a break from their sales meetings and conferences.

'I wish you'd told me, Danners. I might have helped.'

'I didn't tell anyone. Except Hella when we married. She was amazing.' He picked up his glass and drained his orange juice, though there was nothing much left but a couple of ice cubes. Then he set the glass down, carefully, in the exact same spot, back in its circular puddle of condensation. I could see that he'd had enough of the conversation. Danners would be such a great subject for psychotherapy. There's so much locked away in there.

'Have you seen these?' he asked, showing me the latest photos of Ishmael on his phone. Then it was time for us to go – he back to his conference; me to my car, and the drive back to Aber. We hugged goodbye outside the pub.

He said, 'Is it okay, being there?'

'It's really okay. I love it, in fact.'

'Be careful, though?'

'I'm a grown-up now.'

'You're still my little sister.'

I watched him as he walked away. He still believes in Laura's supernatural powers to cause harm.

If he was with us today, he might feel vindicated in that belief. Laura and I are back in the chicken soup café, having a nice discussion about the baby's name. I used to love planning names when Jay and I thought we were going to be parents. Laura still hasn't chosen one, says it's tempting fate to get too attached to the baby. Then she suddenly leaps headlong into a heavy conversation, deliberately rocking the boat.

'What was it like for you, Miff, after we went?'

It's so out of the blue, I can't think what she means. After who went where? Then I realise with a thud that she means after she left Edgware with Olivia and Dad, twenty-odd years ago.

'Do you really want to go over this now, Laura?'

'I thought it might help me understand what Evie's going through.'

I put my spoon down. 'The two situations aren't at all the same.'

'I know. It was so much worse for you. Your dad left with someone you trusted. And you lost your best friend.'

Her eyes are full of concern. I feel my anger threatening to well up. Then I remember the last time I lost my self-control with Laura, and swallow it down.

'Your own parents divorced, Laura. You know what it's like.'

'I was younger when they split, though. I only remember being relieved.'

Trying to divert the conversation, I say, 'Did you ever hear from your dad again after he left?'

353

'Birthday presents for a couple of years, but I haven't heard anything in decades.'

'Your mum mentioned him when you were in hospital. Wondered whether she ought to get in touch with him.'

'God, how weird. Hope she doesn't. Anyway. Please could we talk a little about us, back then?'

I sigh.

Laura says, 'It'll be good for me to hear it. You know. Cleansing.'

'Oh well, if it'd be *cleansing*.'

'Shit, Miffy. I don't mean to piss you off. Sorry. It's just... it's been on my mind so much. I can't stop thinking about it.'

'If we're really going to talk about this, let's go outside. I'll need a cigarette.'

We take our coffees to the outside table, cast iron, grey with lack of use. The sky is white and bright, with no warmth coming through. Laura looks at me expectantly, but I've no idea how to start. I light my cigarette, take a long healing drag, close my eyes and think, as so often, of my beloved Auntie Leila, who died twelve years ago. Lung cancer. She was a heroic smoker, kept it going till the very end. I used to model my smoking style on her: flamboyant, lots of dragon-style snorting through the nostrils, streams of smoke rings.

How do I talk about this without upsetting Laura? Or

myself? A small, dark part of me feels like being very blunt, showing Laura just how much she hurt me. In every sense of the word. Childish, base feelings that all the therapy in the world hasn't shifted. At work, whenever I see children who've been dumped, betrayed, abandoned, it's more than just professional empathy I feel: it's a potent reminder of the pain I once felt myself. That blank, emptied-out feeling. When I look at Evie, I see me, lost and bewildered. An aching hole where my life used to be. A lurch of misery every morning when she wakes, remembering her father is gone. Wondering if I – she – could have done something to prevent it. If she – if I – caused it.

Maybe I am transferring a bit too much of how I felt onto Evie.

What to tell Laura? Where to start? Once upon a time a little girl went to her batmitzvah with two parents, and came back with one. Her mother went to bed and didn't get up for a week. Her brother dumped her unopened presents under the table in the dining room. I can't even remember what happened to them now. So many memories have faded beyond my reach. I know that we ran out of food after a few days, and neither Mum nor Danners seemed able to do anything about it. So I went to buy bread and milk and on the way to the corner shop I saw Mrs Peterson, our next-door neighbour, who'd known me all my life. She crossed the road right in front of me. I was so astonished she hadn't stopped to talk – she *always* stopped to talk – that I turned and watched her. She walked a few more paces, then crossed back again to the side she'd been on in the first place. The side I was on.

I know now that she just didn't know what to say. Divorce was a huge stigma then. Especially divorce in a nice Jewish family. But Mrs Peterson crossing the road was the first time I realised *everything* had changed. Not just the big things: Dad gone; Mum falling apart; losing my best friend. But a million little things. People avoiding us (Mrs Peterson was only the first of many). Eating weird makeshift meals at the oddest hours. Mum abruptly abandoning our bedtimes because she didn't want to be alone, so Danners and I were permanently tired. Mum deciding none of this would have happened if we'd only mixed with Jews. So Danners and I were sent to a Jewish school where we didn't know anyone. I was on crutches for the first term, so that was fun. And then Mum decided our familiar *shul* was too full of nosey parkers, and we started going to a much more religious synagogue. In the midst of all this, Mum's Mum, Booba Preston, died. It was just two months after Dad left, and it finished Mum off completely. After Booba's funeral, Auntie Leila took Danners and me to Pontins in Lowestoft for a week, and I cried every day.

My eyes swim and I blink.

'Are you okay, Miff?'

I nod, take another drag on my cigarette, which has almost burned out, and sip my coffee. 'What do you want to know?'

She looks down at the table. Says quietly, 'I've always wondered. You know. If you and Danny blamed me.'

Well, of course that's what she wants to know: what did we think about *her*? I stub out my cigarette, light another one. 'You're making me a chain-smoker.' I decide, for my sanity, and for our renewed friendship, and because she's been through the wringer lately, to be honest but not harsh. 'Yes. I'm afraid we did blame you.'

She nods, slowly. 'I know you did. I've always known.'

'You were just a kid, though.'

'I'm not fucking well going to cry.' As she says it she starts to sob. 'I don't even know which bit I'm crying about.'

I put my arm round her. 'I don't think you really meant anything. Did you even know what was going on?'

'I just wanted Mama to be happy.'

'We all want our parents to be happy, don't we?'

She straightens up, dabs the mascara under her eyes. 'I want you to know how sorry I was – am – about the...the thing.'

Which of the many things, I wonder? I look quizzically at her.

'The, you know, when you hurt your leg.'

Ah, *that* thing.

'It was an accident, Laura. You just wanted me to get out of the way. You didn't know a car was coming.'

She grips my hand. 'Exactly! Thank you. I think I was still a bit deafened from that alarm; I honestly didn't hear it. What happened? You still limp a tiny bit.'

'I don't know. Something didn't set exactly right. Mum wasn't really paying a huge amount of attention and I just had to get on with it, use my crutches and not make a fuss. I thought the limp was more or less unnoticeable these days.'

'I guess I'm looking out for it. Can I ask one more thing? Did you feel bad that you didn't get back to see Michael before he died?'

'I'll be honest, Laura.' I sit back in my seat. 'I'm not telling Danners this, but I got all his emails. All the ones that said Dad was ill. And I decided not to rush back.'

'Why?'

I blow smoke through my nostrils like Auntie Leila. 'I guess I just thought . . . Well, Dad wasn't there for me. Why should I be there for him?'

Laura sits very still, gazing at me. 'Oh.'

'I'm sorry if that shocks you.'

'It's a relief to find you're not Little Miss Perfect after all.'

'Is that what you think of me?'

'Little Miss Do Everything Right, yeah.'

My coffee's cold now but I drain the cup anyway.

'Even after you know I beat up pregnant women?'

'Ah, well. You had your reasons.'

We smile at each other.

I want to tell Danners that grown-up Laura is a considerable improvement on her younger self. She's still funny, still exciting to be around, but less brittle and a lot less manipulative. I don't want to hurt her, or tell her how bad things were for me in the past. Instead I say, 'Evie will have fun in Spain, won't she? Do you remember when we were there, playing in the garden? Getting covered in mud?'

'Yes, I remember the sheets flapping in the wind.'

'We spent the whole day digging in the back garden because your grandfather told us there was a hidden well.'

'Fancy you remembering that.'

'I remember everything about it.' It was our last family holiday.

'I'm getting a bit cold,' Laura says. 'Shall we go?'

As we walk to the car she says, 'You're right that it's time to name the baby. I've decided to call him Melvin.'

'Melvin?!'

'If he makes it.'

'Of course he'll make it. Why Melvin? It's a bit, er, old-fashioned.'

'I know. But it's so I can call him Mel. After you.'

I stand by the car door, staring at her. Now I start to cry like a baby.

Miffy

1979

Evaporation

I bunked off school today. I'd never done it before, but it was easy. Those kids who were always boasting about bunking weren't so clever after all. This was all there was to it: I didn't get on the bus.

Sasha got on ahead and called my name out of the window, but I pretended not to hear. I looked at the ground till I heard the bus move off. Sasha's voice got fainter and fainter. When I couldn't hear it any more, I looked up. The bus was at the end of the street, and Danners was standing in front of me.

He grinned. 'Saw you not get on. Good idea.'

We didn't discuss where we were going; we just went. I'd never walked there before, but Danners had been there loads on his bike, so it was good he was with me. I'd probably have got lost otherwise. It started raining but we both had our cagoules Dad bought us in Wood Green. We unzipped them out of their pouches. Mine went down to my knees.

I wondered if the school would phone Mum to find out why we weren't in. We passed a man in a beige mac who looked at us as if to say, *Why aren't you at school?* I told Danners we should call home and he said okay, long as I did the talking, so I went into a phone box while he waited outside. Mum always made me keep two pence in my sock for emergencies, so I prised it out and dialled our number.

She picked up straight away. 'Michael?'

I pushed the coin in. 'No, Mum, it's me.'

'Oh, sweetie. Why are you phoning? What's the matter?'

Crappy useless school, they obviously hadn't called her. What was the point of taking that bloody register every day? What if we were dead in a ditch? Then they'd be embarrassed.

'I'm with Danners. We're not at school. We've just come round to...' The rain got really heavy for a minute, drumming on the roof of the phone box, and I could hardly hear my own voice. 'We've come to say goodbye to Daddy.'

The silence went on and on.

Finally I said, 'Mum, I've only got two pence.'

The pips started. Over the top of them, Mum said, 'I'm going to rely on you two from now on. Come straight home after. I'll phone school and tell them you've...' Then the line went dead.

It was still drizzling but the sun came out when we turned into Laura's street, and made my eyes water. There was an enormous lorry parked outside Laura's house. Danners and I sat on a wall a little distance away and watched. Men were putting furniture and boxes into the lorry. I could hear laughter. One man came out of the house carrying Laura's dressing table with the three-way mirror.

The sun started drying up the water on the edge of the wall, and little puffs of steam blew along it. Evaporation. We did it in Science last week.

Danners said, 'I'm going to give Laura a note.' He ripped a piece of paper from the back of his Maths book and started writing. A fat woman came out of the house we were sitting in front of. She didn't say anything about us being on her wall. She got into a blue car with a Chessington Zoo sticker on the back window and drove off.

Danners folded his note and we walked over to the house. Laura was sitting inside the back of the lorry, dangling her bare legs over the edge. She was wearing her white *broderie anglaise* shorts, even though it was cold. When she saw us the smile disappeared from her face.

'Oh! Hi! I'll get your dad.'

She jumped down from the lorry, stumbling a bit as she landed, and ran into the house. One of the removal men called, 'Oi-oi,' but she didn't turn round. We waited on the pavement, watching the men coming and going. Then Dad came out. It felt weird seeing him after all these days. As if he'd died and come back to life, like Jesus. I was doing Luke's Gospel in RE and we'd just got to that bit. When we started the syllabus, Mum wasn't too thrilled I was learning about Christianity, but Dad said, 'After all, Jesus was a good Jewish boy,' and made her laugh. That was only a few weeks ago.

Dad was wearing the blue jumper Danners and I bought him last birthday. He wrapped his arms round us both and squashed us against his chest. No one said anything for what felt like hours but by my digital watch was only one minute and eighteen seconds. When he let us go I saw my tears had made a wet patch on his front.

He said, 'Soon as we've got a permanent address in Norfolk, you'll come and stay for a long holiday.'

Danners shook his head slowly, and kept shaking it.

I said, 'You told me you and Mum don't love each other any more, but I asked her and actually she still loves you.'

'Oh, darling.' Dad reached for my hand.

I looked up at the house and Laura was watching us out of her bedroom window, just as I knew she would be. She ducked away when she realised I'd seen her.

'You're going to be Laura's dad now,' I said.

'You'll always be my daughter, Lissa.' Dad had those black bags he gets under his eyes. 'It's going to rain again. Why don't you both come inside?'

Danners said, 'You must be fucking joking.'

We weren't normally allowed to swear, but Dad didn't tell Dan off.

Mrs Morente appeared in the doorway and called, 'Michael, at least bring them into the hall.'

In my head, I stuck my middle finger up and said, like Colette Fitzgerald once did to Miss Gibbs, 'Swivel on it.'

Dad didn't make any attempt to move, and Mrs Morente went back inside.

I put on a pretend smile. 'Could you ask Laura to come out? I want to tell her we're still friends. Sisters, now.'

He believed me. 'You're an angel. I'll send her out.'

Danners and I went back across the road to the wall. It was drier now; the sun had soaked up more of the rain. In a way, I knew it wasn't her fault. It was the grown-ups. Laura's mother swinging her legs at the table, polished toenails in shiny sandals. Dad drinking whisky and laughing. But I also knew that Laura had helped make it happen. All those times she'd asked me to come round and play. All those times she'd said, 'Get your dad to bring you.' Fiona's party.

Nearly eight minutes by my digital watch. Then she came out of the house and walked over to us.

'Why you sitting here?'

Danners said, 'We're waiting for you to grace us with your presence.'

'Mama says you should come inside. The neighbours will wonder why everyone's outside in the rain.'

'You're moving away,' Danners said. 'What the fuck does she care about the neighbours?'

Laura sat next to me, so I was in the middle of her and Dan. If I turned towards her I could smell her Charlie perfume, and if I turned towards him I could smell his familiar sweaty boy smell. It felt strange, sitting between them.

Laura started picking at the flowers growing behind the wall. Her white shorts had dust marks over them. I thought of all the things I'd planned to say. Walking here this morning; in bed last night; the last few days. I had planned many different ways to tell Laura how much I hated her. But now with her next to me, her shoulder against mine, I just felt sad right through my body. Sad, and very tired. Last night I sat on top of my covers and stared out of the window till midnight. I was freezing but I knew if I moved, Daddy definitely wouldn't come. Actually, he didn't come anyway, so I needn't have bothered.

I wished the wall was my bed and I could just lie down and go to sleep. I opened my mouth to see what would come out. 'Your shorts are dirty.'

She gave a snorting laugh. 'Is that why you wanted to see me? So you could discuss my laundry?'

She was wearing her usual make-up; her hair was in one of the high ponytails she liked. But something about her looked different. She was more like one of the bitchy girls at school than the Laura in my head. Her eyes seemed smaller and narrower. There were three spots on her chin, shining through a layer of brown cover-up stick.

'They've got messed up because of the packing.'

The shorts.

'Mama's making me throw out loads of my things. We won't have room where we're going.'

'How very sad for you,' Danners said.

She went on quickly, 'Look what I've got.' She glanced back at the house, and pulled two battered cigarettes from the pocket of her shorts. She gave me one, then opened a flat packet of matches, the sort you get from a restaurant. It was black and white and the writing said 'Gusti's'. I wondered how she'd got them; if she'd been to a restaurant with my dad. How many more restaurants would she be going to with him? I put the cigarette into the pocket of my cagoule.

She offered the other one to Danners, but he shook his head.

Laura lit it and blew out a stream of smoke. 'You know when we pretended we were sisters?' she said. 'Now we really are. Your dad is my dad too.' She grabbed my hand, and I couldn't get it back without yanking it, so I left it there, my fist scrunched inside her damp palm.

'What about me?' Danners said. 'Are we brother and sister now?'

'Aren't we still going out? Mama said we could.'

'It isn't up to her,' Danners said. He leaned across me and gave her the note. 'Read it later. I'll wait for you outside the phone box, Lissa.'

We watched him walk away, till he disappeared round the corner. Laura looked at me and I remembered something I wanted to say. 'Why didn't you come to my batmitzvah?'

She touched my shoulder. 'I wanted to. I'd bought a new dress. Yellow. From Chelsea Girl. And I was going to wear my gold flats. But Mama didn't think it would be a good idea.'

'I thought you were my friend.'

'I *am*.' She dropped the cigarette butt onto the pavement, then pulled some more red petals off the flowers behind us and held them out to me. I ignored them.

'You're taking my dad off me.' I wish I could have said it in a more mature way. But I didn't know how else to say it.

She crushed up the petals in her palm and scattered them on the ground. 'Silly Miffy-rabbit! It's nothing to do with me. He's fallen in love with Mama.'

I was thirteen now, and officially a grown-up. I was not going to cry. I took such a deep breath I thought my bra would come undone. 'I don't think you were ever really my friend.'

'Of course I was. I still am!' She started doing crocodile tears. 'It's even better now, because we're sisters.'

I undid the silver heart-shaped pendant from round my neck. For a moment, I felt its weight in my hand. Then I held it out to her. 'I don't want this any more.'

She handed it back. 'It's yours.'

I pushed it into her hand. 'I don't want it, Laura.' Then I stood up. 'You know what I think?' I said. 'I think you were friends with me so your mum' – and I had to stop for a moment because my throat filled with lumps. I stepped back, and said in a louder voice – 'so your mum could be with my dad.'

'Shut up.'

'And that's why you went out with Danners too.'

'Shut the fuck up!' She looked really frightening. Her face was blotchy and her mouth was a huge black cave. Her eyes looked red, like the Devil. I thought she was going to hit me, like her dad had hit her mum. She yelled, 'That's total bullshit, and if you believe that you're even more of a stupid cow than I thought you were.' She grabbed my hair and pulled it really hard, so that tears prickled my eyes.

'Let go!'

'You think I want to go away and live in some stupid shit-hole in the middle of nowhere? I don't even know where Norfolk is.'

'Laura, let go, you're really hurting me.'

'You think I want to go to a new school? Leave all my friends? Leave Danny?'

She was crying properly now, and so was I.

'Get off me, Laura!'

'No one told me we'd be moving!'

My fingers closed over the rape alarm in my cagoule pocket, and I pulled the lid off. The siren was unbelievably loud and Laura jumped away, letting go of my hair. She covered her ears with her hands and screamed. Though the noise was dreadful it was exciting too, and I let it go on for a few more seconds before I pushed the lid back on. After the noise, the silence was weird, like I'd suddenly gone deaf. My heart was thudding. I sat down again on the wall.

Laura sat next to me and wiped her eyes on her sleeve. 'Wow, that was loud.'

'Rape alarm.'

She put the necklace on my lap. 'Please keep this. It was a *present*.'

I stood up so it fell onto the ground. I felt as angry as I'd ever felt in my life. I stood over her. For once I was taller, because she was sitting down. I said, 'Don't you understand? I. Don't. Want. It.'

'Don't look at me like that, Miffy.' She snatched the necklace off the ground.

It started to rain again. I put the hood up on my cagoule. I thought how nice it would be to see Jay at *shul*. How safe it had felt, dancing with him.

'I won't ever come to your house,' I said. 'Not while you are there. He is my dad, not yours. I don't want to be your sister and I don't want to share him with you. And I don't want you to go out with Danners any more.'

'That's not what he says!' She pulled the note he'd given her out of her pocket and read it. Then she stared at me, but didn't seem to really see me.

'Where is he?' She turned in the direction that Danners had gone. I stood in front of her.

'Get out of the way, Miffy.'

'Leave him alone.' I held out my hand to stop her.

'I said, get out of the way.' She shoved me aside and started running to the corner. I fell into the road and a car I didn't know was there swerved, and I don't remember anything else apart from Laura screaming, and Dad running from the house in slow motion, shouting my name, and the pain.

Laura

22 June 2003

The weather is perfect: sunny and warm with a gentle breeze. Glynn and Burl, bless their beautiful hides, have dragged every table in the house outside and put them end-to-end. With white sheets for tablecloths and vases of flowers placed at intervals along the length, it looks amazing, like something a family in *The Godfather* might sit round before they have a wedding and bump someone off.

I'm wearing my favourite yellow swirly-skirt sundress, which I'm delighted to tell you I can now get back into, with a bit of help from suck-it-in knickers. Add killer heels and red lipstick and I'm ready. And I need to be, with the fucking guest list I seem to have agreed to. Miffy, that sweet-talker. It's only today, as everyone dashes about poaching salmons, chopping tomatoes, washing strawberries, that the craziness of the thing properly strikes me.

'I'm panicking, Miff.'

She puts down a pile of plates and laughs. 'So am I! We don't have enough spoons.'

'Nineteen people for lunch. Oh my God, what was I thinking?'

'Half of them are kids, though. Everything's under control, Laura. Why don't you sit down and supervise us in comfort.'

I do as she says. I usually do. I sit in the shade of the cherry tree, and peep in at Mel, fast asleep in his Moses basket, one tiny arm flung above his head, oblivious to all the activity. I still can't believe he's home. It was the most amazing day of my life when at last his weight reached five pounds. The nurses and doctors were as delighted as I was. Doctor Massi kissed me, which was nice, apart from his moustache. Five pounds – now five pounds two ounces – is a light year away from where he started, though he's still so little that he's off the bottom of all the charts, and other mums at the clinic gasp when I tell them how old he is. But I think he's perfect. I stroke his cheek, softly, so he doesn't stir, then I sit back and watch my strange, disjointed family work together to prepare for this special occasion. Evie places the name cards she's carefully handwritten; Mama rearranges the flowers; Glynn puts out jugs of Pimm's and homemade lemonade; Huw arrives with six chairs. Thankfully, he's tactful enough not to bring the girlfriend, though part of me is curious to get a proper look at her, especially since Glynn's told me she has wrinkles round her eyes and a fat arse.

Huw sits next to me, gives me an avuncular kiss on the cheek. I missed him so much when he first left, but it's already starting to fade.

'Hey, *cariad*.'

'Oh, still *cariad*, am I? Thanks for bringing the chairs.'

'Not a bother. How's the little fella enjoying being home?' He peers into the basket as though it were some random baby in there, nothing to do with him.

'It's a lot nicer here than that smelly old hospital, isn't it, Melly-baby?'

Mel stirs, wakened by our voices. I pick him up gently and cuddle him. The warmth of him against my body makes tears come into my eyes. I am becoming a right soppy girl.

'Want a go?' I say, offering Mel to Huw, to wind him up. I know Taaa-nee-yah has told Huw to 'remain detached' while we're sorting out money and all that. It's clear who wears the trousers in that relationship; she's a complete ball-breaker. Must be a shock after all these years with little old me. I give them six months.

'No, you're all right, *cariad*; he's just woken up, he'll want you.'

Paige – Dopey Paige, our old baby-sitter – materialises at my side. 'Shall I get the bottle ready, Laura?' She's wisely dropped out of university and is doing an NVQ in child-care. We're letting her practise on us.

'Hey, Paige, how's the world of babies? No regrets about leaving my lovely History classes?'

'None, Dr Ellis,' she says. 'To be honest with you, they was boring as fuck.'

'Not a very forgiving young person, is she?' Huw says mildly, watching Paige stomp into the cottage. He is used to her moral disapproval.

'She's very young, still sees everything in black and white, bless her.'

Paige is an absolute champ at measuring out the formula, heating the milk, testing the temperature on her wrist, all that repetitive shite. She adores it. Soon she'll be lookin-gafter Mel three days a week, while I'm at college.

He nuzzles against my shoulder and starts to whimper. Paige reappears with the bottle, which Mel sucks with the strength of a Dyson, blue eyes watching me through dark lashes. I love him with an intensity I don't remember from Evie's babyhood. It was more of a slow burn with her. With Mel, love at first sight, no question.

Evie comes over and puts her arms round Huw and me. For a fleeting Kodak moment we are a proper little family of four. Then Burl knocks over the sunshade, and Huw gets up to help him. Evie asks me to check the name cards are in the right places. My priority is to be nowhere near Ceri or Heifer. And Miffy would like to be next to Nick. Finally, Miffy and Nick! Though all she keeps saying is, 'Early days.'

Now here *is* Nick, looking handsome in a cream shirt, carrying a huge present for Mel. And then everyone's arriving at once, bringing gifts and wine. Ceri appears, looking meek, as well she might, considering her orange Daisy Duck T-shirt – nice one, Ceri – and the fact that I haven't spoken to her since the Great Sacking. I've deleted all her emails, apart from the most recent, headed 'Bastard', which said she'd split up with Rees. In a weak moment I agreed that Miffy could invite her today. All my favourites, aren't I lucky, because now here's Heifer, swept along on a sea of children. Ah! And Danny, deliciously attractive in a dove-grey suit and festive blue *cuple*, almost hidden behind a pile of beribboned presents and very much avoiding my eye.

Heifer's brought her cousin Jonathan, who's moved in with them, because they've obviously got so much room.

Heifer informed me the other week that Jonathan is the black sheep of the family, which naturally piqued my interest. He's just out of rehab and is supposed to be making a fresh start with the guiding hand of Danny and Heifer, Edgware's moral guardians. Jonathan, thank God, looks nothing like his cousin. In fact, he's quite cute, with a glint of something interesting in his eye. Rather marvellously, I do a little sleight-of-hand name-card rearrangement so that he's sitting opposite me.

Miffy gets everyone seated and the food starts appearing, and Huw goes round topping up glasses and I drink several Pimm's too quickly because of nerves. Burl's in charge of music, and his playlist is sentimental teenage choices such as Ella Fitzgerald and Billie Holiday: the ideal backdrop for his attempt to chat up Atalia, Danny's oldest girl, looking very pretty despite her modest outfit. And talking of cross-culture chatting-ups, Evie and Micah are whispering together, someone's naughty mother having ensured they're sitting next to each other. Evie's had a bloody miserable few months and deserves a bit of a flirt. So does Miffy. You should see the smile she gives Nick as she sits down. I really hope he works out for her.

I do feel bad that I still haven't put her straight about stuff. I honestly keep meaning to, please believe me, but I just haven't found the right time to say it. She's changed her whole life. Got herself a job here, bought a flat just along the coast in Penmaenmawr. All on the understanding that she caused my premature labour. I'm going to tell her tonight, I promise. Then she can yell at me, scream, do whatever she wants. Leave, I suppose, if she's really pissed off. I hope to God she doesn't, though.

Talking of awkward conversations, I'm doing well at avoiding Ceri. She's up the other end of the table next to Huw – ha ha – listening to Heifer list every feature of interest about the Travelodge in Llandudno where they're staying. Did you know you can fit three adults and six children into their biggest family room? Did you know they can get in special kosher food, sent from Manchester? I imagine Ceri wincing every time 'Llandudno' is mentioned, thinking of happy times there with Rees.

I glance at Jonathan, and though he's in conversation with Mama, he winks at me, which makes me laugh. I turn to Danny. 'So how *are* you?'

He smiles past my ear. 'Really good. And how is this little one? May I?' He reaches out for Mel and burbles, 'Who's a sweet little fellow?'

Mama brings out strawberry pavlova and Huw pours more drinks. I think some of the children are getting Pimm's instead of lemonade, but even Heifer doesn't seem to mind; she is drinking Pimm's herself, by accident possibly, and as she's barely eating, nothing being kosher enough, she is squiffy and keeps effusively kissing her kids, making them squirm.

Miffy stands up, taps her glass and calls, 'A toast!' All faces turn to her.

'We have so many things to celebrate,' Miffy says, smiling round the table, 'I hardly know where to start.'

Everyone whoops. Christ, what on earth is in that Pimm's? Other than Pimm's?

'Let's begin with the reason we're all here today. To Mel!'

Everyone turns to Danny, for Mel is cosied up against his chest. Lucky baby.

'Welcome home, Melvin Michael Ellis, you gorgeous boy,' Miffy says. 'Thanks for giving us an excuse to have this party. You were only sprung a week ago, but you've already settled in as if you've always lived here.'

Danny passes Mel back to me and I hold him up high so everyone can see him.

'To Mel!' we chorus. 'Welcome home!'

Heifer leans across to Paige and says, 'The evil eye, you know. Made him come too early.' She straightens up and says more loudly, 'So bonny. When you think how ill he was, the little *bubbeleh*.'

Miffy taps her glass again and says, 'And now Evie.'

Evie gives an embarrassed wave. Micah smiles at her in a way that suggests he is squeezing her hand under the table. I know they still write to each other. I also know

Evie sends her letters to Micah's friend's address, so he doesn't have to explain who his correspondent is at home, because I saw the envelope on her desk the other day. I hope you're impressed I didn't even pick it up. Heifer will never allow them to have a relationship, though. Over her dead body.

I'm willing to risk Heifer's dead body.

'Next week, Evie turns twelve,' says Miffy. 'Has there ever been a more amazing, beautiful, incredible twelve-year-old?'

'Me, next year!' calls Atalia, and everyone laughs.

'This family does have wonderful children,' says Mama.

Ah yes, Mama. This is one big happy family.

'Evie's had a tough time lately,' says Miffy, keeping the toasts a bit more real than I'd like.

The younger children, getting bored, start running round the table. Paige sweeps them off into the house. To my relief, Miffy doesn't elaborate further about Evie's tough times but just sings her praises for somewhat longer than necessary. Then we all cry, 'To Evie!'

'And now a toast to our hostess.'

Oh God, everyone's looking at me. I'm sure my mascara's smudged. How annoying. I pull Mel closer, press my cheek against his. He smells of Danny.

'This hasn't been the easiest of years for Laura. But now she's got her lovely baby, a great business idea, and she's going back to college. And here I am: new home, new job, and I've met some very special people, all because of her.' She smiles at Nick, then turns to me. 'Fate's lent a hand and I love my new life. To Laura!'

I swallow hard as everyone repeats, 'To Laura!' I turn away as I can't bear to see how fondly Miffy looks at me, and catch Danny's eye for the first time today. There is a flicker between us, tiny as a blink. I see it in the widening of his pupils, the tiny beads of sweat on his forehead, the curve of his mouth. Then he puts down his glass, looks away, and the moment is gone. For ever.

'Finally,' Miffy says, 'to my big brother, darling Danners, who turned thirty-nine last week!' She's in a very confessional mood today; starts listing all the support Danny's given her, from her own divorce to, oh God, that of their parents, taking in all points between. I suppose she's a bit plastered. She makes a comment about all the 'additional difficulties' surrounding their parents' split, and I tremble that she might decide to chuck in the abortion as one of the many points of interest on Danny's emotional CV, but thank God she doesn't.

'To Danny!' I say, as I can't stand that 'Danners' name, and smile across at him. Unfortunately, he is mouthing 'I love you' at Heifer. She looks flushed. Slightly pretty. Christ, what am I saying?

I pass Mel to Mama and stand up, to propose my own toast: to Miffy for her excellent party organisation and for supporting me so wonderfully the last few months. When we raise our glasses, her eyes meet mine and she gives me her megawatt Marilyn smile.

Everyone calls her by a different name:

'To Miffy!'

'Melissa!'

'Mel!'

'Lissa!'

After this, Paige and Burl serve coffee, and everyone starts moving around, swapping seats, chatting. Danny goes over to Miffy and they hug each other. Mama sits next to me in Danny's vacated seat and says, 'That went off very well, I thought.'

'Some of those toasts were a bit near the knuckle.'

'Ah, there is no harm in being honest, Laura. You always like to pretend everything is fine all the time.'

'Wonder where I get that from, Mama.'

She laughs. She's lightened up a lot this last couple of months. I'd like to put that down to her love for Mel, but suspect, knowing Mama, it's more likely to be down to having reconnected with my father when she was in Spain at Easter. I'm hoping nothing will come of it, but she's in touch regularly with him, has got Evie to teach her how to use email. She's keen for me to meet him again. 'He's so changed,' she tells me, 'so mellow.' And so available. Mama can't bear her life without a man in it. Some things never change.

'I'm going to take my little *bebita* inside,' she says. 'He is getting too hot.' I watch Mel as she carries him away; he is so gorgeous.

Talking of gorgeous, Jonathan catches my eye and says, 'Terrific party.'

'Really glad you could come,' I say, putting an accidental emphasis on 'come'. Think I'm a bit tiddly myself. 'How are you liking it at Danny and Hella's?'

'I'm hoping it's just a stopgap. I could really do with getting away from London altogether. I can see why Melissa moved here – it's beautiful.'

'Rents are pretty cheap, too.'

'Are they? That's very interesting.'

I offer to pour him some wine but he shakes his head. 'Keeping off everything at the moment.' He indicates his glass of sparkling water. 'Being good.'

'Oh, what a shame.'

'It's a bit boring. Still, you know, in the right company...'

Heifer materialises heftily behind him and gives me her evil eye. 'Johnno, can you give me a hand with the kids?'

'Sure, Hells.' Great new nickname for Heifer. 'I'll be back,' he mouths at me.

A moment later, Ceri slides into the seat next to me, harshing my mellow, as Glynn would say. 'Hi, Laura. Thanks for inviting me.'

'It was Miffy's idea.' I gulp my coffee and burn my throat. 'How's the shop?'

'It's okay. Listen, I've felt so awful since I had to let you go.'

'You didn't "let me go", Ceri. You *sacked* me. Because of your *boyfriend*.'

She stares at her hands. 'I really messed up,' she says. 'You know the Jenny-and-Paul dinner in April. The one you didn't go to?'

'Yeah, well, I had a few minor things going on then – my husband shagging someone else, my premature baby in hospital...Lame excuses, I know, but I just didn't feel like going somehow.'

'God, I'm *so* sorry, Laura.'

'Yeah, yeah.'

I look round the garden. Danny's standing under the cherry tree with Nick; Heifer and Jonathan are swinging small laughing children round; and Miffy and Huw are at the far end of the table, talking intently. Huw glances at me and I look away.

Ceri burbles on. 'You'll never believe what happened. Jenny was in a completely weird mood.'

'When is she not, that bitch.'

'Totally. She went outside with Rees for a cigarette, and when I went out, there they were.'

'Shagging? Jesus, Ceri!'

'NO! Just kissing. It was bad enough. The worst humiliation ever.'

Considering her jumper collection, that really is saying something.

'What did Rees have to say about it?'

'Fuck him. He keeps phoning, writing illiterate letters. It's properly pitiful.'

'Poor you.'

'Laura, I'm so sorry. Please come back, I'll let you do all the windows, proper contract, everything.'

I shake my head. 'Did I tell you I'm starting a beautician course in September? I'm going to open my own salon. Getting some guilt money off Huw for the deposit. I'll be able to give North Wales all the posh London treatments it so desperately needs.'

'Oh. That's great.' Flat monotone.

'I'll give you a free facial when I open.' She could do with one now, to be honest. Look at the size of those pores.

When Ceri eventually buggers off, Miffy sits down on my other side.

'Amazing job,' I say. 'Look at this bizarre group of people. Somehow you turned it into a sparkling event. You should be a party organiser.'

'Think I'll stick to troubled teens, thanks. A lot easier.'

'What were you and Huw talking about? You looked very serious.'

'Ah. Interesting. Huw was asking why I'd decided to move here permanently.'

'Listen, Miff.'

'I told him I felt responsible. Because I'd pushed you over.' Her tone makes me very uncomfortable. 'But Huw told me you'd always been inclined to miscarry. That you've had five miscarriages. Which I didn't know. That you'd had signs of premature labour for several weeks before Mel was born. Which I also didn't know.'

Huw's such a sodding shit-stirrer.

'Miffy, I was going to talk to you about it. This evening, in fact...'

'So it *is* true.' She sits back in her seat and folds her arms. Stares at me.

'It's just...it's been so wonderful having you around. You saved my life, really, after Huw left.'

'I left everything, Laura, to be with you. Because I thought it was my fault.'

'Was it really only because of guilt that you stayed, though? If so, I kind of wish you hadn't. I thought there was more to it than that.'

There's a long pause. She glances in Nick's direction. Though he's looking away, he senses it, in that way lovers do, and he turns towards us.

'There *was* more to it,' Miffy says in a long sigh. 'There were many reasons to stay, and just as many not to go back. If I want you to be honest with me, I'm going to have to be honest myself.'

'Thank you.' I put my hand on hers.

'I suppose me pushing you didn't help. Even if it didn't make a physical difference, the stress of us fighting might have made things worse.'

I shrug. 'It might have. I guess we'll never know for sure.'

Miffy sits back, untangling our hands. 'Laura, from here on out, I need you to be straight with me.'

'I am! Well, I usually am.'

'I love it here. Best thing that ever happened to me. Finally breaking my ties with London, with my mum. With my childhood. I don't want our friendship to be based on lies any more.'

'Oh, Miff, I feel awful.' I want to cry.

She squeezes my arm and says, 'I know you've always had a slightly hazy relationship with the truth, my love. You see things the way you want to see them.'

'Doesn't everyone?'

Miffy leans back in her chair and lights a cigarette.

'I thought you were giving up?'

'First one today. Not bad, given the stress levels.'

'Are you furious with me, Miffy-sister?'

'More resigned, really. I know what you're like, Laura.'

'I reckon you know what I'm like more than anyone else.'

She blows a magnificent series of smoke rings into the

sky. 'I saw Ceri talking to you, looking all contrite. Does she believe you now, and not Rees?'

'Yep.'

We both start laughing.

'Well, more fool her,' says Miffy.

We sit close together, our arms round each other. It's so important to be known properly. Inside out.

Acknowledgements

I really admire writers who go into their studies, don't talk to anyone, and emerge a year later with a novel tucked casually under their arm. I'm not like that. Sometimes I could barely write a sentence without needing feedback. For the most unflinching-yet-supportive critique, thank you to my writing mob: Liz Bahs, Clare Best and Alice Owens. Sorry the massage scene didn't make the final cut, Liz.

The following people all commented helpfully on various drafts: Jo Bloom, Alison Hutchins, Trish Joscelyne, Alex Lahood, Anne Lavender-Jones, Emma Lewis, Nick Lewis, Juliette Mitchell, Rosy Muers-Raby, Gilly Shapiro and Kate Sweetapple. I'd particularly like to thank Saskia Gent and Tim Ward, who each unlocked useful plot points.

For encouragement along the way, thank you to the Literary Consultancy, Tessa West, Chris Taylor at New Writing South, Jim Crace, Suzannah Dunn and Liz Roberts, and my colleagues Emma Chaplin and Katie Moorman. For taking a punt on the book, I'm indebted to my agent Judith Murdoch, and my publisher at Ebury, Gillian Green.

To my children, thanks for making the process much more amusing, if a tad slower. And yes, I will soon write a story featuring your characters, Poshly Posh and Australian Stomach (who is from Brazil).

Finally, John. Even more important than the years of practical support, was your unfaltering belief that this book would be published. You never once hassled me to earn more money/come out of the study/stop using up the printer ink. This is for you.